THE
FANTASTIC SAINT
LESLIE CHARTERIS

A collection of six short stories featuring Simon Templar — that debonair buccaneer — whose name strikes fear into the hearts of the most self-assured villian, excites jealousy among the gumshoes at Scotland Yard, and brings a blush of pleasure to the cheeks of his comely conquests.

In "The Gold Standard," the last words of a dead man bring the Saint back to England, against his better judgement. His chilly reception at customs, the whiz of a slightly off-target bullet past his head, and the knowledge that he is being followed, create a distinctly unfavorable atmosphere for discreet sleuthing. Interference from Scotland Yard and the machinations of his elusive quarry make Templar wonder who is the hunter and who is the hunted in this taut thriller.

The Saint is at his quick-witted best in "The Newdick Helicopter." To the con-

(continued on back flap)

THE FANTASTIC SAINT

THE FANTASTIC
SAINT

LESLIE CHARTERIS

Edited by Martin Harry Greenberg and Charles G. Waugh

DOUBLEDAY & COMPANY, INC.

GARDEN CITY, NEW YORK

1982

28972

ACKNOWLEDGMENTS

"The Gold Standard," copyright 1933 by Leslie Charteris. First appeared,
in *Thriller,* on October 15, 1932, as "The Gold Flood."
"The Newdick Helicopter," copyright 1934. Originally appeared in
Empire News on October 15, 1933, as "The Inventions of Oscar
Newdick."
"The Man Who Liked Ants," copyright 1937 by Leslie Charteris.
"The Questing Tycoon," copyright 1954 by Leslie Charteris.
"The Darker Drink," copyright 1948 by Leslie Charteris. Originally
appeared as "Dawn."
"The Convenient Monster," copyright © 1959 by King-Size Publications
Inc.

ISBN: 0-385-17331-8
Library of Congress Catalog Card Number 81–43614

First Edition

CONTENTS

INTRODUCTION

by

Martin H. Greenberg

The series figure has a long and distinguished history in literature, especially literature for a mass audience. From Tom Swift to Sam Spade, from Sir Arthur Conan Doyle's Sherlock Holmes to Edgar Rice Burroughs' Tarzan and John Carter, the series character has been a staple of popular fiction. This is also true of the electronic media, which have featured hundreds of situation comedies, detective and crime dramas, soap operas, and Western series that have been at the heart of television's commercial success, if not its appeal.

For books and magazines the series has proved to be both popular and vital in a commercial sense. With thousands of books crowding the racks and shelves of newsstands and bookstores, the potential buyer can become bewildered by the variety of choices in front of him. One way to overcome this problem is to seek out the familiar—to look for books by authors that one has enjoyed in the past, with expectations of further satisfaction to come. And while it is true that names do sell books, added inducements are valuable, and this is where the series has proved a commercial success, for the series character provides an identity and a sense of predictability that book buyers have found irresistible. Readers quickly feel at ease with a continuing protagonist who drinks the same drink, drives the same car, carries the same gun, and operates out of the same office in story after story.

Series characters therefore have both commercial and entertainment advantages not found in "single" works. They also have advantages for the writer. The protagonist has a set of characteristics that can be repeated; the background is frequently the same in each book or story; and the cast of characters normally includes many holdovers from previous works. But there are also dangers for readers and authors—a series can become too repetitive or dull and the author can fail to pay attention to detail or may engage in shortcuts that demean and damage the final work. On the other hand, it can be argued that many writers produce the same two or three books throughout their careers, constantly reworking the themes that interest or possess them.

But the truly long-lived and popular series have a special magic that sets them apart. Conan Doyle's Holmes and Burroughs' Tarzan are as popular today as when they were first written. And any list of memorable series characters would have to include Leslie Charteris' Simon Templar—the Saint.

The Saint has achieved tremendous popularity throughout the world. In almost fifty books, in nine motion pictures, in a radio series that started in the late 1930s and ran on and off into the mid-1940s, in one hundred and twenty television episodes (more counting the most recent revival), the exploits of Simon Templar have thrilled and entertained tens of millions of people. From the publication of the first Saint book in 1928, the mystique of the Saint proved to be remarkable.

It was inevitable that Simon Templar would be transferred from the printed page to the movie screen, although the process would take more than ten years. Unlike the case of James Bond, however, the transfer was not a success. Some of the screenplays were adequate, but the real problem was with the casting. Neither the talented (talent largely wasted in his films) Louis Hayward or the grim George Sanders could capture the spirit of Simon Templar, and in the case of Sanders there appears to have been little interest or effort in the attempt. Indeed, the Saint and his creator were both badly treated in Hollywood, the former on the screen and the latter through the efforts of R.K.O. to purloin Simon in the form of "The Falcon," an obvious copy portrayed by both Sanders and his brother Tom Conway. The matter was satisfactorily settled out of court.

Much more successful was the transition to the television screen, both because the (early) scripts tended to follow Saint stories rather faithfully and because of the excellent choice of the charming and handsome Roger Moore for the role. "The Saint" became popular all over the world, and its star has been mobbed by adoring fans as far apart as London and Tel Aviv, the show being a hit in France, Germany, Spain, Latin America, Japan, and elsewhere. As frequently happens, however, the television series began to deviate further and further away from the original inspiration as time went by, and the early faithfulness to original Saint stories began to falter. This was especially true of two of the Saint stories with fantastic elements, "The Newdick Helicopter" and "The Gold Standard." But on the whole, the initial Saint television program was a success and ran for some six years before going into syndication.

In addition to radio and television, the Saint also provided the basis for a long-lived and generally high-quality comic strip that was internationally syndicated by the New York *Herald Tribune* for almost ten years. Its success was due to the fact that Leslie Charteris wrote all of the scripts himself, a task that finally proved too time-consuming.

Simon Templar was also honored with a magazine that carried his name. First called *The Saint Detective Magazine,* then *The Saint Mystery Magazine,* and finally simply *The Saint Magazine,* it ran from 1953 to October 1967, a long life by genre standards. So *The Saint* belongs to a rather limited and illustrious group of magazines named after individuals—*MIKE SHAYNE, ELLERY QUEEN, ALFRED HITCHCOCK,* and most recently *ISAAC ASIMOV*—and while an uneven publication, it ran some excellent stories through the years. But other series characters have appealing features, so what is so special about the Saint?

Simon Templar appeals to so many readers from so many different cultures because he is a *romantic* figure. His motivating spirit is the spirit of Robin Hood, of helping those who cannot help themselves or those that governments, police departments, and established authority will not help. He bends the law but he only breaks it when the good of society will result or when those who are evil will suffer. He is of the law but outside the law—he is inner-directed, with a well-developed sense of justice that is intuitive and compassionate. When the sharp articles in society are outside the reach of the law, indeed, when the law is powerless in the face of evil, the Saint is not. His character is the product of a long literary and cinematic tradition, recently expressed in the figure of Charles Bronson in films like *Chato's Land* (1972) and *Death Wish* (1974), only with a touch of class. In an earlier era, before the word was ripped from common usage, the character would have been described as "gay," the Gay Crusader for justice and good.

The fact that the Saint combines the qualities of good looks, virtue, and upper-class characteristics has enabled him to be popular with both male and female readers, a quality not normally found with series characters (Sherlock Holmes, for example, was and is read overwhelmingly by men). More unusual still is the Saint's popularity across income and occupational spectrums from the poor to the wealthy, from the carpenter to the cabinet minister. After all, Simon Templar is clearly an upper-class person, and he should be difficult for the average person to identify with. It is possible that the British habit of deferring to rather than opposing class distinctions has something to do with this, and as in all great popular fiction, wish-fulfillment probably plays a role here, but it is remarkable nevertheless and does not explain the Saint's success across cultures. Leslie Charteris' character also differs from most others in that his creator is a skillful, at times brilliant writer who employs a large vocabulary without excuses and never writes down to his varied audience. And still they all love the Saint, even if some must occasionally use a dictionary while reading about his adventures.

Some could perhaps argue that the Great Depression and the gathering clouds of war in Europe contributed to the success of a gay romantic hero who could take people's minds off their troubles. However, this does not account for the *continuing* popularity of Simon Templar through good times and bad. No other characters have spanned the range of genres, covering not only whodunit, espionage, pure adventure, but on out to science fiction and fantasy.

THE FANTASTIC SAINT

The Saint experienced his first fantastic adventure in 1930, just two years after beginning his career. The Last Hero (alternate title: The Saint Closes the Case) tells how Simon and his three close friends (Roger Conway, Patricia Holm, and Norman Kent) thwart a mad scientist's attempts to conquer the world. But in accomplishing this feat Simon suffers a serious loss which may have even influenced his subsequent decision to withdraw from a life of crime and devote his entire energies to helping right wrongs. Unfortunately, space limitations prevent the inclusion of this fine work, however all of the other "unusual" Saint adventures are included here, and they present a fascinating thirty-year chronicle of change, travel, and growth.

The first of these shorter works is "The Gold Standard" (1932). Here the Saint's inability to mind his own business involves him in murder, a mystery, and an invention which threatens the world economy. It is a strong story, laced with humor and notable for its revelations about the characters of both the young Saint and his perennial foil, Chief Inspector Claud Eustace Teal.

THE GOLD STANDARD

1

Simon Templar landed in England when the news of Brian Quell's murder was on the streets. He read the brief notice of the killing in an evening paper which he bought in Newhaven, but it added scarcely anything to what he already knew.

Brian Quell died in Paris, and died drunk; which would probably have been his own choice if he had been consulted, for the whole of his unprofitable existence had been wrapped up in the pleasures of the Gay City. He was a prophet who was without honour not only in his own country and among his own family, but even among the long-suffering circle of acquaintances who helped him to spend his money when he had any, and endeavoured to lend him as little as possible when he was broke—

which was about three hundred days out of the year. He had arrived ten years ago as an art student, but he had long since given up any artistic pretensions that were not included in the scope of studio parties and long hair. Probably there was no real vice in him; but the life of the Left Bank is like an insidious drug, an irresistible spell to such a temperament as his, and it was very easy to slip into the stream in those days before the rapacity of Montmartre *patrons* drove the tourist pioneers across the river. They knew him, and charmingly declined to cash his cheques, at the Dôme, the Rotonde, the Select, and all the multitudinous *boïtes-de-nuit* which spring up around those unassailable institutions for a short season's dizzy popularity, and sink back just as suddenly into oblivion. Brian Quell had his fill of them all. And he died.

The evening paper did not say he was drunk; but Simon Templar knew, for he was the last man to see Brian Quell alive.

He heard the shot just as he had removed his shoes, as he prepared for what was left of a night's rest in the obscure little hotel near the Gare du Montparnasse which he had chosen for his sanctuary in Paris. His room was on the first floor, with a window opening on to a well at the back, and it was through this window that the sharp crack of the report came to him. The instinct of his trade made him leap for the nearest switch and snap out the lights without thinking what he was doing, and he padded back to the window in his stockinged feet. By that time he had realised that the shots could be no immediate concern of his, for the shots that kill you are the ones you don't hear. But if Simon Templar had been given to minding his own business there would never have been any stories to write about him.

He swung his legs over the low balustrade and strolled quietly round the flat square of concrete which surrounded the ground-floor skylight that angled up in to it like his own, but all of them except one were in the centre of the well. Other windows opened out on darkness. The lighted window attracted him as inevitably as it would have drawn a moth; and as he went towards it he observed that it was the only one in the courtyard besides his own which had not been firmly shuttered against any breath of the fresh air which, as all the world knows, is instantly fatal to the sleeping Frenchman. And then the light went out.

Simon reached the dark opening, and paused there. He heard a gasping curse; and then a hoarse voice gurgled the most amazing speech that he had ever heard from the lips of a dying man.

"A mos' unfrien'ly thing!"

Without hesitation, Simon Templar climbed into the room. He found his way to the door and turned on the lights; and it was only then that he learned that the drunken man was dying.

Brian Quell was sprawled in the middle of the floor, propping himself up unsteadily on one elbow. There was a pool of blood on the carpet beside him, and his grubby shirt was stained red across the chest. He stared at Simon hazily.

"A mos' unfrien'ly thing!" he repeated.

Simon dropped on one knee at the man's side. The first glance told him that Brian Quell had only a few minutes to live, but the astonishing thing was that Quell did not know he was hurt. The shock had not sobered him at all. The liquor that reeked on his breath was playing the part of an anaesthetic, and the fumes in his brain had fuddled his senses beyond all power of comprehending such an issue.

"Do you know who it was?" Simon asked gently.

Quell shook his head.

"I dunno. Never saw him before in my life. Called himself Jones. Silly sora name, isnit? Jones. . . . An' he tole me Binks can make gold!"

"Where did you meet him, old chap? Can you tell me what he looked like?"

"I dunno. Been all over place. Everywhere you could gerra drink. Man with a silly sora face. Never seen him before in my life. Silly ole Jones." The dying man wagged his head solemnly. "An' he did a mos' unfrien'ly thing. Tried to shoot me! A mos' unfrien'ly thing." Quell giggled feebly. "And he saysh Binks can make gold. Thash funny, isnit?"

Simon looked round the room. There was no trace of the man who called himself Jones—nothing but an ashtray that had been freshly emptied. Obviously the killer had stayed long enough to obliterate all evidence of his visit; obviously too, his victim had been temporarily paralysed, so that the murderer had believed that he was already dead.

There was a telephone by the door, and for a moment Simon Templar gazed at it and wondered if it was his duty to ring for assistance. The last thing on earth that he wanted was an interview even with the most unsuspecting police officer, but that consideration would not have weighed with him for an instant if he had not known that all the doctors in France could have done nothing for the man who was dying in his arms and did not know it.

"Why did Jones try to shoot you?" he asked, and Brian Quell grinned at him vacuously.

"Because he said Binks could——"

The repetition choked off in the man's throat. His eyes wavered over Simon's face stupidly; then they dilated with the first and last stunned realisation of the truth, only for one horrible dumb second before the end. . . .

Simon read the dead man's name from the tailor's tab inside the breast pocket of his coat, and went softly back to his room. The other windows on the courtyard remained shrouded in darkness. If anyone else had heard the shot it must have been attributed to a passing taxi; but there is a difference between the cough of an engine and the crack of an automatic about which the trained ear can never be mistaken. If it had not been for Simon Templar's familiarity with that subtle distinction, a coup might have been inscribed in the annals of crime which would have shaken Europe from end to end—but Simon could not see so far ahead that night.

He left Paris early the following morning. It was unlikely that the murder would be discovered before the afternoon; for it is an axiom of the Quarter that early rising is a purely bourgeois conceit, and one of the few failings of the French hotel-keepers is that they feel none of that divine impulse to dictate the manner of life of their clientéle which has from time immemorial made Great Britain the Mecca of holiday makers from every corner of the globe. Simon Templar had rarely witnessed a violent death about which he had so clear a conscience, and yet he knew that it would have been foolish to stay. It was one of the penalties of his fame that he had no more chance of convincing any well-informed policeman that he was a law-abiding citizen than he had of being elected President of the United States. So he went back to England, where he was more unpopular than anywhere else in Europe.

If it is true that there is some occult urge which draws a murderer back to the scene of his crime, it must have been an infinitely more potent force which brought Simon Templar back across the Channel to the scene of more light-hearted misdemeanours than Scotland Yard had ever before endured from the disproportionate sense of humour of any one outlaw. It was not so many years since he had first formulated the idea of making it his life work to register himself in the popular eye as something akin to a public institution; and yet in that short space of time his dossier in the Records Office had swollen to a saga of debonair lawlessness that made Chief Inspector Claud Eustace Teal speechless to contemplate. The absurd little sketch of a skeleton figure graced with a symbolic halo, that impudent signature with which Simon Templar endorsed all his crimes, had spread the terror of the Saint into every outpost of the underworld and crashed rudely into the placid meandering of all those illustrious members of the Criminal Investigation Department who had hitherto been content to justify their employment as guardians of the Law by perfecting themselves in the time-honoured sport of persuading deluded shop-assistants to sell them a bar of chocolate one minute later than the lawful hours for such transactions. The Robin Hood of Modern Crime they called him in the headlines, and extolled his virtues in the same paragraph as they reviled the C.I.D. for failing to lay him by the heels; which only shows you what newspapers can do for democracy. He had become an accepted incident in current affairs, like Wheat Quotas and the League of Nations, only much more interesting. He stood for a vengeance that struck swiftly and without mercy, for a gay defiance of all dreary and mechanical things.

"It's not my fault, sir," Chief Inspector Teal stated gloomily, in an interview which he had with the Assistant Commissioner. "We aren't in the Saint's class, and some day I suppose we shall have to admit it. If this was a republic we should make him dictator and get some sleep."

The Commissioner frowned. He was one of the last survivors of the old military school of police chiefs, a distinguished soldier of unimpeachable integrity; but he laboured under the disadvantage of expecting professional law-breakers to parade for judgment as meekly as the casual defaulters he had been accustomed to dealing with in Pondicherry.

"About two months ago," he said, "you told me that the Saint's arrest was only a matter of hours. It was something to do with illicit diamonds, wasn't it?"

"It was," Teal said grimly.

He was never likely to forget the incident. Neither, it seemed, were his superiors. Gunner Perrigo was the culprit in that case, and the police had certainly got their man. The only trouble was that Simon Templar had got him first. Perrigo had been duly hanged on the very morning of this conversation, but his illicit diamonds had never been heard of again.

"It should have been possible to form a charge," insisted the Commissioner, plucking his iron-grey moustache nervously. He disapproved of Teal's attitude altogether, but the plump detective was an important officer.

"It might be, if there were no lawyers," said Teal. "If I went into a witness-box and talked about illicit diamonds I should be bawled out of court. We know the diamonds existed, but who's going to prove it to a jury? Frankie Hormer could have talked about them, but Perrigo gave him the works. Perrigo could have talked, but he didn't—and now he's dead. And the Saint got away with them out of England, and that's the end of it. If I could lay my hands on him tomorrow I'd have no more hope of proving he'd ever possessed any illicit diamonds than I'd have of running the Pope for bigamy. We could charge him with obstructing and assaulting the police in the execution of their duty, but what in heaven's name's the use of running the Saint for a milk-and-water rap like that? It'd be the biggest joke that Fleet Street's had on us for years."

"Did you learn all the facts about his last stunt in Germany?"

"Yes. I did. And it just came through yesterday that the German police aren't in a hurry to prosecute. There's some big name involved, and they've got the wind up. If I was expecting anything else, I was betting the Saint would be hustling back here and getting ready to dare them to try and extradite him from his own country—he's pulled that one on me before."

The Commissioner sniffed.

"I suppose if he did come back you'd want me to head a deputation of welcome," he said scathingly.

"I've done everything that any officer could do in the circumstances, sir," said Teal. "If the Saint came back this afternoon, and I met him on the doorstep of this building, I'd have to pass the time of day with him—and like it. You know the law as well as I do. We couldn't ask him any more embarrassing questions than if he had a good time abroad, and how was his aunt's rheumatism when he last heard from her. They don't want detectives here any longer—what they need is a staff of hypnotists and faith healers."

The Commissioner fidgeted with a pencil.

"If the Saint came back, I should certainly expect to see some change in our methods," he remarked pointedly: and then the telephone on his desk buzzed.

He picked up the receiver, and then passed it across to Teal.

"For you, Inspector," he said curtly.

Teal took over the instrument.

"Saint returns to England," clicked the voice on the wire. "A report from Newhaven states that a man answering to Simon Templar's description landed from the *Isle of Sheppy* this afternoon. He was subsequently traced to an hotel in the town——"

"Don't talk to me like a fourth-rate newspaper," snarled Teal. "What have you done with him?"

"On the instructions of the Chief Constable, he is being detained pending advice from London."

Teal put the receiver carefully back on its bracket.

"Well, sir, the Saint *has* come back," he said glumly.

2

The Assistant Commissioner did not head a deputation of welcome to Newhaven. Teal went down alone, with mixed feelings. He remembered that the Saint's last action before leaving England had been to present him with a sheaf of information which had enabled him to clean up several cases that had been racking the brains of the C.I.D. for many months. He remembered also that the Saint's penultimate action had been to threaten him with the most vicious form of blackmail that can be applied to any police officer. But Chief Inspector Teal had long since despaired of reconciling the many contradictions of his endless feud with the man who in any other part of life might have been his closest friend.

He found Simon Templar dozing peacefully on the narrow bed of a cell in Newhaven police station. The Saint rolled up to a sitting position as the detective entered, and smiled at him cheerfully.

"Claud Eustace himself, by the tum-tum of Tutankhamen! I thought I'd be seeing you," Simon looked the detective over thoughtfully. "And I believe you've put on weight," he said.

Teal sank his teeth in a well-worn lump of chewing gum.

"What have you come back for?" he asked shortly.

On the way down he had mapped out the course of the interview minutely. He had decided that his attitude would be authoritative, restrained, distant, perfectly polite but definitely warning. He would tolerate no more nonsense. So long as the Saint was prepared to behave himself, no obstacles would be placed in his way; but if he was contemplating any further misdeeds. . . . The official warning would be delivered thus and thus.

And now, within thirty seconds of his entering the cell, in the first sentence he had uttered, the smooth control of the situation which he had intended to usurp from the start was sliding out of his grasp. It had always been like that. Teal proposed and the Saint disposed. There was something about the insolent self-possession of that scapegrace buccaneer that goaded the detective into *faux pas* for which he was never afterwards able to account.

"As a matter of fact, old porpoise," said the Saint, "I came back for some cigarettes. You can't buy my favourite brand in France, and if you've ever endured a week of Marylands——"

Teal took a seat on the bunk.

"You left England in rather a hurry two months ago, didn't you?"

"I suppose I did," admitted the Saint reflectively. "You see, I felt like having a good bust, and you know what I am. Impetuous. I just upped and went."

"Pity you didn't stay."

The Saint's blue eyes gazed out banteringly from under dark level brows.

"Teal, is that kind? If you want to know, I was expecting a better reception than this. I was only thinking just now how upset

my solicitor would be when he heard about it. Poor old chap—
he's awfully sensitive about these things. When one of his respectable and valued clients comes home to his native land, and he
isn't allowed to move two hundred yards into the interior before
some flat-footed hick cop is lugging him off to the hoosegow for
no earthly reason——"

"Now you listen to me for a minute," Teal cut in bluntly. "I
didn't come here to swap any funny talk of that sort with you. I
came down to tell you how the Yard thinks you'd better behave
now you're home. You're going loose as soon as I've finished with
you, but if you want to stay loose you'll take a word of advice."

"Shall I?"

"That's up to you." The detective was plunging into his big
speech half an hour before it was due, but he was going to get it
through intact if it was the last thing he ever did. It was an amazing thing that even after the two months of comparative calm
which he had enjoyed since the Saint left England, the gall of
many defeats was as bitter on his tongue as it had ever been before. Perhaps he had a clairvoyant glimpse of the future, born out
of the deepest darkness of his subconscious mind, which told him
that he might as well have lectured a sun-spot about its pernicious
influence on the weather. The bland smiling composure of that
lean figure opposite him was fraying the edges of his nerves with
all the accumulated armoury of old associations. "I'm not
suggesting," Teal said tersely. "I'm prophesying."

The Saint acknowledged his authority with the faintest possible
flicker of one eyebrow—and yet the sardonic mockery of that
minute gesture was indescribable.

"Yeah?"

"I'm telling you to watch your step. We've put up with a good
deal from you in the past. You've been lucky. You even earned a
free pardon, once. Anyone would have thought you'd have been
content to retire gracefully after that. You had your own ideas.
But a piece of luck like that doesn't come twice in any man's lifetime. You'd made things hot enough for yourself when you went
away, and you needn't think they've cooled off just because you
took a short holiday. I'm not saying they mightn't cool off a bit if
you took a long one. We aren't out for any more trouble."

"Happy days," drawled the Saint, "are here again. Teal, in an-other minute you'll have me crying."

"You shouldn't have much to cry about," said the detective ag-gressively. "There's some excuse for the sneak-thief who goes on pulling five-pound jobs. He hasn't a chance to retire. You ought to have made a pretty good pile by this time——"

"About a quarter of a million," said the Saint modestly. "I admit it sounds a lot, but look at Rockefeller. He could spend that much every day."

"You've had a good run. I won't complain about it. You've done me some good turns on your way, and the Commissioner is willing to set that in your favour. Why not give the game a rest?"

The bantering blue eyes were surveying Teal steadily all the time he was speaking. Their expression was almost seraphic in its innocence—only the most captious critic, or the most over-wrought inferiority complex could have found anything to com-plain about in their elaborate sobriety. The Saint's face wore the register of a rapt student of theology absorbing wisdom from an archbishop.

And yet Chief Inspector Claud Eustace Teal felt his mouth drying up in spite of the soothing stimulus of spearmint. He had the numbing sensation of fatuity of a man who has embarked on a funny story in the hope of salvaging an extempore after-dinner speech that has been falling progressively flatter with every sen-tence, and who realises in the middle of it that it is not going to get a laugh. His own ears began to wince painfully at the awful dampness of the platitudes that were drooling inexplicably out of his own mouth. His voice sounded like the bleat of a lost sheep crying in the wilderness. He wished he had sent someone else to Newhaven.

"Let me know the worst," said the Saint. "What are you lead-ing up to? Is the Government proposing to offer me a pension and a seat in the House of Lords if I'll retire?"

"It isn't. It's offering you ten years' free board and lodging at Parkhurst if you don't. I shouldn't want you to make any mistake about it. If you think you're——"

Simon waved his hand.

"If you're not careful you'll be repeating yourself, Claud," he murmured. "Let me make the point for you. So long as I carry on like a little gentleman and go to Sunday School every week, your lordships will leave me alone. But if I should get back any of my naughty old ideas—if anyone sort of died suddenly while I was around, or some half-witted policeman lost sight of a packet of illicit diamonds and wanted to blame it on me—then it'll be the ambition of every dick in England to lead me straight to the Old Bailey. The long-suffering police of this great country are on their mettle. Britain has awoken. The Great Empire on which the sun never sets——"

"That's enough of that," yapped the detective.

He had not intended to yap. He should have spoken in a trenchant and paralysing baritone, a voice ringing with power and determination. Something went wrong with his larynx at the crucial moment.

He glared savagely at the Saint.

"I'd like to know your views," he said.

Simon Templar stood up. There were seventy-four steel inches of him, a long lazy uncoiling of easy strength and fighting vitality tapering down from wide square shoulders. The keen tanned face of a cavalier smiled down at Teal.

"Do you really want them, Claud?"

"That's what I'm here for."

"Then if you want the news straight from the stable, I think that speech of yours would be a knockout at the Mothers' Union." The Saint spread out his arms. "I can just see those kindly, wrinkled faces lighting up with the radiant dawn of a new hope—the tired souls wakening again to beauty——"

"Is that all you've got to say?"

"Very nearly, Claud. You see, your proposition doesn't tempt me. Even if it had included the pension and the peerage, I don't think I should have succumbed. It would make life so dull. I can't expect you to see my point, but there it is."

Teal also got to his feet, under the raking twinkle of those very clear blue eyes. There was something in their mockery which he had never understood, which perhaps he would never understand. And against that something which he could not understand his jaw tightened up in grim belligerence.

"Very well," he said. "You'll be sorry."

"I doubt it," said the Saint.

On the way back to London Teal thought of many more brilliant speeches which he could have made but he had not made any of them. He returned to Scotland Yard in a mood of undiluted acid, which the sarcastic comments of the Assistant Commissioner did nothing to mellow.

"To tell you the truth, sir, I never expected anything else," Teal said seriously. "The Saint's outside our province, and he always has been. I never imagined anyone could make me believe in the sort of story-book Raffles who goes in for crime for the fun of the thing, but in this case it's true. I've had it out with Templar before—privately. The plain fact is that he's in the game with a few high-falutin' ideas about a justice above the Law, and a lot of superfluous energy that he's got to get rid of somehow. If we put a psychologist on to him," expounded the detective, who had been reading Freud, "we should be told he'd got an Œdipus Complex. He has to break the law just because it is the law. If we made it illegal to go to church, he'd be heading a revivalist movement inside the week."

The Commissioner accepted the exposition with his characteristic sniff.

"I don't anticipate that the Home Secretary will approve of that method of curtailing the Saint's activities," he said. "Failing the adoption of your interesting scheme, I shall hold you personally responsible for Templar's behaviour."

It was an unsatisfactory day for Mr. Teal from every conceivable angle, for he was in the act of putting on his hat preparatory to leaving Scotland Yard that night when a report was brought to him which made his baby blue eyes open wide with sheer incredulous disgust.

He read the typewritten sheet three times before he had fully absorbed all the implications of it, and then he grabbed the telephone and put through a sulphurous call to the department responsible.

"Why the devil didn't you send me this report before?" he demanded.

"We only received it half an hour ago, sir," explained the offending clerk. "You know what these country police are."

Chief Inspector Claud Eustace Teal slammed back the receiver, and kept his opinion of those country police to himself. He knew very well what they were. The jealousy that exists between the provincial C.I.D.'s and Scotland Yard is familiar to anyone even remotely connected with matters of criminal investigation: on the whole, Teal could have considered himself fortunate in that the provincial office concerned had condescended to communicate with him at all on its own initiative, instead of leaving him to learn the news from a late evening paper.

He sat on in his tiny office for another hour, staring at the message which had filtered the last ray of sunshine out of his day. It informed him that a certain Mr. Wolseley Lormer had been held up in broad daylight in his office at Southend that afternoon and robbed of close on two thousand pounds by an intruder whom he never even saw. It would not have been a particularly remarkable crime by any standards if the caretaker who discovered the outrage had not also discovered a crude haloed figure chalked on the outer door of Mr. Lormer's suite. And the one immutable fact which Chief Inspector Teal could add to the information given him was that at the very time when the robbery was committed the Saint was safely locked up in Newhaven police station—and Mr. Teal was talking to him.

3

One of the charms of London, as against those of more up-to-date and scientific cities, is the multitude of queer little unscientific dwellings which may be found by the experienced explorer who wanders a mere hundred yards out of the broad regular thoroughfares and pries into the secrets of dilapidated alleys and unpromising courtyards. At some time in the more recent history of the city there must have been many adventurous souls who felt the urge to escape from the creeping development of modern steam-heated apartments planned with Euclidean exactitude and geometrically barren of all individuality. Wherever a few rooms with an eccentric entrance could be linked up and made comfortable, a home was established which in the days when there came a boom in such places was to repay a staggering percentage to the originality of its creators.

With his infallible instinct for these things, Simon Templar had
unearthed this very type of ideal home within a matter of hours
after he returned to London. His old stronghold in Upper Berke-
ley Mews which he had fitted up years ago with all the expensive
gadgets essential to a twentieth-century robber baron, had been
the centre of an undue amount of official curiosity just before
he embarked on his last hurried trip abroad. It no longer had any
ingenious secrets to conceal from the inquisitive hostility of Scotland Yard; and the Saint felt in the mood for a change of scene.
He found a suitable change in a quiet cul-de-sac off the lower
end of Queen's Gate, that broad tree-lined avenue which would
be a perfect counterpart of the most Parisian boulevard if its
taxis and inhabitants were less antique and moth-eaten. The home
of his choice was actually situated in a mews which ran across
the end of the cul-de-sac like the crossbar of a T, but some earlier tenant had arranged to combine respectability with a garage
on the premises, and had cut a street door and windows through
the blank wall that closed the cul-de-sac, so that the Saint's new
home was actually an attractive little two-storeyed cottage that
faced squarely down between the houses, while the garage and
mews aspect was discreetly hidden at the rear. It was almost perfectly adapted to the Saint's eccentric circumstances and strategic
requirements; and it is a notable fact that he was able to shift so
much lead out of the pants of the estate agents concerned that
he was fully installed in his new premises within forty-eight hours
of finding that they were to let, which anyone who has ever had
anything to do with London estate agents will agree was no mean
piece of lead-shifting.

Simon was personally supervising the unpacking of some complicated electrical apparatus when Mr. Teal found him at home
on the third day. He had not notified his change of address and it
had taken Mr. Teal some time to locate him; but the Saint's welcome was ingenuous cordiality itself.

"Make yourself at home, Claud," he murmured. "There's a new
packet of gum in the sitting-room, and I'll be with you in two
minutes."

He joined the detective punctually to a second, dusting some
wood shavings from his trousers, and there was nothing whatever
in his manner to indicate that he could anticipate any unpleas-

antness. He found Teal clasping his bowler hat across his stomach and gazing morosely at an unopened package of Wrigley's Three Star which sat up sedately in the middle of the table.

"I just came in," said the detective, "to tell you I liked your alibi."

"That was friendly of you," said the Saint calmly.

"What do you know about Lormer?"

Simon lighted a cigarette.

"Nothing except that he's a receiver of stolen goods, an occasional blackmailer, and a generally septic specimen of humanity. He's quite a small fish, but he's very nasty. Why?"

Teal ignored the question. He shifted a wad of gum meditatively round his mouth, and then swept the Saint's face with unexpectedly searching eyes.

"Your alibi is good enough," he said, "but I am still hoping to learn some more about your friends. You used to work with four of 'em, didn't you? I've often wondered how they all managed to reform so quickly."

The Saint smiled gently.

"Still the same old gang theory?" he drawled. "If I didn't know your playful ways so well, Claud, I'd be offended. It's not complimentary. You must find it hard to believe that so many remarkable qualities can be concentrated under one birth certificate, but as time goes on you may get used to the idea. I was quite a prodigy as a child. From the day when I stole the corsets off my old nannie——"

"If you're getting another gang together, or raking up the old lot," Teal said decisively, "we'll soon know all about it. What about that girl who used to be with you—Miss Holm, wasn't it? What's her alibi?"

"Does she want one? I expect it could be arranged."

"I expect it could. She landed at Croydon the day before we found you at Newhaven. I've only just learned that. Lormer never saw the man who knocked him out and emptied his safe, so just in case it wasn't a man at all——"

"I think you're on the wrong line," said the Saint genially. "After all, even a detective—has got to consider probabilities. In the old days, before all this vulgar publicity, I could put my trademark on every genuine article; but you must admit that times have changed. Now that every half-wit in the British Isles knows who I am, is it likely that if I contemplated any crimes I'd be such a fool as to draw Saints all over 'em? D'you think you could make any jury believe it? I've got a reputation, Claud. I may be wicked, but I'm not waffy. It's obvious that some crook is trying to push his stuff on to me."

Teal hitched himself ponderously out of his chair.

"I had thought of that argument," he said; and then, abruptly: "What's your next job going to be?"

"I haven't decided yet," said the Saint coolly. "Whatever it is, it'll be a corker. I feel that I could do with some good headlines."

"Do you think you're playing the game?"

Simon looked at the detective thoughtfully.

"I suppose my exploits don't improve your standing with the Commissioner. Isn't that it?"

The detective nodded.

"You make it very difficult for us," he said.

He could have said a lot more. Pride kept it back stubbornly behind his official detachment, but the sober glance which he gave the Saint was as near to a confession as he dared to go. It was not in his nature to ask favours of any man.

"I'll have to see what I can do," said the Saint.

He ushered Teal courteously to the door, and opened it to see a slim fair-haired vision of a girl walking up the road towards them. Teal watched her approach with narrowed and expressionless eyes.

The girl reached the door and smiled at him sweetly.

"Good-morning," she said.

"Good-morning," said Teal acridly.

He settled his hat and stepped brusquely past her; and Simon Templar closed the front door and caught the girl in his arms.

"Pat, old darling," he said, "I feel that life has begun all over again. With you around, and Claud Eustace dropping in every other day to have words. . . . If we could only find someone to murder it'd just be perfect!"

Patricia Holm walked into the sitting-room and pulled off her hat. She helped herself to a cigarette from his case and surveyed him with a little smile.

"Don't you think there might be a close season for Teals? I'll

never forget how it was when we left England. I hated you, boy—
the way you baited him."

"It's a rough game," said the Saint quietly. "But I haven't
baited him this time—not yet. The trouble is that the Ass. Com.
holds poor old Claud personally responsible for our brilliance. It
was a brain-wave of yours to raid Lormer directly you found I
was in clink, but that alibi won't work twice. And Teal's just
building up a real case. We'll have to be very careful. Anyway,
we won't murder anyone in public. . . ."

When the Saint went out that afternoon he carried a conspicuously large white envelope in his hand. At the corner of the cul-
de-sac there was a big man patiently manicuring his nails with a
pocket-knife. Simon posted his envelope in full view of the
watcher, and afterwards suffered himself to be painstakingly
shadowed through a harmless shopping expedition in the West
End.

Late that night a certain Mr. Ronald Nilder, whose agency for
vaudeville artists was not above suspicion, received a brief letter
in a large white envelope. It stated quite simply that unless he
made a five-figure donation to the Actors' Orphanage within the
week his relatives might easily suffer an irreparable bereavement;
and it was signed with the Saint's trade-mark. Mr. Nilder, a
public-spirited citizen, immediately rang up the police. Chief Inspector Teal saw him and later had another interview with the
Assistant Commissioner.

"Templar posted a large white envelope yesterday," he said,
"but we can't prove it was the one Nilder received. If I know anything about the Saint, Nilder will get a follow-up message in a
day or two, and we may be able to catch Templar red-handed."

His diagnosis of Saintly psychology proved to be even shrewder
than he knew.

For the next couple of days Simon was busy with the work of
adding to the comfortable furnishings of his house a selection of
electrical devices of his own invention. They were of a type that
he had never expected to find included in the fixtures and fittings
of any ordinary domicile, but he considered them eminently necessary to his safety and peace of mind. He employed no workmen, for workmen are no less inclined to gossip than anyone
else, and the kind of installations which were the Saint's speciality

would have been a fruitful source of conversation to anyone. Wherefore the Saint worked energetically alone, and considered his job well done when at the end of it there were no signs of his activity to be found without a very close investigation. The watcher at the end of the cul-de-sac manicured his nails ceaselessly and had many enjoyable walks at the Saint's heels whenever Simon went out. Simon christened him Fido and became resigned to him as a permanent feature of the landscape.

It was near the end of the week when Simon emerged from his front door with another conspicuously large white envelope similar to the first tucked under his arm; and the plain-clothes man who had definite instructions, closed his penknife with a snap and stepped forward as the Saint came abreast of him.

"Excuse me, sir," he said punctiliously. "May I have a look at your letter?"

The Saint stared at him.

"And who might you be?"

"I'm a police officer," said the man firmly.

"Then why are you wearing an Old Etonian tie?" asked the Saint.

He allowed the envelope to be taken out of his hand. It was addressed to Mr. Ronald Nilder, and the detective ripped it open. Inside he found a flexible gramophone disc, and somewhat to his amazement the label in the centre bore the name of Chief Inspector Teal.

"You'd better come along with me," said the detective.

They went in a taxi to Walton Street police station: and there, after some delay, a gramophone was produced and the record solemnly mounted on the turntable.

The plain-clothes man, the Divisional Inspector, the sergeant on duty, and two constables gathered round to listen. Chief Inspector Teal had already been called on the telephone, and the transmitter was placed close to the gramophone for a limited broadcast. Someone set the needle in its groove and started it off.

"Hullo, everybody," said the disc, in a cracked voice. "This is Chief Inspector Claud Eustace Teal speaking from Scotland Yard. The subject of my lecture to-day is 'How to Catch Criminals Red-Handed'—a subject on which my experience must be almost unique. From the day when I captured Jack the Ripper to the day when I arrested the Saint, my career has been nothing but a series of historic triumphs. Armed with a bottle of red ink, and my three faithful red herrings, Metro, Goldwyn and Mayer, I have never failed to reduce my hands to the requisite colour. Although for many years I suffered from bad legs, eczema, boils, halitosis, superfluous hair, and bunions——"

Simon gave Patricia a graphic account of the incident when he met her at lunch time.

"It was not Teal-baiting," he insisted. "It was a little deed of kindness—a little act of love. After all, is it right that Claud should be encouraged to prod his nose into my private correspondence? If we let him run amok like that, one day he might go too far. We have warned him off for his own good."

They celebrated suitably; and it was late that night when they returned home for a final plate of bacon and eggs before calling it a day. Simon paid off the taxi in Queen's Gate, and they walked up to the house together. The watcher at the corner of the road had gone—the Saint had not expected that Teal would urge him to stay on after that home-made gramophone record had been played.

It was so soon after he had finished installing his electric safety devices that Simon had not even started to anticipate results from them—they were provided for the more strenuous days which he hoped to enjoy before very long, when his return became more widely known and many more guilty consciences began to ask themselves whether their subterranean industries might prosper better if Simon Templar were removed from the catalogue of risks which no insurance company would cover. He had the front door key in his hand before he remembered that the latest product of his defensive genius was now in full working order. Quite casually he slid up a small metal panel under the knocker; and then his face went keen and hard. A tiny bulb set in the woodwork under the panel was glowing red.

Simon dropped the shutter over it again, and drew Patricia aside.

"We've had a visitor," he said. "I didn't think the fun would begin quite so soon."

There was nothing to show whether the visitor had taken his departure. Only one thing was certain—that someone or something had passed across the barrage of invisible alarms that Simon had arranged to cover every door and window in the place. The visitor might have left, but Simon was not disposed to bet on it.

He stood well to the side of the doorway, sheltered by the solid brickwork of the wall, while he reached round and slipped his key soundlessly into the lock at arm's length. Still keeping out of sight, he pushed the door softly back and felt under the jamb for the electric light switch. There was a flicker of fire and a deafening report; and then the light came on and Simon leapt through into the hall. He heard a patter of feet and the slam of a door, and raced through the kitchen to the back entrance on the mews. He got the door open in time to see a running figure fling itself into the back of an open car which was already speeding towards the street, and a second shot came from it before it turned out of the mews. The bullet flew wide and smacked into the wall; and Simon grinned gently and went back to Patricia Holm.

"There's one gunman in London who loses his nerve rather easily, which is just as well for us," he remarked. "But I wonder who it was?"

Curiously enough he had almost forgotten the man named Jones, who had done such an unfriendly thing to Brian Quell that night in Paris.

4

There were no further demonstrations of disapproval that night, although the Saint paid particular attention to the setting of his gadgets before he went to bed, and slept with one ear cocked. He came down to breakfast late the next morning, and was confronted by a shining little cylinder of brass in the middle of his plate. For a moment he stared at it puzzledly, and then he laughed.

"A souvenir?" he murmured, and Patricia nodded.

"I found it in the hall, and I thought you might like to put it in your museum."

Simon spread his napkin cheerfully.

"More 'Weapons I Have Not Been Killed With'?" he suggested.

"There must be quite a trunkful of them." He reached out a hand towards the cartridge case, and then drew it back. "Wait a minute —just how did you pick this thing up?"

"Why—I don't know. I——"

"Surely you can remember. Think for a minute. I want you to show me exactly how you took hold of it, how you handled it, everything that happened to it between the time when you saw it on the carpet and the time when it reached this plate. . . . No— don't touch it again. Use a cigarette."

The girl took up the cigarette endways between her thumb and forefinger.

"That's all I did," she said. "I had the plate in my other hand, and I brought it straight in. Why do you want to know?"

"Because all clever criminals wear gloves when they open safes, but very few of them wear gloves when they're loading a gun." Simon picked up the shell delicately in his handkerchief, rubbed the base carefully where the girl's thumb had touched it, and dropped it into an empty match-box. "Thanks to your fastidious handling, we probably have here some excellent finger-prints of a rotten marksman—and one never knows when they might come in handy."

He returned to a plate of sizzling bacon and eggs with the profound gusto of a man who has slept like a child and woken up like a lion. Patricia allowed him to eat and skim through his morning paper in peace. Whatever schemes and theories were floating through his mercurial imagination, he would never have expounded them before his own chosen time; and she knew better than to try and drag them out of him before he had dealt satisfactorily with his fast.

He was stirring his second cup of coffee when the telephone bell roused him from a fascinating description of the latest woman Atlantic flier's underwear. He reached out a long arm, lifted the receiver, and admitted fearlessly that he was Mr. Simon Templar.

"I trust you are well," said the telephone.

The Saint raised his eyebrows, and felt around for a cigarette.

"I'm very fit, thanks," he said. "How are you? And if it comes to that, who are you?"

A deep chuckle reached him from the other end of the line.

"So long as you don't interfere with me, that need not concern you. I'm sorry that you should have had such an unpleasant shock last night, but if my envoy had kept his head you would have felt nothing at all. On the other hand, his foolishness might still encourage you to accept a friendly warning."

"That's very kind of you," said the Saint thoughtfully. "But I've already got someone to see that my socks are aired, and I always take care not to get my feet wet——"

"I'm talking about more dangerous things than colds, Mr. Templar."

Simon's gaze fell on the sheet of newspaper which he had been reading. Two columns away from the inventory of the lady aviator's wardrobe he saw a headline that he had not noticed before: and the germ of an inspiration suddenly flashed through his mind. "ANOTHER 'SAINT' THREAT," ran the heading of the column, in large black letters; and below it was an account of the letter that had been received by Mr. Ronald Nilder. . . . Patricia was watching him anxiously, but he waved her to silence.

"Dear me! Are you such a dangerous man—Mr. Jones?"

There was a long pause; and the Saint's lips twitched in a faint smile. It had been a shot clear into the dark; but his mind worked like that—flashing on beyond the ordinarily obvious to the fantastically far-fetched that was always so gloriously right.

"My congratulations." The voice on the line was scarcely strained. "How much did Quell tell you?"

"Plenty," said the Saint softly. "I'm sorry you should have had such an unpleasant shock, but if you had kept your head . . ."

He heard the receiver click down at the other end, and pushed the telephone away from him.

"Who was that?" asked Patricia.

"Someone who can think nearly as fast as I can," said the Saint, with a certain artistic admiration. "We know him only as Mr. Jones—the man who shot Brian Quell. And it was one of his pals who disturbed the peace last night." The gay blue eyes levelled themselves on her with the sword-steel intentness that she knew of old. "Shall I tell you about him? He's a rather clever man. He discovered that I was staying in the hotel that night—on Quell's floor, with my window almost opposite his across the well. But he didn't know that before he did his stuff—otherwise he might have thought up something even cleverer. How he found out is more than we know. He may have accidentally seen my name in the register, or he may even have come back for something and listened outside Quell's door—then he'd made inquiries to find out who it could have been. But when he got back to England he heard more about me———"

"How?"

"From the story of your noble assault on Wolseley Lormer. Brother Jones decided to take no chances—hence last night. Also this morning there was another dose for him."

Simon pointed to the headlines that he had seen. It was while Patricia was glancing over them that a name in an adjoining paragraph caught his eye, and he half rose from his chair.

"And that!" His finger stabbed at the news item. "Pat—he can certainly think fast!"

He read the paragraph.

University Professor Missing

SEQUEL TO PARIS SHOOTING TRAGEDY

Birmingham, Thursday.

Loss of memory is believed to be the cause of the mysterious disappearance of Dr. Sylvester Quell, professor of electro-chemistry, who has been missing for twenty-four hours.

The professor's housekeeper, Mrs. E. J. Lane, told a *Daily Express* representative that Dr. Quell left his house as usual at 10:30 A.M. on Wednesday to walk to his lecture-room. He did not arrive there, and he has not been heard of since.

"The professor was very upset by his brother's sudden death," said Mrs. Lane. "He spoke very little about it, but I know that it affected him deeply."

Dr. Quell is acknowledged to be one of the foremost authorities on metallurgy——

Simon sprang out of his chair and began to pace up and down the room.

"Think it out from the angle of Comrade Jones. He knows I was in a position to know something—he knows my reputation—and he knows I'm just the man to pry into his business without saying a word to the police. Therefore he figures I'd be better out of the way. He's a wise guy, Pat—but just a little too wise. A real professional would have bumped me off and said nothing about it. If he failed the first time he'd've just tried again—and still said nothing. But instead of that he had to phone me and tell me about it. Believe it or not, Pat, the professional only does that sort of thing in story-books. Unless——"

"Unless what?" prompted the girl.

The Saint picked up his cigarette from the edge of the ashtray, and fell into his chair again with a slow laugh.

"I wonder! If there's anything more dangerous than being just that little bit too clever, it's being in too much of a hurry to say that very thing of the other man. There's certainly some energetic vendetta going on against the Quell family, and since I've been warned to keep out I shall naturally have to be there."

"Not to-day, if you don't mind," said the girl calmly. "I met Marion Lestrange in Bond Street yesterday, and I promised to drop in for a cocktail this evening."

Simon looked at her.

"I think it might happen about then," he said. "Don't be surprised if you hear my melodious voice on the telephone."

"What are you going to do?" she asked; and the Saint smiled.

"Almost nothing," he said.

He kept her in suspense for the rest of the afternoon, while he smoked innumerable cigarettes and tried to build up a logical story out of the snatches of incoherent explanation that Brian Quell had babbled before he died. It was something about a man called Binks, who could make gold. . . . But no consecutive sense seemed to emerge from it. Dr. Sylvester Quell might have been interested—and he had disappeared. The Saint could get no further than his original idea.

He told Patricia Holm about it at tea-time. It will be remembered that in those days the British Government was still pompously deliberating whether it should take the reckless step of repealing an Act of 1677 which no one obeyed anyhow, and the Saint's feelings on the matter had been finding their outlet in verse when the train of his criminal inspiration faltered. He produced the more enduring fruits of his afternoon's cogitation with some pride.

"Wilberforce Egbert Levi Gupp
Was very, very well brought up,
Not even in his infant crib
Did he make messes on his bib,
Or ever, in his riper years
Forget to wash behind his ears.
Trained from his rawest youth to rule
(At that immortal Public School
Whose playing fields have helped to lose
Innumerable Waterloos),
His brains, his wit, his chin, were all
Infinitesimal,
But (underline the vital fact)
He was the very soul of tact,
And never in his innocence
Gave anyone the least offence:
Can it be wondered at that he
Became, in course of time, M.P."

"Has that got anything to do with your Mr. Jones?" asked Patricia patiently.

"Nothing at all," said the Saint. "It's probably far more important. Posterity will remember Wilberforce Gupp long after Comrade Jones is forgotten. Listen to some more:

"Robed in his faultless morning dress
They voted him a huge success;
The sober drabness of the garb
Fittingly framed the pukka sahib;
And though his many panaceas
Show no original ideas,
Gupp, who could not be lightly baulked,
Just talked, and talked, and talked, and talked,
Until the parliamentary clan
Prophesied him a coming man."

"I seem to have heard something in the same strain before," the girl remarked.

"You probably have," said the Saint. "And you'll probably hear it again. So long as there's ink in my pen, and I can make two words rhyme, and this country is governed by the largest collection of soft-bellied half-wits and doddering grandmothers on earth, I shall continue to castigate its imbecilities—whenever I have time to let go a tankard of old ale. I have not finished with Wilberforce."

"Shall I be seeing you after I leave Marion's?" she asked; and the Saint was persuaded to put away the sheet of paper on which he had been scribbling and tell her something which amazed her.

He expounded a theory which anyone else would have advanced hesitantly as a wild and delirious guess with such vivid conviction that her incredulity wavered and broke in the first five minutes. And after that she listened to him with her heart beating a little faster, helplessly caught up in the simple audacity of his idea. When he put it to her as a question she knew that there was only one answer.

"Wouldn't you say it was worth trying, old Pat? We can only be wrong—and if we are it doesn't cost a cent. If we're right——"

"I'll be there."

She went out at six o'clock with the knowledge that if his theory was right they were on the brink of an adventure that would have startled the menagerie of filleted young men and sophisticated young women whom she had promised to help to entertain. It might even have startled a much less precious audience, if she had felt disposed to talk about it; but Patricia Holm was oblivious of audiences—in which attitude she was the most drastic possible antithesis of Simon Templar. Certainly none of the celebrated or nearly celebrated prodigies with whom it pleased Marion Lestrange to crowd her drawing-room once a month would have believed that the girl who listened so sympathetically to their tedious autobiographies was the partner in crime of the most notorious buccaneer of modern times.

The cocktail party ploughed on through a syrupy flood of mixed alcohols, mechanical compliments, second-hand scandal, vapid criticism, lisps, beards, adolescent philosophy and personal pronouns. Patricia attended with half her mind, while the other half wondered why the egotism which was so delightful and spellbinding in the Saint should be so nauseatingly flatulent in the assorted hominoids around her. She watched the hands of her wrist-

watch creep round to seven and seven-thirty, and wondered if the
Saint could have been wrong.

It was ten minutes to eight when her hostess came and told her
that she was wanted on the telephone.

"Is that you, Pat?" said the Saint's voice. "Listen—I've had the
most amazing luck. I can't tell you about it now. Can you get
away?"

The girl felt a cold tingle run up her spine.

"Yes—I can come now. Where are you?"

"I'm at the May Fair. Hop into a taxi and hurry along—I'll
wait for you in the lounge."

She pulled on her hat and coat with a feeling somewhere between fear and elation. The interruption had come so exactly as
the Saint had predicted it that it seemed almost uncanny. And the
half-dozen bare and uninformative sentences that had come
through the receiver proved beyond doubt that the mystery was
boiling up for an explosion that only Simon Templar would have
gone out of his way to interview at close quarters. As she ran
down the stairs, the fingers of her right hand ran over the invisible outlines of a hard squat shape that was braced securely under
her left arm, and the grim contact gave her back the old
confidence of other dangerous days.

A taxi came crawling along the kerb as she stepped out into
Cavendish Square, and she waved to it and climbed in. The cab
pulled out again with a jerk; and it was then that she noticed that
the glass in the windows was blackened, and was protected
against damage from the inside by a closely-woven mesh of steel
wire.

She leaned forward and felt around in the darkness for a
doorhandle. Her fingers encountered only a smooth metal plate
secured over the place where the handle should have been; and
she knew that the man who called himself Jones was no less fast
a thinker, and not one whit less efficient, than Simon Templar
had diagnosed him to be.

5

Simon Templar refuelled his Duofold and continued with the biography of the coming politician.

> *And down the corridors of fame*
> *Wilberforce Egbert duly came.*
> *His human kindness knew no bounds:*
> *Even when hunting with the hounds*
> *He always had a thought to spare*
> *For the poor little hunted hare;*
> *But manfully he set his lips*
> *And did the bidding of the Whips.*
> *And though at times his motives would*
> *Be cruelly misunderstood,*
> *Wilberforce plodded loyally on*
> *Like a well-bred automaton*
> *Till 1940, when the vote*
> *Placed the Gupp party in the boat,*
> *And Wilberforce assumed the helm*
> *And laboured to defend the realm.*

Simon glanced at his watch, meditated for a few moments, and continued:

> *And through those tense and tedious days*
> *Wilberforce gambolled (in his stays);*
> *The general public got to know*
> *That Gupp, who never answered "No,"*
> *Could be depended on to give*
> *Deft answers in the negative;*
> *And Royal Commissions by the score*
> *Added to Wisdom's bounteous store:*
> *The Simple Foods Commission found*
> *That turnips still grow underground;*
> *The Poultry Farms Commission heard*
> *That turkeys were a kind of bird;*
> *While in an office in the City*

The Famous Vicious Drugs Committee
Sat through ten epic calendars
To learn if women smoked cigars;
And with the help Gupp's party gave
Britannia proudly ruled the wave
(Reported to be wet—but see
Marine Commission, section D.)

It was nearly seven o'clock when the Saint started his car and cruised leisurely eastwards through the Park. He had a sublime faith in his assessment of time limits, and his estimate of Mr. Jones's schedule was almost uncannily exact. He pulled up in the south-west corner of Cavendish Square, from which he could just see the doorway of the Lestranges' house, and prepared himself for a reasonable wait.

He was finishing his third cigarette when a brand-new taxi turned into the square and snailed past the doorway he was watching. It reached the north-east corner, accelerated down the east side and along the south, and resumed its dawdling pace as it turned north again. The Saint bent over a newspaper as it passed him; and when he looked up again the blue in his eyes had the hard glitter of sapphires. Patricia was standing in the doorway; and he knew that Mr. Jones was beyond all doubt a fast mover.

Simon sat and watched the girl hail the taxi; and climb in. The cab picked up speed rapidly; and Simon touched his self-starter and hurled the great silver Hirondel smoothly after it.

The taxi swung away to the north and plunged into the streaming traffic of the Marylebone Road. It had a surprising turn of speed for a vehicle of its type; and the Saint was glad that he could claim to have the legs of almost anything on the road. More than once it was only the explosive acceleration of its silent hundred horse-power that saved him from being jammed in a tangle of slow-moving traffic which would have wrecked his scheme irretrievably. He clung to the taxi's rear number-plate like a hungry leech, snaking after it past buses, drays, lorries, private cars of every size and shape under the sun, westwards along the main road and then to the right around the Baker Street Crossing, following every twist of his unconscious quarry as faithfully as if he had been merely steering a trailer linked to it by an invisible steel coupling. It was the only possible method of making certain that no minor accident of the route could leave him sandwiched behind while the taxi slipped round a corner and vanished for ever; and the Saint concentrated on it with an ice-cold singleness of purpose that shut every other thought out of his head, driving with every trick of the road that he knew and an inexorable determination to keep his radiator nailed to a point in space precisely nine inches aft of the taxi's hind-quarters.

There was always the risk that his limpet-like attachment would attract the attention of the driver of the taxi, but it was a risk that had to be ignored. Fortunately it was growing dark rapidly after a dull and rainy afternoon; they raced up the Finchley Road in a swiftly deepening dusk, and as they passed Swiss Cottage Underground the Saint took the first chance of the chase—fell far behind the taxi, switched on his lights, tore after it again, and picked up the red glow-worm eye of its tail light after thirty breathless seconds. That device might have done something to allay any possible suspicions; and the lights of one car look very much like the lights of any other when the distinctive features of its coachwork are hidden behind the diffused rays of a few statutory candlepower.

So far the procession had led him through familiar highways; but a little while after switching on his lights he was practically lost. His bump of locality told him that they were somewhere to the east of the Finchley Road and heading roughly north; but the taxi in front of him whizzed round one corner after another until his bearings were boxed all round the compass, and the names of streets which occasionally flashed past the tail of his eye were unknown to him.

Presently they were running down a broad avenue of large houses set well back from the road, and the taxi ahead was slowing up. In a moment of intuitive understanding, the Saint held his own speed and shot past it; keeping the cab in his driving mirror, he saw it turning in through a pair of gates set in a high garden wall twenty yards behind him.

Simon locked his wheels round the next corner and pulled up dead. In a second he was out of the car and walking quickly back towards the driveway into which the taxi had disappeared.

He strolled quietly past the gates and took in as much of the lie

of the land as he could in one searching survey under the slanted
brim of his hat. The house was a massively gloomy three-storeyed
edifice in the most pompous Georgian style, reminiscent of a fat
archdeacon suffering an attack of liver with rhinoscerine forti-
tude; and the only light visible on that side of it was a pale pink
bulb that hung in the drab portico like a forlorn plum in an orchard that the pickers have finished with. The neglected front garden was dappled with the shadows of a few laurel bushes and
unkempt flower-beds. Of the taxi there was no sign; but a dim
nimbus of light was discernible beyond the shrubbery on the
right.

The Saint's leisured step eased up gradually and reached a
standstill. After all, Mr. Jones was the man he wanted to meet:
this appeared to be Mr. Jones's headquarters: and there were no
counter-attractions in the way of night life to be seen in that part
of Hampstead. The main idea suffered no competition; and a
shrewd glance up and down the road revealed no other evening
prowlers to notice what happened.

Simon dropped his hands into his pockets and grinned gently at
the stars.

"Here goes," he murmured.

The dense shadows inside the garden swallowed him up like a
ghost. A faint scraping of gears came to him as he skirted a
clump of laurels and padded warily along the grass border of a
part of the drive which circled round towards the regions where
he had seen the light; and he rounded the corner of the house in
time to see the taxi's stern gliding through the doors of a garage
that was built on to the side of Mr. Jones's manor. Simon halted
again, and stood like a statue while he watched a vague figure
scrunch out of the darkness and pull the doors shut behind the
cab—from the inside. He surmised that there was a direct communication from the garage through into the house, but he heard
a heavy bolt grating into its socket as he drew nearer to investigate.

The Saint sidled on past the garage to the back of the house
and waited. After a time he saw two parallel slits of subdued radi-
ance blink out around the edges of a drawn blind in a first-floor
window; they were no more than hair-lines of almost imper-

ceptible luminance etched in the blackness of the wall, but they were enough to give him the information he needed.

Down on the ground level, almost opposite where he stood, he made out another door—obviously a kitchen entrance for the convenience of servants, tradesmen, and policemen with ten minutes to spare and a sheik-like style with cooks. He moved forward and ran his fingers over it cautiously. A gentle pressure here and there told him that it was not bolted and he felt in his pocket for a slim pack of skeleton keys. At the third attempt the heavy wards turned solidly over and Simon replaced the keys in his pocket and pushed the door inwards by fractions of an inch, with the blade of his penknife pressing against the point where it would first be able to slip through. He checked the movement of the door at the instant when his knife slid into the gap, and ran the blade delicately up and down the minute opening. At the very base of the door it encountered an obstruction; and the Saint flicked the burglar alarm aside with a neat twist and an inaudible sigh of satisfaction, and stepped in.

Standing on the mat, with his back to the closed door, he put away the knife and snapped a tiny electric flashlight from its clip in his breast pocket. It was no longer than a fountain pen, and a scrap of tinfoil with a two-millimetre puncture in it was gummed over the bulb so that the beam it sent out was as fine as a needle. A three-inch ellipse of concentrated light wisked along the wall beside him, and rounded itself off into a perfect circle as it came to rest on another door facing the one by which he had entered.

Simon Templar's experience as a burglar was strictly limited. On the rare occasions when he had unlawfully introduced himself into the houses of his victims, it had nearly always been in quest of information rather than booty. And he set out to explore the abode of the man called Jones with the untainted zest of a man to whom the crime was still an adventure.

With one hand still resting lightly on the side pocket of his coat he opened the opposite door soundlessly and admitted himself to a large dimly illuminated central hall. A broad marble staircase wound up and around the sides of the hall, climbing from gallery to gallery up the three floors of the house until it was indistinguishable against the great shrouded emptiness of what was probably an ornate stained-glass skylight in the roof. Everything around was wrapped in the silence of death, and the atmosphere had the damply naked feel of air that has not been breathed for many months. A thin smear of dust came off on his fingers from everything he touched; and when he flashed his torch over the interior of one of the ground-floor rooms he found it bare and dilapidated, with the paint peeling off the walls and cobwebs festooning an enormous dingy gilt chandelier.

"Rented for the job," he diagnosed. "They wouldn't bother about the ground floor at all—not with kidnapped prisoners."

He flitted up the staircase without so much as a tap from his feather-weight crêpe-soled shoes. A strip of cheap carpet had been roughly laid round the gallery which admitted to the first-floor rooms; and the Saint walked softly over it, listening at door after door.

Then he heard with startling clarity, a voice that he recognised.

"You have nothing to be afraid of, Miss Holm, so long as you behave yourself. I'm sorry to have had to take the liberty of abducting you, but you doubtless know one or two reasons why I must discourage your friend's curiosity."

He heard the girl's calm reply:

"I think you could have invented a less roundabout way of committing suicide."

The man's bass chuckle answered her. Perhaps only the Saint's ears could have detected the iron core of ruthless menace that hardened the overtones of its full-throated heartiness.

"I'm glad you're not hysterical." A brief pause. "If there's anything within reason that you want, I hope you'll ask for it. Are you feeling hungry?"

"Thanks," said the girl coolly. "I should like a couple of sausages, some potatoes, and a cup of coffee."

Simon darted along the gallery and whipped open the nearest door. Through the gap which he left open he saw a heavily-built grey-haired man emerge from the next room, lock the door after him, and go down the stairs. As the man bent to the key, the Saint had a photographic impression of a dark, large-featured, smooth-shaven face; then he could only see the broad well-tailored back passing downwards out of view.

The man's footsteps died away; and Simon returned to the

landing. He stood at the door of Patricia's room and tapped softly on the wood with his fingernails.

"Hullo, Pat!"

Her dress rustled inside the room.

"Quick work, boy. How did you do it?"

"Easy. Are you all right?"

"Sure."

"How's the window in there?"

"There's a sort of cage over it—I couldn't reach the glass. The taxi was the same. There's a divan bed and a couple of wicker arm-chairs. The table's very low—the legs wouldn't reach through the bars. He's thought of everything. Wash-basin and jug of water on the floor—some towels—cigarettes——"

"What happened to the taxi-driver?"

"That was Mr. Jones."

The Saint drew a thoughtful breath.

"Phew! And what a solo worker! . . . Can you hold on for a bit? I'd like to explore the rest of the establishment before I start any trouble."

"Go ahead, old chap. I'm fine."

"Still got your gun?"

"Sure."

"So long, lass."

The Saint tip-toed along the landing and prowled up the second flight of stairs.

6

There were no lights burning on the upper gallery, but a dull glimmer of twilight flittered up from the lamps below and relieved the darkness sufficiently for him to be able to move as quickly as he wanted to. With his slim electric flash in his hand he went around the storey from room to room, turning the door-handles with infinite care, and probing the apartments with the dancing beam of his torch. The first one he opened was plainly but comfortably furnished as a bedroom: it was evidently occupied, for the bed had not been made since it was last slept in, and a shav-

ing brush crested with a mound of dried lather stood on the mantelpiece. The second room was another bedroom, tidier than the
first, but showing the ends of a suit of silk pyjamas under the pil-
low as proof that it also was used. The door of the third room
was locked; and Simon delved in his pocket again for a skeleton
key. The lock was of the same type as that on the back door by
which he had entered the house—one of those ponderously use-
less contraptions which any cracksman can open with a bent pin
—and in a second or two it gave way.

Simon pushed the door ajar, and saw that the room was in
darkness. He stepped boldly in, quartering the room with his
weaving pencil of light. The flying disc of luminance danced
along the walls and suddenly stopped, splashing itself in an irregular pool over the motionless form of a man who lay quietly on
the floor as if asleep. But the Saint knew that he was dead.

He knelt down and made a rapid examination. The man had
been dead about forty-eight hours—there was no trace of a
wound but with his face close to the dead man's mouth he detected the unmistakable scent of prussic acid. It was as he was rising to go that he accidentally turned over the lapel of the dead
man's coat, and saw the thin silver badge underneath—the silver
greyhound of a King's Messenger.

The Saint came to his feet again rather slowly. The waters were
running deeper than he had ever expected, and he felt an odd
sense of shock. That slight silver badge had transformed the adventure at one glance from a more or less ordinary if still mysterious criminal problem to an intrigue that might lead anywhere.

As he left the room he heard the man called Jones coming up
the stairs again. Peeping over the wooden balustrade, he saw that
the man carried a tray—the catering arrangements in that house
appeared to be highly commendable, even if nothing else was.

Simon slipped along the gallery without a sound. He opened
two more rooms and found them both empty; then he paused outside another and saw a narrow line of light under the door.

He stood still for a few seconds, listening. He heard an occasional faint chink of glass or metal, and the shuffling of slippered
feet over the carpet; but there were no voices. Almost mechanically he tried the door, and had one of the biggest surprises of his
life when he felt it opening.

The Saint froze up motionless, with a dry electric tingle glissading over the surface of his skin. The way the door gave back under his light touch disintegrated the very ground from under his nebulous theory about the occupant of that room. In the space of four seconds his brain set up, surveyed, and bowled over a series of possible explanations that were chiefly notable for their complete uselessness. In the fifth second that ultimate fact impressed itself unanswerably on his consciousness, and he acknowledged it with a wry shrug and the decimal point of a smile. Theories were all very well in their place; but he had come to the house of Mr. Jones on a quest for irrefutable knowledge, and an item of irrefutable knowledge was awaiting his attention inside that room. It remained for him to go in and get introduced—and that was what he had given up a peaceful evening in his own home to do.

He glanced downwards into the hall. There was no sound or movement from below. For a minute or two he might consider he had the field to himself—if he was quick and quiet about taking it over.

The door of the lighted room opened further, inch by inch, against the steady persuasion of his fingers, while his nerves were keyed up to check its swing at the first faint hint of a squeak out of the hinges. Gradually the strip of light at the edge widened until he could see part of the room. A grotesque confusion of metal and glass, tangled up with innumerable strands and coils of wire, was heaped over all the floor space that he could see like the scrap-heap of one of those nightmare laboratories of the future which appear in every magazine of pseudo-scientific fiction. The Saint's unscientific mind could grasp nothing but the bare visual impression of it—an apparently aimless conglomeration of burnished steel spheres and shining crystal tubes that climbed in and out of each other like a futurist sculptor's rendering of two all-in wrestlers getting acquainted. Back against the far wall ran a long work-bench of wood and porcelain surmounted by racks and shelves of glass vessels and bottles of multi-coloured mixtures. It was the most fantastic collection of incomprehensible apparatus that Simon Templar had ever seen; and yet in some ridiculously conventional way it seemed to have its perfect focus and presiding genius in the slender white-haired man in a stained and grimy white overall who stood at the bench with his back to the open door.

Simon Templar walked very quietly into the room and closed the door noiselessly behind him. He stood with his back leaning against it and his right hand circling comfortably round the butt of the automatic in his pocket, and cleared his throat apologetically.

"Hullo," he said.

The figure at the bench turned round sharply. He was a mild-faced man with a pair of thick gold-rimmed *pince-nez* perched slantwise on the end of a long fleshy nose; and his response was pitched in the last key on earth that the Saint had expected to hear.

"What the devil do you want?" he demanded.

To say that the Saint was taken aback means nothing. The effect on his emotional system was much the same as it would have been if the aged scientist had uttered a shrill war-whoop and begun to turn cartwheels over the test-tubes. Even in these days of free thought and speech the greeting seemed singularly unusual. When you have been at considerable pains, without appreciable hope of reward, to hunt along the trail of a kidnapped professor—when, in the process, you have been warned off the course with a couple of bullets, and have found it necessary to let yourself in for a charge of vulgar burglary in the good cause— you are definitely entitled to expect a fairly cordial welcome from the object of your rescue expedition.

Once before the Saint had been greeted something like that in rather similar circumstances, and the memory of that adventure was still fresh with him. It cut short the involuntary upward jerk of his eyebrows; and when he found an answer his voice was absolutely level and natural. Only an ear that was listening for it would have sensed the rapier points that stroked in and out of its casual syllables.

"I just came to see how you were getting on, Dr. Quell."

"Well, why can't you leave me alone? How do you expect me to get any work done while I'm being pestered with your absurd questions every ten minutes?" The old man was gesticulating his disgust with everything from his feet to his forehead, till the glasses on his nose quivered with indignation. "What d'you think

I am—a lazy schoolboy? Eh? Dammit, haven't you any work of your own?"

"You see, we don't want you to have a breakdown, professor," said the Saint, soothingly. "If you took a little rest now and then——"

"I had seven hours' rest last night. I'm not an invalid. And how would I get this done in time if I lay in bed all day? Think it would get done by itself? Eh?"

Simon took out a cigarette case and moved over to sit down on a conveniently shaped dome of metal.

"All the same, professor, if you wouldn't mind——"

The old man leapt towards him with a kind of yelp. Simon drew back hurriedly; and the professor glared at him, breathing heavily.

"Dammit, if you want to commit suicide, must you come and do it here?"

"Suicide?" repeated the Saint vaguely. "I hadn't——"

"Pish!" squawked the professor.

He snatched up a loose length of wire and tossed it on to the dome on which Simon had been preparing to rest himself. There was a momentary crackle of hot blue flame—and the wire ceased to resemble anything like wire. It simply trickled down the side of the dome in the shape of a few incandescent drops of molten metal; and Simon Templar mopped his brow.

He retreated towards the clear space around the door with some alacrity.

"Thanks very much, professor," he remarked. "Have you any more firework effects like that?"

"Bah!" croaked the professor huffily.

He went back to his bench and wiped his hands on a piece of rag, with every symptom of a society welfare worker removing the contamination of an afternoon with the deserving poor.

"Is there anything else you want to know?" he barked; and the Saint braced himself for the shot that had to be taken in the dark.

"When are we going to see some gold?"

The professor seemed on the verge of an outburst beside which his former demonstrations would pale into polite tea-table chatter. And then with a tremendous effort he controlled himself. He addressed the Saint with the dreadfully laboured restraint of a doting mother taking an interest in the precocities of a rival parent's prodigy and thinking what an abominable little beast he is.

"When you can use your eyes. When you can get some glasses powerful enough to show you something smaller than a haystack. Or else when you can improve on my methods and make gold run out of the bathroom tap. That's when." The old man stalked across to a cupboard and flung it open. "There. Look again. Try to see it. Borrow a microscope if you have to. But for heaven's sake, young man"—the quavering voice lost some of its self-control and rose two shrill notes—"for heaven's sake, don't utter any more blithering idiocies like that in my laboratory."

Simon stared into the cupboard.

He had never dreamed of seeing wealth like that concentrated in tangible form under his eyes. From floor to ceiling the cupboard was stacked high with it—great glittering yellow ingots the size of bricks reflecting the lamplight in one soaring block of tawny sleekness like the realisation of a miser's dream. The sight of it dazed him. There must have been over a million pounds' worth of the metal heaped carelessly into that tall rectangular cavity in the wall. And back and forth across his memory flashed the inane repetition of the dying young roué in Paris: "He says Binks can make gold . . ."

The professor's cracked voice broke in on him through a kind of fog.

"Well? Can you see it? Have you found your eyes at last? Eh? Does it begin to satisfy you?"

Simon had to fight for the smooth use of his tongue.

"Naturally, that's—er—very satisfactory, Dr. Quell; but——"

"Very satisfactory. I should think so." The professor snorted. "Half a hundredweight every hour. Very satisfactory. Faugh! You're a fool—that's what you are. Dammit, if the rest of the Secret Service are as thick-headed as you, I don't know why the country should bother to have a Secret Service."

The Saint stood very still.

But he felt as if a light-bomb had exploded inside him. The mystery was opening out before his eyes with a suddenness that could only be compared with an explosion. The detached items of it whirled around like scattered aircraft in the beam of a searchlight, and fell luminously into formation with a precision that was uncanny. Everything fitted in its place: the murder of Brian Quell, the King's Messenger who lay dead in an adjoining room, the man who could make gold . . . the man called "Binks"—a queer nickname to be given to such a brilliant and irritable old magician by his dissolute young brother! And that last mordant reference to the Secret Service: an idea that was worthy of the genius of Mr. Jones—so much simpler, so much more ingenious and effective than the obvious and hackneyed alternative of threats and torture. . . . Most astounding of all, the proof that the essential pivot of the thing was true. Sylvester Quell—"Binks" —*could* make gold. He had made it—hundredweights of it. He was making more.

Simon heard him grousing on in the same cracked querulous voice.

"I don't know why I came here. I could have done better in my own laboratory. Look after me, eh? With the intelligence you've got, you couldn't look after yourself. What use d'you think you are? Why don't you go away and let me do my work? You're worse than that other man, with his stupid questions and his school-room tests. Does he think I don't know real gold when I make it?"

It was all quite clear to the Saint. The only question left was how he should act. He could give very little time now to arguments and discussions—escape from that house had become one of the paramount considerations of his life, a thing more vitally important than he had ever thought it could be.

His hand went back to his pocket, his thumb feeling around for the safety-catch of his automatic and pressing it gently out of engagement. Under straight dark brows the blue Saintly eyes centred on Quell like spear-points.

"Of course not, professor. But about the notes of your process——"

He was so intent on the scientist that the movement of the door behind him missed his ears. The crack of an automatic fired at close quarters battered and stung his ear-drums, and the bullet plucked at his coat. Somehow he was untouched—it is much easier to miss with an automatic than any inexperienced person would believe, and perhaps Mr. Jones's haste made him snatch at the pull-off. The Saint spun round and fired from his pocket; his nerves were steadier, and he scored where he meant to score—on the gun in the big man's hand. The weapon dropped to the floor, and Simon stepped closer.

"Keep still."

The big man's face was twisted with fury. Behind him, Simon heard Quell's shrill whine.

"What does this mean, sir? Eh? Dammit——"

The Saint smiled.

"I'm afraid you've been taken in, professor. Our friend no more belongs to the Secret Service——"

"Than you do!" The big man's voice snarled in viciously. His fists were clenched and his eyes murderous—only the Saint's gun held him where he stood. "This is one of the men I warned you about, professor—he's trying to steal your secret, that's what it means! The damned traitor!—if I could only get my hands on him. . . . For God's sake why don't you do something? He's probably one of the gang that killed your brother——"

"Stop that!"

The Saint's voice cracked through the room like a blade of lightning; but he saw where the big man's desperate clatter of words was leading to a fraction of a second too late. Quell leapt at him suddenly with a kind of sob, before Simon had time to turn. The professor's skinny hand wrestled with his gun wrist and hate-crazed talons clawed at his throat. Simon stumbled sideways under the berserk fury of the scientist's onslaught, and his aim on the man called Jones was hopelessly lost. They swayed together in the corner. Quell's hysterical breathing hissed and moaned horribly in the Saint's ears; and over the demented man's shoulder he saw Jones stooping with his left hand for the fallen gun.

The Saint saw certain and relentless death blazing across his path like an express train. With a savage gathering of all his muscles he shook the professor off and sent him reeling back like a rag doll. Quell's dreadful shriek rang in his ears as Simon leapt across the dividing space and kicked away the automatic that the big man's fingers were within an inch of touching.

The gun clanged heavily into a piece of metal on the far side of the room, and Simon caught the big man by one lapel of his coat and spun him round. The Saint's gun rammed into the big man's ribs with a brutal forcefulness that made the other wince.

"Don't try that again."

Simon's whisper floated into the other's ears with an arctic gentleness that could not have been driven deeper home by a hundred megaphones. It carried a rasping huskiness of meaning that only a fool could have mistaken. And Mr. Jones was no fool. He stood frozen into stone; but the sweat stood out in glistening beads on his forehead.

The Saint flashed one glance sideways, and saw what Mr. Jones had seen first.

Sylvester Quell was sitting on the floor with his back to the shining dome-like contrivance that Simon had seen in action. One hand still rested on the dome, as if by some kind of spastic attraction, exactly as it had involuntarily gone out to save himself when the Saint's frantic struggle sent him stumbling back against the machine; but the hand was stiff and curiously blackened. The professor's upturned face was twisted in a hideous grin. . . . Whilst Simon looked, the head slipped sideways and lolled over on one shoulder. . . .

7

A twitch of expression tensed over the face of the man who called himself Jones. His eyebrows were drawn down at the bridge of his nose, and strained upwards at the outside corners; the eyes under them were swollen and bloodshot.

"You killed him," he rasped.

"I'm afraid I did," said the Saint. "An unfortunate result of my efforts at self-defence—for which you were entirely responsible."

"You'll have a job to prove it."

The Saint's gentlest smile plucked for an instant at thin-drawn lips.

"I don't know whether I shall try."

He grasped the big man's shoulder suddenly and whirled him half round again, driving him back towards the door.

"Move on, comrade."

"Where are you going?"

"Downstairs. I've got a friend of mine waiting with claustrophobia, and I guess she's been locked up long enough for one day. And if she couldn't eat all those sausages I might find a home for one."

They went down the stairs step by step, in a kind of tango style that would have been humorous to anyone who was insensitive to the deadly tension of it. But Simon Templar was giving no more chances. His forefinger was curled tightly over the trigger for every foot of the way, and the big man kept pace with him in a silence that prickled with malignant vigilance. They came to the door of the room below, and the Saint stopped.

"Open it."

The big man obeyed, turning the lock with a key which he took from his trouser pocket. Simon kicked the door wider.

"This way, Pat."

He waited on the landing while the girl came out, never shifting his eyes from the big man's venomous stillness. Patricia touched his sleeve, and he smiled.

"Simon—then it wasn't you I heard. . . ."

"That scream?" Simon slipped an arm round her and held her for a moment. "Why—did you think my voice was as bad as that, old darling? . . . No, but it wasn't Brother Jones either, which is a pity."

"Then who was it?"

"It was Dr. Quell. Pat, we've struck something a little tougher than I expected, and it hasn't turned out too well. This is just once in our lives that Claud Eustace will be useful. Once upon a time we might have handled it alone, but I think I promised to be careful."

He looked at his prisoner.

"I want your telephone," he said.

The big man hesitated, and Simon's gun screwed in his ribs.

"C'mon. You can have indigestion afterwards." Simon released the girl. "And that reminds me—if you did leave one of those sausages . . ."

Again they descended step by step towards the hall, with the Saint using his free hand to feed himself in a manner that is rarely practised in the best circles. The telephone was in the hall, on a small table by the front door; and Simon turned his gun over to

Patricia and walked across to it, chewing. He leaned a chair against the door and sat in it. The dial buzzed and clicked.

"Hullo. . . . I want Chief Inspector Teal. . . . Yeah—and nobody else. Simon Templar speaking. And make it snappy!"

The big man took a step towards him, his face yellow and his hands working. And immediately the girl's finger took up the slack of the trigger. It was an almost imperceptible movement; but Mr. Jones saw it, and the steady deliberateness of it was more significant than anything that had entered his imagination since the gun changed hands. He halted abruptly; and the Saint grinned.

"Hullo. Is that you, Claud? . . . Well, I want you. . . . Yeah —for the first time in my life I'll be glad to see you. Come right over, and bring as many friends as you like. . . . I can't tell you on the phone, but I promise it'll be worth the trip. There's any amount of dead bodies in the house, and. . . . Well, I suppose I can find out for you. Hold on."

He clamped a hand over the mouthpiece and looked across the table.

"What's the address, Jones?"

"You'd better go on finding out," retorted the big man sullenly.

"Sure." The Saint smile was angelic. "I'll find out. I'll go to the street corner and see. And before I go I'll just kick you once round the hall—just to see my legs are functioning."

He lounged round the table, and their eyes met.

"This is two hundred and eight Meadowbrook Road," said the man grimly.

"Thanks a lot." Simon dropped into his chair again and picked up the telephone. "Two-o-eight, Meadowbrook Road, Hampstead —I'll be here when you come. . . . O.K., Eustace."

He rose.

"Let's climb stairs again," he said brightly.

He took over the gun and shepherded the party aloft. The show had to be seen through, and his telephone call to Chief Inspector Teal had set a time limit on the action that could not be altered. It was a far cry from that deserted house to the hotel in Paris where Brian Quell had died, and yet Simon knew that he was watching the end of a coherent chain of circumstances that had moved with the inscrutable remorselessness of a Greek tragedy.

Fate had thrust him into the story again and again, as if resolved that there should be no possibility of a failure in the link that bore his name; and it was ordained that he should write the end of the story in his own way.

The laboratory upstairs stood wide open. Simon pushed the big man in, and followed closely behind. Patricia Holm came last: she saw the professor huddled back against his machine with his face still distorted in the ghastly grimace that the death-agony of high-voltage electricity had stamped into his features, and bit her lip. But she said nothing. Her questioning eyes searched the Saint's countenance of carved brown granite; and Simon backed away a little from his captive and locked the door behind him.

"We haven't a lot of time, Jones," he remarked quietly; and the big man's lips snarled.

"That's your fault."

"Doubtless. But there it is. Chief Inspector Claud Eustace Teal is on his way, and we have one or two things to settle before he comes. Before we start, may I congratulate you?"

"I don't want any congratulations."

"Never mind, you deserve them." The Saint fished out his cigarette case with his left hand. Quite naturally he extracted and lighted a cigarette, and stole a glance at his wrist-watch while he did so. His brain worked like a taximeter, weighing out miles and minutes. "I think I've got everything taped but you can check me up if I go wrong anywhere. Somehow or other—we won't speculate how—you got to know that Dr. Quell had just perfected a perfectly sound commercial method of transmuting metals. It's been done already on a small scale, but the expense of the process ruled it right out as a get-rich-quick proposition. Quell had worked along a new line, and made it a financial cinch."

"You must have had a long talk with him," said the big man sardonically.

"I did. . . . However—your next move, of course, was to get the process for yourself. You're really interesting, Jones—you work on such original lines. Where the ordinary crook would have tried to capture the professor and torture him, you thought of subtler methods. You heard of Quell's brother, a good-for-nothing idler who was always drunk and usually broke. You went over to Paris and tried to get him in with you, figuring that he could get Sylvester's confidence when no one else could. But Brian Quell had a streak of honesty in him that you hadn't reckoned with. He turned you down—and then he knew too much. You couldn't risk him remembering you when he sobered up. So you shot him. I was there. A rotten shot, Jones—just like the one you took at me this evening, or that other one last night. Gun work is a gift, brother, and you simply haven't got it."

The big man said nothing.

"You knew I knew something about Brian Quell's murder, so you tried to get me. That talk about an 'envoy' of yours was the bunk—you were playing the hand alone, because you knew there wasn't a crook on earth who could be trusted on a thing as big as this." The Saint never paused in his analysis; but his eyes were riveted to the prisoner's face, and he would have known at once if his shot in the dark went astray. Not the faintest change of expression answered him, and he knew he was right. Jones was alone. "By the way, I suppose you wouldn't like to tell me exactly how you knew something had gone wrong in Paris?"

"If you want to know, I thought I heard someone move in the corridor outside, and I went out to make sure. The door blew shut behind me, on an automatic lock. I had to stand outside and listen. Then someone really did come along the passage——"

"And you had to beat it." Simon nodded. "But I don't think you rang me up this morning just to make out how much I heard. What you wanted was to hear my voice, so that you could imitate it."

"He did it perfectly," said Patricia.

The Saint smiled genially.

"You see, Jones. If you couldn't have made your fortune as a gun artist, you might have had a swell career as a ventriloquist. But you wouldn't have it. You wanted to be a Master Mind, and that's where the sawdust came out. My dear old borzoi, did you think we'd never heard that taxi joke before? Did you think poor little Patricia with all her experience of sin, was falling for a gag like that? Jones, that was very silly of you—quite irreparably silly. We've let you have your little joke just because it seemed the easiest way to get a close-up of your beautiful whiskers. If you'd left us your address before you rang off this morning we'd have been saved the trouble but as it was——"

"Well, what are you getting at?" grated the big man.

"Just checking up," said the Saint equably. "So you know how we got here. And I found that King's Messenger in the other room—that's what first confirmed what we were up against. Anyone making gold is one of the things the Secret Service sits and waits for all year round: one day the discovery is going to be genuine, and the first news of it would send the international exchanges crazy. There'd be the most frightful panic in history, and any Government has got to be watching for it. That King's Messenger had the news—you were lucky to get him."

The big man was silent again, but his face was pale and pasty.

"Two murders, Jones, that were your very own handiwork," said the Saint. "And then—the professor. Accidental, of course. But very unfortunate. Because it means that you're the only man left alive who knows this tremendous secret."

Simon actually looked away. But he had no idea what he looked at. The whole of his faculties were concentrated on the features which were still pinned in the borders of his field of vision, watching with every sense in his body for the answer to the question that he could not possibly ask. That one thing had to be known before anything else could be done, and there was only one way to know it. He bluffed, as he had bluffed once before, without a tremor of his voice or a flicker of his eyes. . . .

And the most impressive thing about the big man's expression was that it did not change. The big man took the Saint's casual assertion into his store of knowledge without the slightest symptom of surprise. It signified nothing more to him than one more superfluous blow on the head of a nail that was already driven deep enough. He glared at the Saint, and the gun in the Saint's hand, without any movement beyond a mechanical moistening of his lips, intent only on watching for the chance to fight that seemed infinitely improbable. . . . And the Saint tapped the ash from his cigarette and looked at the big man again.

"I got nearly everything out of Dr. Quell before you interrupted us," he said, clinching the assertion of utter certainty. "It was clever of you to wheedle Quell's process out of him bit by bit —and very useful that you had enough scientific knowledge to understand it. I suppose Quell's sphere of service was running out about this time, anyway—you'd have got rid of him yourself even if there'd been no accident. A very sound and prudent policy for a Master Mind, Jones, but just a shade too dangerous when the scheme springs a leak like me."

"Cut it short," snarled the big man. "What more d'you want? The gold's there——"

"Yes, the gold's certainly there," said the Saint dispassionately. "And in about ten minutes the police will be here to gape at it. I'm afraid that can't be helped. I'd like to get rich quick myself, but I've realised to-night that there's one way of doing it which is too dangerous for any man to tackle. And you don't realise it, Jones—that's the trouble. So we can't take any risks."

"No?"

"No." Simon gazed at the big man with eyes that were very clear, and hard as polished flints. "You see, that secret's too big a thing to be left with you. There's too much dynamite tied up in it. And yet the police couldn't do anything worth a damn. They're bound by the law, and it's just possible you might beat a murder rap. I don't know how the evidence might look in front of a jury; and of course my reputation's rather shop-soiled, and you may be a member of parliament for all I know. . . . Are you following me, Jones? The police couldn't make you part with your secret——"

"Neither could you."

"Have your own way. As it happens, I'm not trying. But with a reputation like mine it'd be a bad business for me to shoot you. On the other hand, there could always be another accident—before the police arrived."

The man called Jones stood with his arms hanging loosely at his sides, staring at the Saint unblinkingly. In those last few minutes he had gone suddenly quiet: the snarl had faded out of his voice and left a more restrained level of grim interrogation. His chin was sunken tensely on his powerful chest, and under the thick black eyebrows his eyes were focusing on the Saint with the stony brightness of brown marble.

He hunched his muscular shoulders abruptly—it was the only movement he made.

"Is that a threat?" he asked.

"No." Simon was just as quiet. "It's a promise. When the police arrive they're going to find that there's been another accident.

And the fact will be that you, Jones, also fell against that machine."

8

The big man leapt forward as he finished speaking. Simon knew that that was coming—he was ready and waiting for it. There was no other way about it; and he had been prepared for it ever since one question had been answered. He had never intended to shoot after they returned to the laboratory, whatever happened; but he snatched his gun away out of range of the wild grab that Jones made for it, and tossed it neatly across to Patricia. She caught it at her knees; and the Saint slipped under the big man's arms and jammed him against the door. For an instant they strained against each other face to face; and the Saint drew a deep breath and spoke over his shoulder.

"Don't shoot, Pat," he said. "Get over in the corner and stay out of the way. The gun's for you to get out with if anything goes wrong."

The big man heaved up off the door in a mighty jerk, and hurled the Saint back with all the impetus of his superior weight. He shook off the Saint's grip with a writhing effort of his arms— Simon felt the man's biceps cording under his hands before the grip was broken, and knew that he was taking on nothing easy. The force of his opponent's rush drove him to within a yard of the deadly steel dome; then he recovered his balance, and stopped the man with a couple of half-arm jolts to the stomach that thudded into their mark like pistons hitting a sandbag. Jones grunted, and went back on his heels, dropping his hands to guard; and the Saint shot out a snake-like left for the exposed chin. The big man took it on the side of his jaw, deliberately, and snatched at the flying wrist as the blow landed.

His fingers closed on it like iron clamps, twisting spitefully. He had every ounce of the strength that his build indicated, and he was as hard as teak all over—the Saint had felt that when he landed with those two staggering blows that would have broken most men in the middle. What was more, he had been trained in a school of fighting that knew its stuff: he never gave the Saint a chance to make a boxing match of it. Simon swerved away from the dome and kicked up his knee, but the big man edged back. The Saint's left arm was clamped in an agonising arm-lock, and he was wrenched ruthlessly round again towards the dome. The leverage of the hold was bearing him down to his knees; then with a swift, terrific kick he straightened his legs under him and swung his right fist over in a smashing blow at the back of the man's neck. The man coughed, and crumpled to his hands and knees; and Simon tore his wrist out of the grip and fell on top of him.

They rolled over together, with the Saint groping for a toe-hold. One of the big man's insteps came under the palm of his hand, and he hauled it up and bent it over with a brutal efficiency that made his victim gasp. But the big man was wise to that one —the hold only hurt him for a couple of seconds, before he flung it off with a mighty squirm of his body that pitched the Saint over on his face. In an instant the big man's legs were scissoring for a clasp round the Saint's neck and shoulders, and his hands were clamping again on the Saint's wrist. Simon heard his muscles creaking as he strained against the backward pressure that was slowly straightening his arm. Once that arm was locked out straight from the shoulder, with the elbow over the big man's knee-joint, he would have to move like a supercharged eel to get away before a bone was snapped like dry wood. He fought it desperately, but it was his one arm against the big man's two; and he knew he was losing inch by inch. His free hand clawed for a nerve centre under one of the thighs that were crushing his chest: he found it, and saw the big man wince, but the remorseless straightening of his arm went on. In the last desperate moment that he had, he struggled to break the nutcracker grip around his upper body. One of the big man's shoes came off in his hand, and with a triumphant laugh he piled all his strength into another toe-twist. The man squeaked and kicked, and Simon broke away. As he came up on all fours, the other rolled away. They leapt up simultaneously and circled round each other, breathing heavily.

"Thanks for the fight," said the Saint shortly. "I never cared for cold-blooded killings."

For answer the big man came forward off his toes like a charging bull; but he had not moved six inches before the Saint's swift dash reached him. Again those pile-driving fists jarred on the weak spot just below the other's breast-bone. Jones grabbed for a strangle-hold, but the drumming of iron knuckles on his solar plexus made him stagger backwards and cover up with his elbows. His mouth opened against the protest of his paralysed lungs, and his face went white and puffy. Simon drove him to the door, and held off warily. He knew that the big man was badly hurt, but perhaps his helplessness looked a little too realistic. . . . The Saint feinted with a left to the head, and in a second the big man was bear-hugging him in a wild rush that almost carried him off his feet.

They went back towards the gleaming dome in a fighting tangle. Simon looked over his shoulder and saw it a yard away, with its brilliant surface shining like silver around the charred blackness of the professor's hand. The strip of wire that he had seen melted on it had left streaky trails of smeared metal down the curved sides, like the slime of a fantastic snail. The Saint saw them in an instant of photographically vivid vision in which the minutest details of that diabolical apparatus were printed for ever on his memory. There must have been tens of thousands of volts pulsing invisibly through that section of the secret process, hundreds of amperes of burning annihilation waiting to scorch through the first thing that tapped them with that crackle of blue flame and hiss of intolerable heat which he had seen once and heard again. His shoes slipped over the floor as he wrestled superhumanly against the momentum that was pressing him back towards certain death: the big man's face was cracked in a fiendish grin, and he heard Patricia cry out. . . . Then one of his heels tripped over the professor's outstretched legs, and he was thrown off his balance. He put all his strength into a frantic twist of his body as he fell, and saw the dome leap up beside him, a foot away. The fall knocked half the wind out of his body, and he fought blindly away to one side. Suddenly his hands grasped empty air, and he heard Patricia cry out again.

The splitting detonation of a shot racketed in his ears as he rolled up on one elbow. Patricia had missed, somehow, and the big man was grappling for the gun.

Simon crawled up and flung himself forward. As he did so, the big man saw his own gun lying in the corner where the Saint had kicked it, and dived for it. Simon caught him from behind in a circling sweep, locking the big man's arms to his sides at the elbows: but the big man had the gun. The Saint saw it curling round for a backward shot that could not help scoring somewhere: he made a wild grab at the curving wrist and caught it, jerking it up as the trigger tightened, and the shot smashed through the floor. Simon flung his left leg forward, across the big man's stance. The steel dome was a yard away on his left. He heaved sideways, across the leverage of his thigh, and sprang back. . . .

The man's scream rang in his ear as he staggered away. Once again that spurt of eye-aching blue flame seared across his eyes, and turned suddenly orange. The big man had hit the dome with his shoulder, and his coat was burning: the smell of singeing cloth stung the Saint's nostrils, and the crack of cordite sang through his head as the galvanic current clamped a dead finger convulsively on the trigger and held it there rigidly in one last aimless shot. . . .

"And we still don't know his real name," murmured the Saint.

He pushed a handkerchief across his brow, and looked at Patricia with a crooked grin. Patricia was fingering her wrist tenderly, where the big man's crushing grip had fastened on it. She looked back at the Saint with a pale face that was still hopelessly puzzled.

"That's your fault," she said.

"I know." The Saint's eyes had a mocking twist in their inscrutable blue that she couldn't understand. "You see, when you've made up your mind about a thing like Brother Jones's demise, the only way is to get it over quickly. And Claud Eustace will be along soon. But I promise you, Pat, I've never hated killing anyone so much—and there was never anyone who'd've been so dangerous to my peace of mind if he'd stayed alive. If you want any excuses for it, he'd got two deliberate murders on his own hands and one more for which he was deliberately responsible, so he only got what was coming to him."

She waited alone in the room of death while the Saint vanished along the landing towards one of the bedrooms. It took the Saint a few minutes to repair the damage which the fight had done to his immaculate elegance, but when he had finished there was hardly a trace of it—nothing but a slight disorder that could have been caused by a brief scuffle. He used the dead man's hair-brushes and clothes brush and wrapped a handkerchief round his hand before he touched anything. Everything went back on the dressing-table exactly as he had found it; and he returned to the girl with a ready smile.

"Let's finish the clean up, Pat—I don't know that we've a lot of time."

He went over the floor with keen restless eyes. Two cartridge cases he picked up from odd corners where they had rolled away after the snap action of the recoil had spewed them out of a pistol breech. He identified them as the products of his own gun, for he had marked each of them with a nick in the base. They went into his pocket: the others, which testified to the shots which Jones had fired, he left where they lay, and added to them the souvenir which he had preserved in a match-box from his breakfast-table that morning. He searched the room once more for any other clues which he might have overlooked, and was satisfied.

His hand fell on Patricia's shoulder.

"Let's go," he said.

They went down to the hall. Simon left her again while he went out into the garden. His automatic, and the shells he had picked up, went deep under the earth of a neglected flower-bed; and he uprooted a clump of weeds and pressed them into a new berth where they would hide the marks of freshly-turned earth.

"Don't you ever want me to know what you're up to?" asked Patricia, when he came back; and the Saint took her by the arm and led her to a chair.

"Lass, don't you realise I've just committed murder? And times is not what they was. I've known much bigger things than this which were easy enough to get away with before Claud Eustace had quite such a life-and-death ambition to hang my scalp on his belt; but this is not once upon a time. We might have run away and left the mystery to uncover itself, but I didn't think that was such a hot idea. I'd rather know how we stand from the start. Now sit down and let me write some more about Wilberforce Gupp—this is a great evening for brain work."

He propelled her gently into the chair, and sat himself down in another. An envelope and a pencil came out of his pocket; and with perfect calm and detachment, as if he were sitting in his own room at home with a few minutes to spare, the amazing Saint proceeded to scribble down and read aloud to her the epilogue of his epic.

> *"Thus, on good terms with everyone,*
> *Nothing accomplished, nothing done,*
> *Sir Wilberforce, as history knows,*
> *Earned in due course a k-night's repose,*
> *And with his fellow pioneers,*
> *Rose shortly to the House of Peers,*
> *Which nearly (but not quite) woke up*
> *To greet the noble Baron Gupp,*
> *Citizens, praise careers like his,*
> *Which have made England what she is,*
> *And prove that only Lesser Breeds*
> *Follow where a stuffed walrus leads."*

He had just finished when they both heard a car swing into the drive. Feet crunched over the gravel, and heavy boots grounded on the stone outside the front door. The resonant clatter of a brass knocker curtly applied echoed through the house.

Simon opened the door.

"Claud Eustace himself!" he murmured genially. "It seems years since I last saw you, Claud. And how's the ingrowing toenail?" He glanced past the detective's bulky presence at the four other men who were unloading themselves and their apparatus from the police car and lining up for the entrance. "I rather thought you'd be bringing a party with you, old dear, but I don't know that the caviare will go all the way round."

The detective stepped past him into the hall, and the other men followed. They were of various shapes and sizes, deficient in sex appeal but unconversationally efficient. They clumped themselves together on the mat and waited patiently for orders.

Mr. Teal faced the Saint with a certain grimness. His round pink face was rather more flushed than usual, and his baby blue eyes were creased up into the merest slits, though which pinpoints of red danger-lights glinted like scattering embers. He knew that he had taken a chance in coming to that house at all, and the squad he had brought with him multiplied his potential regrets by more factors than he cared to think about. If this was

one of the Saint's practical jokes, Chief Inspector Teal would
never hear the last of it. The whole C.I.D. would laugh itself sick
—there were still giggles circulating over the gramophone record
incident—and the Assistant Commissioner's sniff would flay him
till he wanted to find a quiet place to die. And yet he had had no
choice. If he was told about a murder he had to go out and investigate it, and his private doubts did not count.

"Well?" he barked.

"Fairly," said the Saint. "I see you brought the homicide
squad."

Teal nodded briefly.

"I gathered from what you told me that a murder had been
committed. Is that the case?"

"There are certainly some dead bodies packed about the
house," admitted the Saint candidly. "In fact, the place is making
a great start as a morgue. If you're interested——"

"Where are these bodies?"

Simon gestured impressively heavenwards.

"Upstairs—at least, so far as the mortal clay is concerned, Eustace."

"We'll go up and see them."

Curtly Teal gave his orders to the silent squad. One man was
left in the hall, and Patricia stayed with him. The others, who included a finger-print expert with a little black bag, and a photographer burdened with camera and folding tripod, followed behind. They went on a tour that made every member of it stare
more incredulously from stage to stage, until the culminating revelation left their eyeballs bulging as if they were watching the
finale of a Grand Guignol drama coming true under their noses.

9

Chief Inspector Teal twiddled his pudgy fingers on his knees
and studied the Saint's face soberly, digesting what he had heard.

"So after that you allowed this man Jones to kidnap Miss Holm
so that you could follow him and find out his address?" he murmured; and the Saint nodded.

"That's about it. Can you blame me? The guy Jones was obviously a menace to the community that we ought to know more about, and it was the only way. I hadn't the faintest idea at that time what his graft was, but I figured that anything which included wilful murder in its programme must be worth looking into. I was all bubbling over with beans after that bust I told you about—talking of busts, Claud, if you ever go to the Folies-Bergère——"

"Yes, yes," interrupted the detective brusquely. "I want you to tell me exactly what happened when you got here."

"Well, naturally I had to break into the house. I went up to the first floor and heard Jones talking to Miss Holm in the room where he'd taken her. I hid in another room when he came out to get her some food; then I went and spoke to Miss Holm through the door—which Brother J. had remembered to lock. We exchanged some bright remarks about the weather and the Test Match prospects, and then I carried on with the exploration. On the way I found that King's Messenger. Then Jones came upstairs again and I lay low for quite a while, cautious like. After a time I got tired standing about, and I went in search of him. I came up outside this laboratory door and listened. That's when I heard what it was all about. Jones was just wheedling what sounded like the last details of the process out of Quell—the science I know wouldn't cover a pinhead, but Jones seemed quite happy about it."

"Can you remember any part of what you heard?"

"Not a thing that'd make sense—except the out-standing bit about the gold. Quell *was* making gold, there's not a doubt about it. You can see it for yourself. I gathered that Jones had told the old man some yarn about saving England from going off the gold standard—manufacturing an enormous quantity of the stuff under the auspices of the Secret Service, and unloading it quietly in a way that'd put new life into the Bank of England—and Quell, who probably wasn't so wise to the ways of crime as he was to the habits of electrons and atoms, had fallen for it like a dove. Anyway, Jones was happy."

"And then?"

"There was a frightful yell. I've never heard anything like it. I burst in—the door wasn't locked—and saw the professor doing a last kick beside that machine. Jones must have pushed him on to it in cold blood. The old man had told him everything he wanted to know, and made him a lot of specimen gold as well, and Jones hadn't any further use for him. Jones heard me come in, and spun round, pulling a gun. He tripped over the professor's legs and put out a hand to save himself—then he saw his hand was going on the machine, and he pulled it away. He fell on his shoulder, and it burned him just the same. I suppose the current jiggered his muscles like it does on those electric machines, and he went on shooting all round the place for a second or two."

Teal looked round at the finger-print expert, who was busy at the bench.

"Have you done those shells?" he asked.

"Just finished, sir."

Simon raised his eyebrows.

"What's the idea?" he inquired.

"I don't know whether you've thought of wearing gloves when you're loading a gun," said the detective blandly; and the Saint did not smile.

He allowed the expert to take impressions of his finger-tips on a special block, and waited while the man squinted at them through a magnifying-glass and checked them against the marks which he had developed on the spent cartridge cases which had been picked up. Teal went over to his side and stood there with a kind of mountainous placidity which was not the most convincing thing Simon Templar had ever seen.

"There's no similarity, sir," pronounced the expert at length, and a glimmer of blank disbelief crossed the detective's round face.

"Are you sure?"

"It's quite obvious, sir. The prints are of totally different types. You can see for yourself. The prints on the shells are spirals, and this gentleman's prints——"

"Don't call him 'this gentleman'," snapped the detective. "This is Simon Templar, known as the Saint—and you know it too."

"Why not try Jones's finger-prints?" suggested the Saint mildly. "It seems simpler than suspecting me automatically. I've told you —I'm not in this party. That's why I sent for you."

Teal regarded the two contorted bodies thoughtfully. The photographer had finished his work and he was packing his exposed plates away in a satchel. The detective took a step forward.

"I should take a lot of care, if I were you," murmured the Saint. "I'd hate you to have an accident, and I suppose the juice is still functioning."

They went round the room circumspectly. Someone discovered a collection of switches, and reversed them. A likely looking terminal was disconnected by a man who donned rubber gloves for the purpose. Finally they approached the dome again, and one of the men tossed bits of wire on to it from various angles. Nothing happened; and eventually Teal knelt down and tried to detach the gun from the dead man's hand. He remained alive, but it took the efforts of two other men to unlock the terrific clutch of the dead man's fingers.

Teal straightened up and clicked out the magazine.

"Two shots here." He jerked the sliding jacket. "One in the breech. . . . We picked up four shells, and four shots have been fired in this room." Teal turned the figures over in his head as if he loathed them. The chagrin showed on his face; and Simon Templar relaxed gently. It was the one risk that he had to take—if Jones's gun had contained more shells it would have been a tougher proposition, but seven was a possible load. "You're lucky," Teal said venomously.

He turned the gun over in his hand, and suddenly he stiffened.

"What's that?"

He displayed a thin silvery scratch on the blue-black steel, and Simon gazed at the mark along with the other detectives.

"It looks as if it had hit something," said one of them.

"I'll say it does," grunted Mr. Teal.

He crawled round the room on his hands and knees, studying the bullet scars that had already been discovered. One of them occupied him for some time, and he called over one of the other men to join him. There was a low-voiced colloquy; and then Teal rose again and dusted the knees of his trousers. He faced the Saint again.

"That shot there was a ricochet," he said, "and it could have come off Jones's gun."

"Shooting round corners and hitting itself?" drawled the Saint mildly. "You know, you're a genius—or rather Jones must have been. That's an invention that's been wanted for years. Damned useful thing in a tight corner, Claud—you aim one way, and the bullet comes back and hits the man standing behind you——"

"I don't think that was it," said the detective short-windedly. "What kind of gun are you carrying these days?"

Simon spread out his hands.

"You know I haven't got a licence."

"Never mind. We'll just look you over."

The Saint shrugged resignedly, and held out his arms. Teal frisked him twice, efficiently, and found nothing. He turned to the odd man.

"You'd better get busy and dig out all the bullets. We'll be able to tell from the marks of the rifling whether they were all fired from the same gun."

A trickle of something like ice-cold water fluttered down Simon Templar's spine. That was the one possibility that he had overlooked—the one inspiration he had not expected the plump detective to produce. He hadn't even thought that Teal's suspicions would have worked so hard. That gramophone record must have scored a deeper hit than he anticipated—deeper perhaps than he had ever wanted it to be. It must have taken something that had rubbed salt viciously into an old and stubbornly unhealed wound to kindle an animosity that would drive itself so far in the attempt to pin guilt on a quarter where there was so much prima facie innocence.

But the Saint schooled himself to a careless shrug. The least trace of expression would have been fatal. He had never acted with such intensity in his life as he did at that moment, keeping unruffled his air of rather bored protest. He knew that Teal was watching him with the eyes of a lynx, with his rather soft mouth compressed into a narrow line which symbolised that unlooked-for streak of malice. "I can't help it if you want to waste time making a damned fool of yourself," he said wearily. "If there's a scratch on that gun it's probably there because Jones *did* happen to bang it on something. If there's a ricco anywhere, it's probably one that bounced off some of the apparatus—there's any amount of solid metal about, and I told you how Jones was thrashing around when the current got him. Why go trying to fix something on me?"

"Only because I'm curious," said the detective inflexibly. "You've had quite a lot of jokes at our expense, so I'm sure you won't mind us having a harmless little fun at yours."

Simon took out his cigarette case.

"Am I to consider myself under arrest—is that the idea?"

"Not yet," said Teal, with a vague note of menace sticking out of the way he said it.

"No? Well, I'm just interested. This is the first time in my life I ever behaved like a respectable citizen and gave you your break according to the rules, and I'm glad to know how you take it. It'll save me doing anything so damned daft again."

Teal stripped the wrapping from a wafer of spearmint with a sort of hard-strung gusto.

"I hope you'll have the opportunity of doing it again," he said. "But this looks like the kind of case that would have interested you in other ways, and I shouldn't be doing my duty if I took everything for granted."

Simon looked at him.

"You're wrong," he said soberly. "I tell you, Teal, when I saw that guy Jones dying all that went through my mind in a flash. Before he killed Quell—before I came through the door—I'd heard enough to know what it meant. I knew I could have taken him prisoner, made him work the process for me—had all the wealth I wanted. You know what one can do with a bit of persuasion. I could have taken him away from this house and left everything as it was—Quell and the King's Messenger mightn't have been found for weeks, and there'd have been nothing in the world to show that I'd ever been near the place. I could have done in real earnest what Jones was trying to kid Quell he was doing. I could have manufactured gold until I'd built up a balance in the Bank of England that would have been the sensation of the century. I could have played fairy godmother in a way that would have made me safe for ever from your well-meant persecutions, Claud. I could have paid off the National Debt with one cheque —my own free gift to Great Britain. With love and kisses from the Saint. Think of it! I could have named my own price. I might have been dictator—and then there might have been some more sense in the laws of this nit-witted community than there is now. Certainly you'd never have dared to touch me so long as I lived

—there'd have been a revolution if you'd tried it. Simon Templar
—the man who abolished income tax. My God, Teal, I don't
think anyone's ever been able to dream a miracle like that and
see it within his reach!"

"Well?"

Teal was chewing steadily, but his eyes were fixed on the
Saint's face with a solid attentiveness that had not been there before. Something in the Saint's speech commanded the respect that
he was unwilling to give—it was drawn from him in spite of himself. Simon's sincerity was starkly irresistible.

"You know what happened. I passed up the idea. And I don't
mind telling you, Claud, quite honestly, that if Jones hadn't died
as he did, I should have killed him. There you are. You can use
that as evidence against me if you like, because this time I haven't
a thing on my conscience—just for once."

"What made you pass up the idea?" asked Teal.

Simon took the cigarette from his mouth, and answered with an
utter frankness that could have been nothing but the truth.

"It would have made life too damned dull!"

Teal scratched his chin and stared at the toe-cap of one shoe.
The odd man had finished digging out bullets: he dropped them
into a match-box and stood by, listening like the others.

"You know me, Claud," said the Saint. "I was just tempted—
just in imagination—for that second or two while I watched Jones
die and his bullets were crashing round me. And I saw what a
deadly frost it would have been. No more danger—no more risk
—no more duels with Scotland Yard—no more of your very jolly
backchat and bloody officiousness as per this evening. Claud, I'd
have died of boredom. So I gave you your break. I left everything
as it was, and phoned you straight away. There was no need to,
but that's what I did. Jones was dead of his own accord, and I'd
nothing to be afraid of. I haven't even touched an ounce of the
gold—it's there for you to take away, and I suppose if the Quell
family's extinct the Government will get it and I won't even be
offered a rebate on my income tax. But naturally, like the poor
dumb boobs you are, you have to sweat blood trying to make me
a murderer the one time in my life I'm innocent. Why, you sap, if
I'd wanted to get away with anything——"

"It's a pity you couldn't have saved Jones and done what you thought of all the same," said Teal; and the change in his manner was so marked that the Saint smiled. "It might have done the country some good."

Simon drew at his cigarette and hunched his shoulders.

"Why the hell should I bother? The country's got its salvation in its own hands. While a nation that's always boasting about its outstanding brilliance can put up with a collection of licensing laws, defence of the realm Acts, seaside councillors, Lambeth conventions, sweepstake laws, Sunday observance Acts, and one fatuity after another that's nailed on it by a bunch of blathering maiden aunts and pimply hypocrites, and can't make up its knock-kneed mind to get rid of 'em and let some fresh air and common sense into its life—when they can't do anything but dither over things that an infant in arms would know its own mind about—how the devil can they expect to solve bigger problems? And why the blazes should I take any trouble to save them from the necessity of thinking for themselves . . . ? Now, for heaven's sake make up your mind whether you want to arrest me or not, because if you don't I'd like to go home to bed."

"All right," said Teal. "You can go."

The Saint held out his hand.

"Thanks," he said. "I'm sorry about that gramophone record. Maybe we can get on better in the future—if we're both very good."

"I'll believe that of you when I see it," said Teal; but he smiled.

Simon pushed his way through the knot of waiting men to the door.

At the foot of the stairs the detective who had been left with Patricia barred his way. Teal looked over the gallery rail and spoke down.

"It's all right, Peters," he said. "Mr. Templar and Miss Holm can go."

Simon opened the front door and turned to wave the detective a debonair good-bye. They went out to where the Saint had left his car, and Simon lighted another cigarette and waited in silence for the engine to warm. Presently he let in the clutch and they slid away southwards for home.

"Was it all right?" asked Patricia.

"Just," said the Saint. "But I don't want such a narrow squeak again for many years. There was one vital piece of evidence I'd overlooked, and Teal thought of it. I had to think fast—and play for my life. But I collared the evidence as I went out, and they'll never be able to make a case without it. And do you know, Pat? —Claud Eustace ended up by really believing me."

"What did you tell him?"

"Very, very nearly the whole truth," said the Saint, and hummed softly to himself for a long while.

He drove home by a roundabout route that took them over Westminster Bridge. In the middle of the bridge he dipped into his pocket and flung something sideways, far out over the parapet.

It was a small box that weighed heavily and rattled.

Back at Scotland Yard, a puzzled detective-sergeant turned his coat inside out for the second time.

"I could have sworn I put the match-box with those bullets in my pocket, sir," he said. "I must have left it on the bench or something. Shall I go back and fetch it?"

"Never mind," said Mr. Teal. "We shan't be needing it."

Many of Simon Templar's escapades involve flimflams, but "The Newdick Helicopter" (1933) is the only time he pulls a con by allowing himself to be conned. And despite his assertions of an unscientific mind, he proves to be a quick student of the then emerging field of helicopter technology.

THE NEWDICK HELICOPTER

"I'm afraid," said Patricia Holm soberly, "you'll be getting into trouble again soon."

Simon Templar grinned, and opened another bottle of beer. He poured it out with a steady hand, unshaken by the future predicted for him.

"You may be right, darling," he admitted. "Trouble is one of the things that sort of happen to me, like other people have colds."

"I've often heard you complaining about it," said the girl sceptically.

The Saint shook his head.

"You wrong me," he said. "Posterity will know me as a maligned, misunderstood, ill-used victim of a cruel fate. I have tried to be good. Instinctive righteousness glows from me like an inward light. But nobody gives it a chance. What do you suggest?"

"You might go into business."

"I know. Something safe and respectable, like manufacturing woollen combinations for elderly ladies and lorgnettes. We might throw in a pair of lorgnettes with every suit. You could knit them, and I'd do the fitting—the fitting of the lorgnettes, of course." Simon raised his glass and drank deeply. "It's an attractive idea, old darling, but all these schemes involve laying out a lot of capital on which you have to wait such a hell of a long time for a return. Besides, there can't be much of a profit in it. On a rough estimate, the amount of wool required to circumnavigate a fifty-four-inch bust——"

Monty Hayward, who was also present, took out a tobacco-pouch and began to fill his pipe.

"I had some capital once," he said reminiscently, "but it didn't do me much good."

"How much can you lend me?" asked the Saint hopefully.

Monty brushed stray ends of tobacco from his lap and tested the draught through his handiwork cautiously.

"I haven't got it any more, but I don't think I'd lend it to you if I had," he said kindly. "Anyway, the point doesn't arise, because a fellow called Oscar Newdick has got it. Didn't I ever tell you about that?"

The Saint moved his head negatively, and settled deeper into his chair.

"It doesn't sound like you, Monty. D'you mean to say you were hornswoggled?"

Monty nodded.

"I suppose you might call it that. It happened about six years ago, when I was a bit younger and not quite so wise. It wasn't a bad swindle on the whole, though." He struck a match and puffed meditatively. "This fellow Newdick was a bloke I met on the train coming down from the office. He used to get into the same compartment with me three or four times a week, and naturally we took to passing the time of day—you know the way one does. He was an aeronautical engineer and a bit of an inventor, apparently. He was experimenting with autogiros, and he had a little one-horse factory near Walton where he was building them. He used to talk a lot of technical stuff about them to me, and I talked technical stuff about make-up and dummies to him—I don't suppose either of us understood half of what the other was talking about, so we got on famously."

With his pipe drawing satisfactorily, Monty possessed himself of the beer-opener and executed a neat flanking movement towards the source of supply.

"Well, one day this fellow Newdick asked me if I'd like to drop over and have a look at his autogiros, so the following Saturday afternoon I hadn't anything particular to do and I took a run out to his aerodrome to see how he was getting along. All he had there was a couple of corrugated-iron sheds and a small field which he used to take off from and land at, but he really had got a helicopter effect which he said he'd made himself. He told me all about it and how it worked, which was all double-Dutch to me; and then he asked me if I'd like to go up in it. So I said 'Thank you very much, I should simply hate to go up in it.' You know what these things look like—an ordinary aeroplane with the wings taken off and just a sort of large fan business to hold you up in the air—I never thought they looked particularly safe even when they're properly made, and I certainly didn't feel like risking my neck in this home-made version that he'd rigged up out of old bits of wood and angle iron. However, he was so insistent about it and seemed so upset when I refused that eventually I thought I'd better gratify the old boy and just keep on praying that the damn thing wouldn't fall to pieces before we got down again."

The Saint sighed.

"So that's what happened to your face," he remarked, in a tone of profound relief. "If you only knew how that had been bothering me——"

"My mother did that," said Monty proudly. "No—we didn't crash. In fact, I had a really interesting flight. Either it must have been a very good machine, or he was a very good flier, because he made it do almost everything except answer questions. I don't know if you've ever been up in one of these autogiros—I've never been up in any other make, but this one was certainly everything that he claimed for it. It went up exactly like going up in a lift, and came down the same way. I never have known anything about the mechanics of these things, but after having had a ride in this bus of his I couldn't help feeling that the Air Age had arrived—I mean, anyone with a reasonable sized lawn could have kept one of 'em and gone tootling off for week-ends in it."

"And therefore," said the Saint reproachfully, "when he asked you if you'd like to invest some money in a company he was forming to turn out these machines and sell them at about twenty pounds a time, you hauled out your cheque-book and asked him how much he wanted."

Monty chuckled good-humouredly.

"That's about it. The details don't really matter, but the fact is that about three weeks later I'd bought above five thousand quids' worth of shares."

"What was the catch?" Simon asked; and Monty shrugged.

"Well, the catch was simply that this helicopter wasn't his invention at all. He had really built it himself, apparently, but it was copied line for line from one of the existing makes. There wasn't a thing in it that he'd invented. Therefore the design wasn't his, and he hadn't any right at all to manufacture it. So the company couldn't function. Of course, he didn't put it exactly like that. He told me that he'd 'discovered' that his designs 'overlapped' the existing patents—he swore that it was absolutely a coincidence, and nearly wept all over my office because his heart was broken because he'd found out that all his research work had already been done before. I told him I didn't believe a word of it, but that wasn't any help towards getting my money back. I hadn't any evidence against him that I could have brought into a court of law. Of course he'd told me that his design was patented and protected in every way, but he hadn't put any of that in writing, and when he came and told me the whole thing was smashed he denied it. He said he'd told me he was getting the design patented. I did see a solicitor about it afterwards, but he told me I hadn't a chance of proving a deliberate fraud. Newdick would probably have been ticked off in court for taking money without reasonable precautions, but that wouldn't have brought any of it back."

"It was a private company, I suppose," said the Saint.

Monty nodded.

"If it had been a public one, with shares on the open market, it would have been a different matter," he said.

"What happened to the money?"

"Newdick had spent it—or he said he had. He told me he'd paid off all the old debts that had run up while he was experimenting, and spent the rest on some manufacturing plant and machinery for the company. He did give me about six or seven hundred back, and told me he'd work like hell to produce another invention that would really be original so he could pay me back the rest, but that was the last I heard of him. He's probably caught several other mugs with the same game since then." Monty grinned philosophically, looked at the clock, and got up. "Well, I must be getting along. I'll look in and see you on Saturday—if you haven't been arrested and shoved in clink before then."

He departed after another bottle of beer had been lowered; and when he had gone Patricia Holm viewed the Saint doubtfully. She had not missed the quiet attention with which he had followed Monty Hayward's narrative; and she had known Simon Templar a long time. The Saint had a fresh cigarette slanting from the corner of his mouth, his hands were in his pockets, and he was smiling at her with a seraphic innocence which was belied by every facet of the twinkling tang of mockery in his blue eyes.

"You know what I told you," she said.

He laughed.

"About getting into trouble? My darling, when will you stop thinking these wicked thoughts? I'm taking your advice to heart. Maybe there is something to be said for going into business. I think I should look rather fetching in a silk hat and a pair of white spats with pearl buttons; and you've no idea how I could liven up a directors' meeting if I set my mind to it."

Patricia was not convinced.

She was even less convinced when the Saint went out the next morning. From his extensive wardrobe he had selected one of his most elegant suits, a creation in light-hued saxony of the softest and most expensive weave—a garment which could by no possible chance have been worn by a man who had to devote his day to honest toil. His tie was dashing, his silk socks would have made a Communist's righteous indignation swell to bursting point, and over his right eye he had tilted a brand new Panama which would have made one wonder whether the strange shapeless headgear of the same breed worn by old gents whilst pottering around their gardens could conceivably be any relation whatsoever of such a superbly stylish lid. Moreover he had taken out the car which was the pride of his stable—the new cream and red Hirondel which was in itself the hallmark of a man who could afford to pay five thousand pounds for a car and thereafter watch a gallon of petrol blown into smoke every three or four miles.

"Where's the funeral?" she asked; and the Saint smiled blandly.

"I'm a young sportsman with far more money than sense, and I'm sure Comrade Newdick will be pleased to see me," he said; and he kissed her.

Mr. Oscar Newdick was pleased to see him—Simon Templar would have been vastly surprised if he hadn't been. That aura of idle affluence which the Saint could put on as easily as he put on a coat was one of his most priceless accessories, and it was never worn for any honest purpose.

But this Mr. Oscar Newdick did not know. To him, the arrival of such a person was like an answer to prayer. Monty Hayward's guess at Mr. Newdick's activities since collecting five thousand pounds from him was fairly accurate, but only fairly. Mr. Newdick had not caught several other mugs, but only three; and one of them had only been induced to invest a paltry three hundred pounds. The helicopter racket had been failing in its dividends, and the past year had not shown a single pennyworth of profit. Mr. Newdick did not believe in accumulating pennies: when he made a touch, it had to be a big one, and he was prepared to wait for it—the paltry three hundred pound investor had been an error of judgment, a young man who had grossly misled him with fabulous accounts of wealthy uncles, which when the time came to make the touch had been discovered to be the purest fiction—but recently the periods of waiting had exceeded all reasonable limits. Mr. Newdick had travelled literally thousands of miles on the more prosperous suburban lines in search of victims—the fellow-passenger technique really was his own invention, and he practised it to perfection—but many moons had passed since he brought a prospective investor home from his many voyages.

When Simon Templar arrived, in fact, Mr. Newdick was gazing mournfully over the litter of spars and fabric and machinery in one of his corrugated-iron sheds, endeavouring to estimate its value in the junk market. The time had come, he was beginning to feel, when that particular stock-in-trade had paid the last percentage that could be squeezed out of it; it had rewarded him handsomely for his initial investment, but now it was obsolete. The best solution appeared to be to turn it in and concentrate his varied talents on some other subject. A fat insurance policy, of course, followed by a well-organized fire, would have been more profitable; but a recent sensational arson trial and the consequent publicity given to such schemes made him wary of taking that way out. And he was engrossed in these uninspiring meditations when the bell in his "office" rang and manna fell from Heaven.

Mr. Oscar Newdick, it must be acknowledged, did not instantly recognise it as manna. At first he thought it could only be the rate collector, or another summons for his unpaid electric light bill. He tiptoed to a grimy window which looked out on the road, with intent to escape rapidly across the adjacent fields if his surmise proved correct; and it was thus that he saw the imposing automobile which stood outside.

Mr. Newdick, a man of the world, was jerry to the fact that rate collectors and servers of summonses rarely arrive to their grim work in five-thousand-pound Hirondels; and it was with an easy conscience, if not yet admixed with undue optimism, that he went to open the door.

"Hullo, old bean," said the Saint.

"Er—hullo," said Mr. Newdick.

"I blew in to see if you could tell me anything about your jolly old company," said the Saint.

"Er—yes," said Mr. Newdick. "Er—why don't you come inside?"

His hesitation was not due to any bashfulness or even to offended dignity. Mr. Newdick did not mind being called an old bean. He had no instinctive desire to snub wealthy-looking young men with five-thousand-pound Hirondels who added jollity to his old company. The fact was that he was just beginning to recognise the manna for what it was, and his soul was suffering the same emotions as those which had afflicted the Israelites in their time when they contemplated the miracle. The Saint came in. Mr. Newdick's "office" was a small roughly-fashioned cubicle about the size of a telephone booth, containing a small table littered with papers and overlaid with a thin film of dust—it scarcely seemed in keeping with the neatly engraved brass plate on the door which proclaimed it to be the registered offices of the New-dick Helicopter Company, Limited, but his visitor did not seem distressed by it.

"What did you want to know?" asked Mr. Newdick.

Simon observed him to be a middle-aged man of only vaguely military appearance, with sharp eyes that looked at him unwaveringly. That characteristic alone might have deceived most men; but Simon Templar had moved in disreputable circles long enough to know that the ability to look another man squarely in the eye is one of the most fallacious indices of honesty.

"Well," said the Saint amiably, tendering a platinum cigarette-case, "the fact is that I'm interested in helicopters. I happen to have noticed your little place several times recently when I've been passing, and I got the idea that it was quite a small show, and I wondered if there might by any chance be room for another partner in it."

"You mean," repeated Mr. Newdick, checking back on the incredible evidence of his ears, "that you wanted to take an interest in the firm?"

Simon nodded.

"That was the jolly old idea," he said. "In fact, if the other partners felt like selling out, I might take over the whole blinkin' show. I've got a good deal of time on my hands, and I like pottering about with aeroplanes and what not. A chap's got to do something to keep out of mischief, what? Besides, it doesn't look as if you were doing a lot of business here, and I might be able to wake the jolly old place up a bit. Sort of aerial roadhouse, if you know what I mean. Dinners—drinks—dancing—pretty girls. . . . What?"

"I didn't say anything," said Mr. Newdick.

"All right. What about it, old bean?"

Mr. Newdick scratched his chin. The notion of manna had passed into his cosmogony. It fell from Heaven. It was real. Miracles happened. The world was a brighter, rosier place.

"One of your remarks, of course," he said, "is somewhat uninformed. As a matter of fact, we are doing quite a lot of business. We have orders, negotiations, tenders, contracts. . . ." The eloquent movement of one hand, temporarily released from massaging his chin, indicated a whole field of industry of which the uninitiated were in ignorance. "However," he said, "if your proposition were attractive enough, it would be worth hearing."

Simon nodded.

"Well, old bean, who do I put it to?"

"You may put it to me, if you like," said Mr. Newdick. "I am Oscar Newdick."

"I see. But what about the other partners, Oscar, old sprout?"

Mr. Newdick waved his hand.

"They are largely figureheads," he explained. "A few friends, with very small interests—just enough to meet the technical requirements of a limited company. The concern really belongs to me."

Simon beamed.

"Splendid!" he said. "Jolly good! Well, well, well, dear old Newdick, what d'you think it's worth?"

"There is a nominal share value of twenty-five thousands pounds," said Mr. Newdick seriously. "But, of course, they are worth far more than that. Far more. . . . I very much doubt," he said, "whether fifty thousand would be an adequate price. My patents alone are worth more than fifty thousand pounds. Sixty thousands pounds would scarcely tempt me. Seventy thousand would be a poor price. Eighty thousand——"

"Is quite a lot of money," said the Saint, interrupting Mr. Newdick's private auction.

Mr. Newdick nodded.

"But you haven't seen the place yet—or the machine we turn out. You ought to have a look round, even if we can't do business."

Mr. Newdick suffered a twinge of horror at the thought even while he uttered it.

He led the Saint out of his "office" to the junk shed. No one who had witnessed his sad survey of that collection of lumber a few minutes before would have believed that it was the same man who now gazed on it with such enthusiasm and affection.

"This," said Mr. Newdick, "is our workshop. Here you can see the parts of our machines in course of construction and assembly. Those lengths of wood are our special longerons. Over there are stay and braces. . . ."

"By Jove!" said the Saint in awe. "I'd no idea helicopters went in for all those things. They must be quite dressed up when you've finished with them, what? By the way, talking of longerons, a girl friend of mine has the neatest pattern of step-ins . . ."

Mr. Newdick listened patiently.

Presently they passed on to the other shed. Mr. Newdick opened the door as reverently as if he had been unveiling a memorial.

"And this," he said, "is the Newdick helicopter."

Simon glanced over it vacuously, and looked about him.

"Where are all your workmen today?" he asked.

"They are on holiday," said Mr. Newdick, making a mental note to engage some picturesque mechanics the next day. "An old custom of the firm. I always give them a full day's holiday on the anniversary of my dear mother's death." He wiped away a tear and changed the subject. "How would you like to take a flight?"

"Jolly good idea," agreed the Saint.

The helicopter was wheeled out, and while it was warming up, Simon revealed that he also was a flier and possessed a license for helicopters. Mr. Newdick complimented him gravely. They made a ten-minute flight, and when they had landed again the Saint remained in his seat.

"D'you mind if I try her out myself?" he said. "I won't ask you to take the flight with me."

The machine was not fitted with dual control, but it was well insured. Mr. Newdick only hesitated a moment. He was very anxious to please.

"Certainly," he said. "Give her a thorough test yourself, and you'll see that she's a good bus."

Simon took the ship off and climbed towards the north. When Mr. Newdick's tiny aerodrome was out of sight he put the helicopter through every test he could think of, and the results amazed him even while they only confirmed the remarkable impression he had gained while Mr. Newdick was flying it.

When he saw the London Air Park below him he shut off the engine and came down in a perfect vertical descent which set him down outside the Cierva hangars. Simon climbed out and buttonholed one of the company's test pilots.

"Would you like to come on a short hop with me?" he asked. "I want to show you something."

As they walked back towards the Newdick helicopter the pilot studied it with a puzzled frown.

"Is that one of our machines?" he said.

"More or less," Simon told him.

"It looks as if it had been put together wrong," said the pilot worriedly. "Have you been having trouble with it?"

The Saint shook his head.

"I think you'll find," he answered, "that it's been put together right."

He demonstrated what he meant, and when they returned the test pilot took the machine up again himself and tried it a second time. Other test pilots tried it. Engineers scratched their heads over it and tried it. Telephone calls were made to London. A whole two hours passed before Simon Templar dropped the machine beside Mr. Newdick's sheds and relieved the inventor of the agonies of anxiety which had been racking him.

"I was afraid you'd killed yourself," said Mr. Newdick with emotion; and indeed the thought that his miraculous benefactor might have passed away before being separated from his money had brought Mr. Newdick out in several cold sweats.

The Saint grinned.

"I just buzzed over to Reading to look up a friend," he said untruthfully. "I like your helicopter. Let us go inside and talk business."

When he returned to Patricia, much later that day, he was jubilant but mysterious. He spent most of the next day with Mr. Newdick, and half of the Saturday which came after, but he refused to tell her what he was doing. It was not until that evening, when he was pouring beer once more for Monty Hayward, that he mentioned Mr. Newdick again; and then his announcement took her breath away.

"I've bought that helicopter company," he said casually.

"You've *what?*" spluttered Monty.

"I've bought that helicopter company and everything it owns," said the Saint, "for forty thousand pounds."

They gaped at him for a while in silence, while he calmly continued with the essential task of opening bottles.

"The man's mad," said Patricia finally. "I always thought so."

"When did you do this?" asked Monty.

"We fixed up the last details of the deal today," said the Saint. "Oscar is due here at any minute to sign the papers."

Monty swallowed beer feverishly.

"I suppose you wouldn't care to buy my shares as well?" he suggested.

"Sure, I'll buy them," said the Saint affably. "Name your price. Oscar's contribution gives me a controlling interest, but I can al-

ways handle a bit more. As ordered by Patricia, I'm going into
business. The machine is to be rechristened the Templar helicopter. I shall go down to history as the man who put England in the
air. Bevies of English beauty, wearing their Templar longerons—
stays, braces, and everything complete——"

The ringing of his door-bell interrupted the word-picture and
took him from the room before any of the questions that were
howling through their bewildered minds could be asked.

Mr. Newdick was on the mat, beaming like a delighted fox.
Simon took his hat and umbrella, took Mr. Newdick by the arm,
and led him through into the living-room.

"Boys and girls," he said cheerfully, "this is our fairy godmother, Mr. Oscar Newdick. This is Miss Holm, Oscar, old toad-
stool; and I think you know Mr. Hayward——"

The inventor's arm had stiffened under his hand, and his smile
had vanished. His face was turning pale and nasty.

"What's the game?" he demanded hoarsely.

"No game at all, dear old garlic-blossom," said the Saint innocently. "Just a coincidence. Mr. Hayward is going to sell me
his shares too. Now, all the papers are here, and if you'll just sign
on the dotted line——"

"I refuse!" babbled Newdick wildly. "It's a trap!"

Simon stepped back and regarded him blandly.

"A trap, Oscar? What on earth are you talking about? You've
got a jolly good helicopter, and you've nothing to be ashamed of.
Come, now, be brave. Harden the Newdick heart. There may be a
wrench at parting with your brainchild, but you can cry afterwards. Just a signature or two on the dotted line, and it's all over.
And there's a cheque for forty thousand pounds waiting for
you. . . ."

He thrust a fountain-pen into the inventor's hand; and, half-
hypnotised, Mr. Newdick signed. The Saint blotted the signatures
carefully and put the agreements away in a drawer, which he
locked. Then he handed Mr. Newdick a cheque. The inventor
grasped it weakly and stared at the writing and figures on it as if
he expected them to fade away under his eyes. He had the quite
natural conviction that his brain had given way.

"Th-thank you very much," he said shakily, and was conscious
of little more than an overpowering desire to remove himself

from those parts—to camp out on the doorstep of a bank and wait there with his head in his hands until morning, when he could pass the cheque over the counter and see crisp banknotes clicking back to him in return to prove that his sanity was not entirely gone. "Well, I must be going," he gulped out; but the Saint stopped him.

"Not a bit of it, Oscar," he murmured. "You don't intrude. In fact, you ought to be the guest of honour. Your class as an inventor really is A 1. When I showed the Cierva people what you'd done, they nearly collapsed."

Mr. Newdick blinked at him in a painful daze.

"What do you mean?" he stammered.

"Why, the way you managed to build an autogiro that would go straight up and down. None of the ordinary ones will, of course—the torque of the vanes would make it spin round like a top if it didn't have a certain amount of forward movement to hold it straight. I can only think that when you got hold of some Cierva parts and drawings and built it up yourself, you found out that it didn't go straight up and down as you'd expected and thought you must have done something wrong. So you set about trying to put it right—and somehow or other you brought it off. It's a pity you were in such a hurry to tell Mr. Hayward that everything in your invention had been patented before, Oscar, because if you'd made a few more inquiries you'd have found that it hadn't." Simon Templar grinned, and patted the stunned man kindly on the shoulder. "But everything happens for the best, dear old bird; and when I tell you that the Cierva people have already made me an offer of a hundred thousand quid for the invention you've just sold me, I'm sure you'll stay and join us in a celebratory bottle of beer."

Mr. Oscar Newdick swayed slightly, and glugged a strangling obstruction out of his throat.

"I—I don't think I'll stay," he said. "I'm not feeling very well."

"A dose of salts in the morning will do you all the good in the world," said the Saint chattily, and ushered him sympathetically to the door.

"The Man Who Liked Ants" (1937) *finds Simon Templar in Florida, visiting an old friend and once again stumbling over a mad scientist. This time it is a biologist (Dr. Sardon) who is determined to expiate a traumatic childhood memory by providing his insect friends an opportunity to take revenge against all humanity.*

THE MAN WHO LIKED ANTS

"I wonder what would have happened if you had gone into a respectable business, Saint," Ivar Nordsten remarked one afternoon.

Simon Templar smiled at him so innocently that for an instant his nickname might almost have seemed justified—if it had not been for the faint lazy twinkle of unsaintly mockery that stirred at the back of his blue eyes. "The question is too farfetched, Ivar. You might as well speculate about what would have happened if I'd been a Martian or a horse."

They sat on the veranda of the house of Ivar Nordsten—whose name was not really Ivar Nordsten, but who was alive that day and the master of fabulous millions only because the course of one of the Saint's lawless escapades had once crossed his path at a time when death would have seemed a happy release. He of all living men should have had no wish to change the history of that twentieth-century Robin Hood, whose dark reckless face and gay impudence of outlawry had in its time set the underworlds of five continents buzzing like nests of infuriated wasps. But in that mood of idle fantasy which may well come with the after-lunch contentment of a warm Florida afternoon, Nordsten would have put forward almost any preposterous premise that might give him the pleasure of listening to his friend. "It isn't as farfetched as that," he said. "You will never admit it, but you have many respectable instincts."

"But I have so many more disreputable ones to keep them

under control," answered the Saint earnestly. "And it's always been so much more amusing to indulge the disreputable instincts. . . . No, Ivar, I mustn't let you make a paragon out of me. If I were quite cynically psychoanalyzing myself, I should probably say that the reason why I only soak the more obvious excrescences on the human race is because it makes everything okay with my respectable instincts and lets them go peacefully to sleep. Then I can turn all my disreputable impulses loose on the mechanical problem of soaking this obvious excrescence in some satisfyingly novel and juicy manner, and get all the fun of original sin out of it without any qualms of conscience."

"But you contradict yourself. The mere fact that you speak in terms of what you call 'an obvious excrescence on the human race' proves that you have some moral standards by which you judge him, and that you have some idealistic interest in the human race itself."

"The human race," said the Saint sombrely, "is a repulsive, dull, bloated, ill-conditioned and ill-favoured mass of dimly conscious meat, the chief justification for whose existence is that it provides a contrasting background against which my beauty and spiritual perfections can shine with a lustre only exceeded by your own."

"You have a natural modesty which I had never suspected," Nordsten observed gravely, and they both laughed. "But," he added, "I think you will get on well with Dr. Sardon."

"Who is he?"

"A neighbour of mine. We are dining with him tonight."

Simon frowned. "I warned you that I was travelling without any dress clothes," he began, but Nordsten shook his head maliciously.

"Dr. Sardon likes dress clothes even less than you do. And you never warned me that you were coming here at all. So what could I do? I accepted his invitation a week ago, so when you arrived I could only tell Sardon what had happened. Of course he insisted that you must come with me. But I think he will interest you."

The Saint sighed resignedly and swished the highball gently around in his glass so that the ice clinked. "Why should I be interested in any of your neighbours?" he protested. "I didn't come here to commit any crimes; and I'm sure all these people are as respectable as millionaires can be."

"Dr. Sardon is not a millionaire. He is a very brilliant biologist."

"What else makes him interesting?"

"He is very fond of ants," said Nordsten seriously, and the Saint sat up.

Then he finished his drink deliberately and put down the glass. "Now I know that this climate doesn't agree with you," he said. "Let's get changed and go down to the tennis court. I'll put you in your place before we start the evening."

Nevertheless he drove over to Dr. Sardon's house that evening in a mood of open-minded curiosity. Scientists he had known before, men who went down thousands of feet into the sea to look at globigerina ooze and men who devised complicated electrical gadgets in laboratories to manufacture gold; but this was the first time that he had heard of a biologist who was fond of ants. Everything that was out of the ordinary was prospective material for the Saint. It must be admitted that in simplifying his own career of elementary equations by which obvious excrescences on the human race could be soaked, he did himself less than justice.

But there was nothing about the square smooth-shaven man who was introduced to him as Dr. Sardon to take away the breath of any hardened outlaw. He might perhaps have been an ordinary efficient doctor, possibly with an exclusive and sophisticated practice; more probably he could have been a successful stockbroker, or the manager of any profitable commercial business. He shook hands with them briskly and almost mechanically, seeming to summarize the Saint in one sweeping glance through his crisp-looking rimless pince-nez. "No, you're not a bit late, Mr. Nordsten. As a matter of fact I was working until twenty minutes ago. If you had come earlier I should have been quite embarrassed."

He introduced his niece, a dark slender girl with a quiet and rather aloof beauty which would have been chilling if it had not been relieved by the friendly humour of her brown eyes. About her, Simon admitted, there might certainly have been things to attract the attention of a modern buccaneer. "Carmen has been assisting me. She has a very good degree from Columbia."

He made no other unprompted reference to his researches, and

Simon recognized him as the modern type of scientist whose carefully cultivated pose of matter-of-fact worldliness is just as fashionable an affectation as the mystical and bearded eccentricity of his predecessors used to be. Dr. Sardon talked about politics, about his golf handicap and about the art of Otto Soglow. He was an entertaining and effective conversationalist but he might never have heard of such a thing as biology until towards the close of dinner Ivar Nordsten skilfully turned a discussion of gardening to the subject of insect pests. "Although, of course," he said, "you would not call them that."

It was strange to see the dark glow that came into Sardon's eyes. "As a popular term," he said in his deep vibrant voice, "I suppose it is too well established for me to change it. But it would be much more reasonable for the insects to talk about human pests."

He turned to Simon. "I expect Mr. Nordsten has already warned you about the—bee in my bonnet," he said; but he used the phrase without smiling. "Do you by any chance know anything about the subject?"

"I had a flea once," said the Saint reminiscently. "I called him Goebbels. But he left me."

"Then you would be surprised to know how many of the most sensational achievements of man were surpassed by the insects hundreds of years ago without any artificial aids." The finger-tips of his strong nervous hands played a tattoo against each other. "You talk about the Age of Speed and Man's Conquest of the Air; and yet the fly *Cephenomia,* the swiftest living creature, can outpace the fastest of your boasted airplanes. What is the greatest scientific marvel of the century? Probably you would say radio. But Count Arco, the German radio expert, has proved the existence of a kind of wireless telegraphy, or telepathy, between certain species of beetle, which makes nothing of a separation of miles. Lakhovsky claims to have demonstrated that this is common to several other insects. When the *Redemanni* termites build their twenty-five-foot conical towers topped with ten-foot chimneys they are performing much greater marvels of engineering than building an Empire State Building. To match them, in proportion to our size, we should have to put up skyscrapers four thousand feet high—and do it without tools."

"I knew the ants would come into it," said Nordsten sotto voce.

Sardon turned on him with his hot piercing gaze. "Termites are not true ants—the term 'white ants' is a misnomer. Actually they are related to the cockroach. I merely mentioned them as one of the most remarkable of the lower insects. They have a superb social organization, and they may even be superior strategists to the true ants, but they were never destined to conquer the globe. The reason is that they cannot stand light and they cannot tolerate temperatures below twenty degrees centigrade. Therefore, their fields of expansion are forever limited. They are one of Nature's false beginnings. They are a much older species than man, and they have evolved as far as they are likely to evolve. . . . It is not the same with the true ants."

He leaned forward over the table, with his face white and transfigured as if in a kind of trance. "The true ant is the destined ruler of the earth. Can you imagine a state of society in which there was no idleness, no poverty, no unemployment, no unrest? We humans would say that it was an unattainable Utopia; and yet it was in existence among the ants when man was a hairy savage scarcely distinguishable from an ape. You may say that it is incompatible with progress—that it could only be achieved in the same way that it is achieved by domestic cattle. But the ant has the same instincts which have made man the tyrant of creation in his time. *Lasius fuliginosus* keeps and milks its own domestic cattle, in the form of plant lice. *Polyergus rufescens* and *Formica sanguinea* capture slaves and put them to work. *Messor barbarus,* the harvesting ant, collects and stores grain. The *Attini* cultivate mushrooms in underground forcing houses. And all these things are done, not for private gain, but for the good of the whole community. Could man in any of his advances ever boast of that?"

"But if ants have so many advantages," said the Saint slowly, "and they've been civilized so much longer than man, why haven't they conquered the earth before this?"

"Because Nature cheated them. Having given them so much, she made them wait for the last essential—pure physical bulk."

"The brontosaurus had enough of that," said Nordsten, "and yet man took its place."

Sardon's thin lips curled. "The difference in size between man and brontosaurus was nothing compared with the difference in size between man and ant. There are limits to the superiority of brain over brawn—even to the superiority of the brain of an ant, which in proportion to its size is twice as large as the brain of a man. But the time is coming . . ." His voice sank almost to a whisper, and in the dim light of candles on the table the smouldering luminousness of his eyes seemed to leave the rest of his face in deep shadow. "With the ant, Nature overreached herself. The ant was ready to take his place at the head of creation before creation was ready for him—before the solar system had progressed far enough to give him the conditions in which his body, and his brain with it, his brain which in all its intrinsic qualities is so much finer than the brain of man, could grow to the brute size at which all its potentialities could be developed. Nevertheless, when the solar system is older, and the sun is red because the white heat of its fire is exhausted, and the red light which will accelerate the growth of all living cells is stronger, the ant will be waiting for his turn. Unless Nature finds a swifter instrument than Time to put right her miscalculation . . ."

"Does it matter?" asked the Saint lightly, and Sardon's face seemed to flame at him.

"It matters. That is only another thing which we can learn from the ant—that individual profit and ambition should count for nothing beside more enduring good. Listen. When I was a boy I loved small creatures. Among them I kept a colony of ants. In a glass box. I watched them in their busy lives, I studied them as they built their nest, I saw how they divided their labor and how they lived and died so that their common life could go on. I loved them because they were so much better than everyone else I knew. But the other boys could not understand. They thought I was soft and stupid. They were always tormenting me. One day they found my glass box where the ants lived. I fought them, but there were so many of them. They were big and cruel. They made a fire and they put my box on it, while they held me. I saw the ants running, fighting, struggling insanely——" The hushed voice tightened as he spoke until it became thin and shrill like a suppressed scream. "I saw them curling up and shriveling, writhing, tortured. I could hear the hiss of their seething agony in the flames. I saw them going mad, twisting—sprawling—blackening —*burning alive before my eyes*——"

"Uncle!"

The quiet voice of the girl Carmen cut softly across the muted shriek in which the last words were spoken, so quietly and normally that it was only in the contrast that Simon realized that Sardon had not really raised his voice.

The wild fire died slowly out of Sardon's eyes. For a moment his face remained set and frozen, and then, as if he had only been recalled from a fleeting lapse of attention, he seemed to come awake again with a slight start. "Where was I?" he said calmly. "Oh yes. I was speaking about the intelligence of ants. . . . It is even a mistake to assume, because they make no audible sounds, that they have not just as excellent means of communication as ourselves. Whether they share the telepathic gifts of other insects is a disputed point, but it is certain that in their antennae they possess an idiom which is adequate to all ordinary needs. By close study and observation it has even been possible for us to learn some of the elementary gestures. The work of Karl Escherich . . ."

He went into details, in the same detached incisive tone in which he had been speaking before his outburst.

Simon Templar's fingers stroked over the cloth, found a crumb of bread and massaged it gradually into a soft round pellet. He stole a casual glance at the girl. Her aloof oval face was pale, but that might have been its natural complexion; her composure was unaltered. Sardon's outburst might never have occurred, and she might never have had to interrupt it. Only the Saint thought that he saw a shadow of fear moving far down in her eyes.

Even after Carmen had left the table, and the room was richening with the comfortable aromas of coffee and liqueur brandy and cigars, Sardon was still riding his hobbyhorse. It went on for nearly an hour, until at one of the rare lulls in the discussion Nordsten said: "All the same, Doctor, you are very mysterious about what this has to do with your own experiments."

Sardon's hands rested on the table, white and motionless, the fingers spread out. "Because I was not ready. Even to my friends I should not like to show anything incomplete. But in the last few weeks I have disposed of my uncertainty. Tonight, if you like, I could show you a little."

"We should be honoured."

The flat pressure of Sardon's hands on the table increased as he pushed back his chair and stood up. "My workshops are at the end of the garden," he said, and blew out the four candles.

As they rose and followed him from the room, Nordsten touched the Saint's arm and said in a low voice: "Are you sorry I dragged you out?"

The girl Carmen rejoined them as they left the house. Simon found her walking beside him as they strolled through the warm moonlight. He dropped the remains of his cigar and offered his cigarette case; they stopped for a moment while he gave her a light. Neither of them spoke, but her arm slipped through his as they went on.

The blaze of lights which Sardon switched on in his laboratory wiped the dim silvery gloom out of their eyes in a crash of harsh glaring illumination. In contrast with the tasteful furnishings of the house, the cold white walls and bare tiled floor struck the Saint's sensitive vision with the hygienic and inhuman chill which such places always gave him. But Sardon's laboratory was not like any other place of that kind in which he had ever been.

Ranged along the walls were rows of big glass-fronted boxes, in which apparently formless heaps of litter and rubble could be dimly made out. His eye was caught by a movement in one of the boxes, and he stepped up to look at it more closely. Almost in the same moment he stopped, and nearly recoiled from it, as he realized that he was looking at the largest ant that he had ever seen. It was fully six inches long; and, magnified in that proportion, he could see every joint in its shiny armor-plated surface and the curious bifurcated claws at the ends of its legs. It stood there with its antennae waving gently, watching him with its bulging eyes . . . "*Tetramorium cespitum*," said Dr. Sardon, standing beside him. "One of my early experiments. Its natural size is about three tenths of an inch, but it did not respond very well to treatment."

"I should say it had responded heroically," said the Saint. "You don't mean you can do better than that?"

Sardon smiled. "It was one of my early experiments," he repeated. "I was then merely trying to improve on the work of Ludwig and Ries of Berne, who were breeding giant insects almost comparable with that one, many years ago, with the aid of red light. Subsequently I discovered another principle of growth

which they had overlooked, and I also found that an artificial se-
lective cross-breeding between different species not only improved
the potential size but also increased the intelligence. For instance,
here is one of my later results—a combination of *Oecophylla
smaragdina* and *Prenolepsis imparis*."

He went to one of the longer and larger boxes at the end of the
room. At first Simon could see nothing but a great mound of
twigs and leaves piled high in one corner. There were two or
three bones, stripped bare and white, lying on the sandy floor of
the box. . . . Then Sardon tapped on the glass, and Simon saw
with a sudden thrill of horror that what had been a dark hole in
the mound of leaves was no longer black and empty. There was a
head peering out of the shadow—dark bronze-green, iridescent,
covered with short sparse bristly hairs. . . . "*Oecophylla* is, of
course, one of the more advanced species," Sardon was saying, in
his calm precise manner. "It is the only known creature other
than man to use a tool. The larvae secrete a substance similar to
silk, with which the *ants* weave leaves together to make their
nests, holding the larvae in their jaws and using them as shuttles.
I don't yet know whether my hybrid has inherited that instinct."

"It looks as if it would make a charming pet, anyway," murmured the Saint thoughtfully. "Sort of improved lap dog, isn't it?"

The faint sly smile stayed fixed on Sardon's thin lips. He took
two steps further, to a wide sliding door that took up most of the
wall at the end of the laboratory, and looked back at them sidelong. "Perhaps you would like to see the future ruler of the
world," he said, so very softly that it seemed as if everyone else
stopped breathing while he spoke.

Simon heard the girl beside him catch her breath, and Nordsten
said quickly: "Surely we've troubled you enough already——"

"I should like to see it," said the Saint quietly.

Sardon's tongue slid once over his lips. He put his hand up and
moved a couple of levers on the glittering panels of dials and
switches beside the door. It was to the Saint that his gaze returned, with that rapt expression of strangely cunning and yet
childish happiness.

"You will see it from where you stand. I will ask you to keep
perfectly still, so as not to draw attention to yourselves—there is
a strain of *Dorylina* in this one. *Dorylina* is one of the most intel-

ligent and highly disciplined species, but it is also the most savage. I do not wish it to become angry——" His arm stretched out
to the handle of the door. He slid it aside in one movement,
standing with his back to it, facing them.

The girl's cold hand touched the Saint's wrist. Her fingers
slipped down over his hand and locked in with his own, clutching
them in a sudden convulsive grip. He heard Ivar Nordsten's
suppressed gasp as it caught in his throat, and an icy tingle ran up
his spine and broke out in a clammy dew on his forehead.

The rich red light from the chamber beyond the door spilled
out like liquid fire, so fierce and vivid that it seemed as if it could
only be accompanied by the scorching heat of an open furnace;
but it held only a slight appreciable warmth. It beat down from
huge crimson arcs ranged along the cornices of the inner room
among a maze of shining tubes and twisted wires; there was a
great glass hall opposite in which a pale yellow streak of lightning
forked and flickered with a faint humming sound. The light struck
scarlet highlights from the gleaming bars of a great metal cage
like a gigantic chicken coop which filled the centre of the room to
within a yard of the walls. And within the cage something monstrous and incredible stood motionless, staring at them. Simon
would see it sometimes, years afterwards, in uneasy dreams.
Something immense and frightful, glistening like burnished cop-
per, balanced on angled legs like bars of plated metal. Only for a
few seconds he saw it then, and for most of that time he was held
fascinated by its eyes, understanding something that he would
never have believed before. . . .

And then suddenly the thing moved, swiftly and horribly and
without sound; and Sardon slammed the door shut, blotting out
the eye-aching sea of red light and leaving only the austere cold
whiteness of the laboratory. "They are not all like lap dogs," Sardon said in a kind of whisper.

Simon took out a handkerchief and passed it across his brow.
The last thing about that weird scene that fixed itself consciously
in his memory was the girl's fingers relaxing their tense grip on
his hand, and Sardon's eyes, bland and efficient and businesslike
again, pinned steadily on them both in a sort of secret sneer. . . .

"What do you think of our friend?" Ivar Nordsten asked, as
they drove home two hours later.

Simon stretched out a long arm for the lighter at the side of the car. "He is a lunatic—but of course you knew that. I'm only wondering whether he is quite harmless."

"You ought to sympathize with his contempt for the human race."

The red glow of the Saint's cigarette end brightened so that for an instant the interior of the car was filled with something like a pale reflection of the unearthly crimson luminescence they had seen in Dr. Sardon's forcing room. "Did you sympathize with his affection for his pets?"

"Those great ants?" Nordsten shivered involuntarily. "No. That last one—it was the most frightful thing I have ever seen. I suppose it was really alive?"

"It was alive," said the Saint steadily. "That's why I'm wondering whether Dr. Sardon is harmless. I don't know what you were looking at, Ivar, but I'll tell you what made my blood run cold. It wasn't the mere size of the thing—though any common or garden ant would be terrifying enough if you enlarged it to those dimensions. It was worse than that. It was the proof that Sardon was right. That ant was looking at me. Not like any other insect or even animal that I've ever seen, but like an insect with a man's brain might look. That was the most frightful thing to me. *It knew!*"

Nordsten stared at him. "You mean that you believe what he was saying about it being the future ruler of the world?"

"By itself, no," answered Simon. "But if it were not by itself——"

He did not finish the sentence; and they were silent for the rest of the drive. Before they went to bed he asked one more question. "Who else knows about these experiments?"

"No one, I believe. He told me the other day that he was not prepared to say anything about them until he could show complete success. As a matter of fact, I lent him some money to go on with his work, and that is the only reason he took me into his confidence. I was surprised when he showed us his laboratory tonight—even I had never seen it before."

"So he is convinced now that he can show a complete success," said the Saint quietly, and was still subdued and preoccupied the next morning. In the afternoon he refused to swim or play tennis.

He sat hunched up in a chair on the veranda, scowling into space and smoking innumerable cigarettes, except when he rose to pace restlessly up and down like a big nervous cat.

"What you are really worried about is the girl," Nordsten teased him.

"She's pretty enough to worry about," said the Saint shamelessly. "I think I'll go over and ask her for a cocktail."

Nordsten smiled. "If it will make you a human being again, by all means do," he said. "If you don't come back to dinner I shall know that she is appreciating your anxiety. In any case, I shall probably be very late myself. I have to attend a committee meeting at the golf club and that always adjourns to the bar and goes on for hours."

But the brief tropical twilight had already given way to the dark before Simon made good his threat. He took out Ivar Nordsten's spare Rolls-Royce and drove slowly over the highway until he found the turning that led through the deep cypress groves to the doctor's house. He was prepared to feel foolish; and yet as his headlights circled through the iron gates he touched his hip pocket to reassure himself that if the need arose he might still feel wise. The trees arching over the drive formed a ghostly tunnel down which the Rolls chased its own forerush of light. The smooth hiss of the engine accentuated rather than broke the silence, so that the mind even of a hardened and unimaginative man might cling to the comfort of that faint sound in the same way that the mind of a child might cling to the light of a candle as a comfort against the gathering terrors of the night. The Saint's lip curled cynically at the flight of his own thoughts. . . .

And then, as the car turned a bend in the drive, he saw the girl, and trod fiercely on the brakes. The tires shrieked on the macadam and the engine stalled as the big car rocked to a standstill. It flashed through the Saint's mind at that instant, when all sound was abruptly wiped out, that the stillness which he had imagined before was too complete for accident. He felt the skin creep over his back, and had to call on an effort of will to force himself to open the door and get out of the car.

She lay face downwards, halfway across the drive, in the pool of illumination shed by the glaring headlights. Simon turned her over and raised her head on his arm. Her eyelids twitched as he did so; a kind of moan broke from her lips, and she fought away from him, in a dreadful wildness of panic, for the brief moment before her eyes opened and she recognized him.

"My dear," he said, "what has been happening?"

She had gone limp in his arms, the breath jerking pitifully through her lips, but she had not fainted again. And behind him in that surround of stifling stillness, he heard quite clearly the rustle of something brushing stealthily over the grass beside the drive. He saw her eyes turning over his shoulder, saw the wide horror in them. *"Look!"*

He spun around, whipping the gun from his pocket, and for more than a second he was paralyzed. For that eternity he saw the thing, deep in the far shadows, dimly illumined by the marginal reflections from the beam of the headlights—something gross and swollen, a dirty grey-white, shaped rather like a great bleached sausage, hideously bloated. Then the darkness swallowed it again, even as his last shot smashed the silence into a hundred tiny echoes.

The girl was struggling to her feet. He snatched at her wrist. "This way."

He got her into the car and slammed the door. Steel and glass closed around them to give an absurd relief, the weak unreasoning comfort to the naked flesh which men under a bombardment find in cowering behind canvas screens. She slumped against his shoulder, sobbing hysterically. "Oh, my God. My God!"

"What was it?" he asked.

"It's escaped again. I knew it would. He can't handle it——"

"Has it got loose before?"

"Yes. Once."

He tapped a cigarette on his thumbnail, stroked his lighter. His face was a beaten mask of bronze and granite in the red glow as he drew the smoke down into the mainsprings of his leaping nerves. "I never dreamed it had come to that," he said. "Even last night, I wouldn't have believed it."

"He wouldn't have shown you that. Even when he was boasting, he wouldn't have shown you. That was his secret. . . . And I've helped him. Oh God," she said. "I can't go on!"

He gripped her shoulders. "Carmen," he said quietly. "You must go away from here."

"He'd kill me."

"You must go away."

The headlamps threw back enough light for him to see her face, tear-streaked and desperate. "He's mad," she said. "He must be. Those horrible things . . . I'm afraid. I wanted to go away but he wouldn't let me. I can't go on. Something terrible is going to happen. One day I saw it catch a dog . . . Oh, my God, if you hadn't come when you did——"

"Carmen." He still held her, speaking slowly and deliberately, putting every gift of sanity that he possessed into the level dominance of his voice. "You must not talk like this. You're safe now. Take hold of yourself."

She nodded. "I know. I'm sorry. I'll be all right. But——"

"Can you drive?"

"Yes."

He started the engine and turned the car around. Then he pushed the gear lever into neutral and set the hand brake. "Drive this car," he said. "Take it down to the gates and wait for me there. You'll be close to the highway, and there'll be plenty of other cars passing for company. Even if you do see anything, you needn't be frightened. Treat the car like a tank and run it over. Ivar won't mind—he's got plenty more. And if you hear anything, don't worry. Give me half an hour, and if I'm not back go to Ivar's and talk to him."

Her mouth opened incredulously. "You're not getting out again?"

"I am. And I'm scared stiff." The ghost of a smile touched his lips, and then she saw that his face was stern and cold. "But I must talk to your uncle."

He gripped her arm for a moment, kissed her lightly, and got out. Without a backward glance he walked quickly away from the car, up the drive towards the house. A flashlight in his left hand lanced the darkness ahead of him with its powerful beam, and he swung it from left to right as he walked, holding his gun in his right hand. His ears strained into the gloom which his eyes could not penetrate, probing the silence under the soft scuff of his own footsteps for any sound that would give him warning; but he forced himself not to look back. The palms of his hands were moist.

The house loomed up in front of him. He turned off to one side of the building, following the direction in which he remembered that Dr. Sardon's laboratory lay. Almost at once he saw the squares of lighted windows through the trees. A dull clang of sound came to him, followed by a sort of furious thumping. He checked himself; and then as he walked on more quickly some of the lighted windows went black. The door of the laboratory opened as the last light went out, and his torch framed Dr. Sardon and the doorway in its yellow circle.

Sardon was pale and dishevelled, his clothes awry. One of his sleeves was torn, and there was a scratch on his face from which blood ran. He flinched from the light as if it had burned him. "Who is that?" he shouted.

"This is Simon Templar," said the Saint in a commonplace tone. "I just dropped in to say hullo."

Sardon turned the switch down again and went back into the laboratory. The Saint followed him. "You just dropped in, eh? Of course. Good. Why not? Did you run into Carmen, by any chance?"

"I nearly ran over her," said the Saint evenly.

The doctor's wandering glance snapped to his face. Sardon's hands were shaking, and a tiny muscle at the side of his mouth twitched spasmodically. "Of course," he said vacantly. "Is she all right?"

"She is quite safe." Simon had put away his gun before the other saw it. He laid a hand gently on the other's shoulder. "You've had trouble here," he said.

"She lost her nerve," Sardon retorted furiously. "She ran away. It was the worst thing she could do. They understand, these creatures. They are too much for me to control now. They disobey me. My commands must seem so stupid to their wonderful brains. If it had not been that this one is heavy and waiting for her time ——" He checked himself.

"I knew," said the Saint calmly.

The doctor peered up at him out of the corners of his eyes.

"You knew?" he repeated cunningly.

"Yes. I saw it."

"Just now?"

92 THE FANTASTIC SAINT

Simon nodded. "You didn't tell us last night," he said. "But it's what I was afraid of. I have been thinking about it all day."

"You've been thinking, have you? That's funny." Sardon chuckled shrilly. "Well, you're quite right. I've done it. I've succeeded. I don't have to work any more. They can look after themselves now. That's funny, isn't it?"

"So it is true. I hoped I was wrong."

Sardon edged closer to him. "You hoped you were wrong? You fool! But I would expect it of you. You are the egotistical human being who believes in his ridiculous conceit that the whole history of the world from its own birth, all the species and races that have come into being and been discarded, everything—everything has existed only to lead up to his own magnificent presence on the earth. Bah! Do you imagine that your miserable little life can stand in the way of the march of evolution? Your day is over! Finished! In there"—his arms stiffened and pointed—"in there you can find the matriarch of the new ruling race of the earth. At any moment she will begin to lay her eggs, thousands upon thousands of them, from which her sons and daughters will breed—as big as she is, with her power and her brains." His voice dropped. "To me it is only wonderful that I should have been Nature's chosen instrument to give them their rightful place a million years before Time would have opened the door to them."

The flame in his eyes sank down as his voice sank and his features seemed to relax so that his square clean-cut efficient face became soft and beguiling like the face of an idiot child. "I know what it feels like to be God."

Simon held both his arms.

"Dr. Sardon," he said, "you must not go on with this experiment."

The other's face twisted. "The experiment is finished," he snarled. "Are you still blind? Look—I will show you."

He was broad-shouldered and powerfully built, and his strength was that of a maniac. He threw off the Saint's hands with a convulsive wrench of his body and ran to the sliding door at the end of the room. He turned with his back to it, grasping the handle, as the Saint started after him. "You shall meet them yourself," he said hoarsely. "They are not in their cage any more. I will let them out here, and you shall see whether you can stand against them. Stay where you are!"

A revolver flashed in his hand; and the Saint stopped four paces from him. "For your own sake, Dr. Sardon," he said, "stand away from that door."

The doctor leered at him crookedly. "You would like to burn my ants," he whispered.

He turned and fumbled with the spring catch, his revolver swinging carelessly wide from its aim; and the door had started to move when Simon shot him twice through the heart.

Simon was stretched out on the veranda, sipping a highball and sniping mosquitoes with a cigarette end, when Nordsten came up the steps from his car. The Saint looked up with a smile. "My dear fellow," said Nordsten, "I thought you would be at the fire."

"Is there a fire?" Simon asked innocently.

"Didn't you know? Sardon's whole laboratory has gone up in flames. I heard about it at the club, and when I left I drove back that way thinking I should meet you. Sardon and his niece were not there, either. It will be a terrible shock for him when he hears of it. The place was absolutely gutted—I've never seen such a blaze. It might have been soaked in gasoline. It was still too hot to go near, but I suppose all his work has been destroyed. Did you miss Carmen?"

The Saint pointed over his shoulder. "At the present moment she's sleeping in your best guest room," he said. "I gave her enough of your sleeping tablets to keep her like that till breakfast time."

Nordsten looked at him. "And where is Sardon?" he asked at length.

"He is in his laboratory."

Nordsten poured himself out a drink and sat down. "Tell me," he said.

Simon told him the story. When he had finished, Nordsten was silent for a while. Then he said: "It's all right, of course. A fire like that must have destroyed all the evidence. It could all have been an accident. But what about the girl?"

"I told her that her uncle had locked the door and refused to let me in. Her evidence will be enough to show that Sardon was not in his right mind."

"Would you have done it anyhow, Simon?"

The Saint nodded. "I think so. That's what I was worried about, ever since last night. It came to me at once that if any of those brutes could breed——" He shrugged a little wearily. "And when I saw that great queen ant, I knew that it had gone too far. I don't know quite how rapidly ants can breed, but I should imagine that they do it by thousands. If the thousands were all the same size as Sardon's specimens, with the same intelligence, who knows what might have been the end of it?"

"But I thought you disliked the human race," said Nordsten.

Simon got up and strolled across the veranda. "Taken in the mass," he said soberly, "it will probably go on nauseating me. But it isn't my job to alter it. If Sardon was right, Nature will find her own remedy. But the world has millions of years left, and I think evolution can afford to wait."

His cigarette spun over the rail and vanished into the dark like a firefly as the butler came out to announce dinner; and they went into the dining room together.

Years later (1954), in "The Questing Tycoon," the Saint's vacation in Haiti is ended when his too active curiosity lands him in trouble once again. The story features a vivid and detailed account of voodoo lore and a narrow escape in which Simon's life depends on the tin heart of a young woman.

THE QUESTING TYCOON

It was intolerably hot in Port-au-Prince; for the capital city of Haiti lies at the back of a bay, a gullet twenty miles deep beyond which the opening jaws of land extend a hundred and twenty miles still farther to the west and northwest, walled in by steep high hills, and thus perfectly sheltered from every normal shift of the trade winds which temper the climate of most parts of the Antilles. The geography which made it one of the finest natural harbors in the Caribbean had doubtless appealed strongly to the French buccaneers who founded the original settlement; but three centuries later, with the wings of Pan American Airways to replace the sails of a frigate, a no less authentic pirate could be excused for being more interested in escaping from the sweltering heat pocket than in dallying to admire the anchorage.

As soon as Simon Templar had completed his errands in the town, he climbed into the jeep he had borrowed and headed back up into the hills.

Knowing what to expect of Port-au-Prince at that time of year, he had passed up the ambitious new hotels of the capital in favor of the natural air-conditioning of the Châtelet des Fleurs, an unpretentious but comfortable inn operated by an American whom he had met on a previous visit, only about fifteen miles out of the city but five thousand feet above the sea-level heat. He could feel it getting cooler as the road climbed, and in a surprisingly short time it was like being in another latitude. But the scenery did not seem to become any milder to correspond with

the relief of temperature: the same brazen sun bathed rugged
brownish slopes with few trees to soften their parched contours.
Most of the houses he passed, whether a peasant's one-room cottage or an occasional expensive château, were built of irregular
blocks of the same native stone, so that they had an air of being
literally carved out of the landscape; but sometimes in a sudden
valley or clinging to a distant hillside there would be a palm-
thatched cabin of rough raw timbers that looked as if it had been
transplanted straight from Africa. And indisputably transplanted
from Africa were the straggling files of ebony people, most of
them women, a few plutocrats adding their own weight to the already fantastic burdens of incredibly powerful little donkeys, but
the majority laden fabulously themselves with great baskets balanced on their heads, who bustled cheerfully along the rough
shoulders of the road.

He came into the little town of Pétionville, drove past the
pleasant grass-lawned square dominated by the very French-look-
ing white church, and headed on up the corkscrew highway towards Kenscoff. And six kilometers further on he met Sibao.

As he rounded one of the innumerable curves he saw a little
crowd collected, much as some fascinating obstruction would
create a knot in a busy string of ants. Unlike other groups that he
had passed before where a few individuals from one of the ant-
lines would fall out by the wayside to rest and gossip, this cluster
had a focal point and an air of gravity and concern that made
him think first of an automobile accident, although there was no
car or truck in sight. He slowed up automatically, trying to see
what it was all about as he went by, like almost any normal
traveller; but when he glimpsed the unmistakable bright color of
fresh blood he pulled over and stopped, which perhaps few
drivers on that road would have troubled to do.

The chocolate-skinned young woman whom the others were
gathered around had a six-inch gash in the calf of one leg. From
the gestures and pantomime of her companions rather than the
few basic French word-sounds which his ear could pick out of
their excited jabber of Creole, he concluded that a loose stone
had rolled under her foot as she walked, taking it from under her
and causing her to slip sideways down off the shoulder, where another sharp pointed stone happened to stick out at exactly the

right place and angle to slash her like a crude dagger. The mechanics of the accident were not really important, but it was an ugly wound, and the primitive first-aid efforts of the spectators had not been able to stanch the bleeding.

Simon saw from the tint of the blood that no artery had been cut. He made a pressure bandage with his handkerchief and two strips ripped from the tail of his shirt; but it was obvious that a few stitches would be necessary for a proper repair. He picked the girl up and carried her to the jeep.

"Nous allons chercher un médecin," he said; and he must have been understood, for there was no protest over the abduction as he turned the jeep around and headed back towards Pétionville.

The doctor whom he located was learning English and was anxious to practise it. He contrived to keep Simon around while he cleaned and sewed up and dressed the cut, and then conveniently mentioned his fee. Simon paid it, although the young woman tried to protest, and helped her back into the jeep.

His good-Samaritan gesture seemed to have become slightly harder to break off than it had been to get into; but with nothing but time on his hands he was cheerfully resigned to letting it work itself out.

"Where were you going?" he asked in French, and she pointed up the road.

"Là-haut."

The reply was given with a curious dignity, but without presumption. He was not sure at what point he had begun to feel that she was not quite an ordinary peasant girl. She wore the same faded and formless kind of cotton dress, perhaps cleaner than some, but not cleaner than all the others, for it was not uncommon for them to be spotless. Her figure was slimmer and shapelier than most, and her features had a patrician mould that reminded him of ancient Egyptian carvings. They had remained masklike and detached throughout the ministrations of the doctor, although Simon knew that some of it must have hurt like hell.

He drove up again to the place where he had found her. Two other older women were sitting there, and they greeted her as the jeep stopped. She smiled and answered, proudly displaying the new white bandage on her leg. She started to get out.

He saw that there were three baskets by the roadside where the two women had waited. He stopped her, and said: "You should not walk far today, especially with a load. I can take you all the way."

"Vous êtes très gentil."

She spoke French very stiffly and shyly and correctly, like a child remembering lessons. Then she spoke fluently to the other women in Creole, and they hoisted the third basket between them and put it in the back of the jeep. Her shoes were still on top of its miscellany of fruits and vegetables, according to the custom of the country, which regards shoes as too valuable to be worn out with mere tramping from place to place, especially over rough rocky paths.

Simon drove all the way to the Châtelet des Fleurs, where the road seems to end, but she pointed ahead and said: *"Plus loin."*

He drove on around the inn. Not very far beyond it the pavement ended, but a navigable trail meandered on still further and higher towards the background peaks. He expected it to become impassable at every turn, but it teased him on for several minutes and still hadn't petered out when a house suddenly came in sight, built out of rock and perched like a fragment of a medieval castle on a promontory a little above them. A rutted driveway branched off and slanted up to it, and the young woman pointed again.

"La maison-là."

It was not a mansion in size, but on the other hand it was certainly no native peasant's cottage.

"Merci beaucoup," she said in her stilted schoolgirl French, as the jeep stopped in front of it.

"De rien," he murmured amiably, and went around to lift out the heavy basket.

A man came out on to the verandah, and she spoke rapidly in Creole, obviously explaining about her accident and how she came to be chauffeured to the door. As Simon looked up, the man came down to meet him, holding out his hand.

"Please don't bother with that," he said. "I've got a handy man who'll take care of it. You've done enough for Sibao already. Won't you come in and have a drink? My name's Theron Netlord."

Simon Templar could not help looking a little surprised. For Mr. Netlord was not only a white man, but he was unmistakably an American; and Simon had some vague recollection of his name.

II

It can be assumed that the birth of the girl who was later to be called Sibao took place under the very best auspices, for her father was the *houngan* of an *houmfort* in a valley that could be seen from the house where Simon had taken her, which in terms of a more familiar religion than voodoo would be the equivalent of the vicar of a parish church; and her mother was not only a *mambo* in her own right, but also an occasional communicant of the church in Pétionville. But after the elaborate precautionary rituals with which her birth was surrounded, the child grew up just like any of the other naked children of the hills, until she was nearly seven.

At that time, she woke up one morning and said: "Mama, I saw Uncle Zande trying to fly, but he dived into the ground."

Her mother thought nothing of this until the evening, when word came that Uncle Zande, who was laying tile on the roof of a building in Léogane, had stumbled off it and broken his neck. After that much attention was paid to her dreams, but the things that they prophesied were not always so easy to interpret until after they happened.

Two years later her grandfather fell sick with a burning fever, and his children and grandchildren gathered around to see him die. But the young girl went to him and caressed his forehead, and at that moment the sweating and shivering stopped, and the fever left him and he began to mend. After that there were others who asked for her touch, and many of them affirmed that they experienced extraordinary relief.

At least it was evident that she was entitled to admission to the *houmfort* without further probation. One night, with a red bandanna on her head and gay handkerchiefs knotted around her neck and arms, with a bouquet in one hand and a crucifix in the other, she sat in a chair between her four sponsors and watched the *hounsis-canzo*, the student priests, dance before her. Then her father took her by the hand to the President of the congregation, and she recited her first voodoo oath:

"*Je jure, je jure,* I swear, to respect the powers of the *mystères de Guinée,* to respect the powers of the *houngan,* of the President of the Society, and the powers of all those on whom these powers are conferred."

And after she had made all her salutations and prostrations, and had herself been raised shoulder high and applauded, they withdrew and left her before the altar to receive whatever revelation the spirits might vouchsafe to her.

At thirteen she was a young woman, long-legged and comely, with a proud yet supple walk and prematurely steady eyes that gazed so gravely at those whom she noticed that they seemed never to rest on a person's face but to look through into the thoughts behind it. She went faithfully to school and learned what she was told to, including a smattering of the absurdly involved and illogical version of her native tongue which they called "French"; but when her father stated that her energy could be better devoted to helping to feed the family, she ended her formal education without complaint.

There were three young men who watched her one evening as she picked pigeon peas among the bushes that her father had planted, and who were more interested by the grace of her body than by any tales they may have heard of her supernatural gifts. As the brief mountain twilight darkened they came to seize her; but she knew what was in their minds, and ran. As the one penitent survivor told it, a cloud suddenly swallowed her: they blundered after her in the fog, following the sounds of her flight: then they saw her shadow almost within reach, and leapt to the capture, but the ground vanished from under their feet. The bodies of two of them were found at the foot of the precipice; and the third lived, though with a broken back, only because a tree caught him on the way down.

Her father knew then that she was more than qualified to become an *hounsis-canzo,* and she told him that she was ready. He took her to the *houmfort* and set in motion the elaborate seven-day ritual of purification and initiation, instructing her in all the mysteries himself. For her *loa,* or personal patron deity, she had chosen Erzulie; and in the baptismal ceremony of the fifth day she received the name of Sibao, the mystic mountain ridge where Erzulie mates with the Supreme Gods, the legendary place of eternal love and fertility. And when the *houngan* made the invocation, the goddess showed her favor by possessing Sibao, who uttered prophecies and admonitions in a language that only *houngans* can interpret, and with the hands and mouth of Sibao accepted and ate of the sacrificial white pigeons and white rice; and the *houngan* was filled with pride as he chanted:

> *"Les Saints mandés mangés.*
> *Genoux-terre!*
> *Parce que gnou loa nan govi pas capab mangé,*
> *Ou gaingnin pour mangé pour li!"*

Thereafter she hoed the patches of vegetables that her father cultivated as before, and helped to grate manioc, and carried water from the spring, and went back and forth to market, like all the other young women; but the tale of her powers grew slowly and surely, and it would have been a reckless man who dared to molest her.

Then Theron Netlord came to Kenscoff, and presently heard of her through the inquiries that he made. He sent word that he would like her to work in his house; and because he offered wages that would much more than pay for a substitute to do her work at home, she accepted. She was then seventeen.

"A rather remarkable girl," said Netlord, who had told Simon some of these things. "Believe me, to some of the people around here, she's almost like a living saint."

Simon just managed not to blink at the word.

"Won't that accident this afternoon shake her pedestal a bit?" he asked.

"Does a bishop lose face if he trips over something and breaks a leg?" Netlord retorted. "Besides, *you* happened. Just when she needed help, you drove by, picked her up, took her to the doctor, and then brought her here. What would you say were the odds against her being so lucky? And then tell me why it doesn't still look as if *something* was taking special care of her!"

He was a big thick-shouldered man who looked as forceful as the way he talked. He had iron-grey hair and metallic grey eyes, a blunt nose, a square thrusting jaw, and the kind of lips that even look muscular. You had an inevitable impression of him at the first glance; and without hesitation you would have guessed him to be a man who had reached the top ranks of some competitive business, and who had bulled his way up there with ruthless disregard for whatever obstructions might have to be trodden down or jostled aside. And trite as the physiognomy must seem, in this instance you would have been absolutely right.

Theron Netlord had made a fortune from the manufacture of bargain-priced lingerie.

The incongruity of this will only amuse those who know little about the clothing industry. It would be natural for the uninitiated to think of the trade in fragile feminine frotheries as being carried on by fragile, feminine and frothy types, but in fact, at the wholesale manufacturing level it is as tough and cut-throat a business as any legitimate operation in the modern world. And even in a business which has always been somewhat notorious for lack of tenderness towards its employees, Mr. Netlord had been a perennial source of ammunition for socialistic agitators. His long-standing vendetta against organized labor was an epic of its kind; and he had been named in one Congressional investigation as the man who, with a combination of gangster tactics and an icepick eye for loopholes in union contracts and government regulations, had come closest in the last decade to running an old-fashioned sweatshop. It was from casually remembered references to such things in the newspapers that Simon had identified the name.

"Do you live here permanently?" Simon asked in a conversational way.

"I've been here for a while, and I'm staying a while," Netlord answered equivocally. "I like the rum. How do you like it?"

"It's strictly ambrosial."

"You can get fine rum in the States, like that Lemon Hart from Jamaica, but you have to come here to drink Barbancourt. They don't make enough to export."

"I can think of worse reasons for coming here. But I might want something more to hold me indefinitely."

Netlord chuckled.

"Of course you would. I was kidding. So do I. I'll never retire. I *like* being in business. It's my sport, my hobby, and my recreation. I've spent more than a year all around the Caribbean, having what everyone would say was a nice long vacation. Nuts. My mind hasn't been off business for a single day."

"They tell me there's a great future in the area."

"And I'm looking for the future. There's none left in America. At the bottom, you've got your employees demanding more wages and pension funds for less work every year. At the top, you've got a damned paternalistic Government taxing your profits to the bone to pay for all its utopian projects at home and abroad. The man who's trying to literally mind his own business is in the middle, in a squeeze that wrings all the incentive out of him. I'm sick of bucking that set-up."

"What's wrong with Puerto Rico? You can get a tax exemption there if you bring in an employing industry."

"Sure. But the Puerto Ricans are getting spoiled, and the cost of labor is shooting up. In a few more years they'll have it as expensive and as organized as it is back home."

"So you're investigating Haiti because the labor is cheaper?"

"It's still so cheap that you could starve to death trying to sell machinery. Go visit one of the factories where they're making wooden salad bowls, for instance. The only power tool they use is a lathe. And where does the power come from? From a man who spends the whole day cranking a big wheel. Why? Because all he costs is one dollar a day—and that's cheaper than you can operate a motor, let alone amortizing the initial cost of it!"

"Then what's the catch?"

"This being a foreign country: your product hits a tariff wall when you try to import it into the States, and the duty will knock you silly."

"Things are tough all over," Simon remarked sympathetically.

The other's sinewy lips flexed in a tight grin.

"Any problem is tough till you lick it. Coming here showed me how to lick this one—but you'd never guess how!"

"I give up."

"I'm sorry, I'm not telling. May I fix your drink?"

Simon glanced at his watch and shook his head.

"Thanks, but I should be on my way." He put down his glass and stood up. "I'm glad I needn't worry about you getting ulcers, though."

Netlord laughed comfortably, and walked with him out on to the front verandah.

"I hope getting Sibao back here didn't bring you too far out of your way."

"No, I'm staying just a little below you, at the Châtelet des Fleurs."

"Then we'll probably run into each other." Netlord put out his hand. "It was nice talking to you, Mr.——"

"Templar. Simon Templar."

The big man's powerful grip held on to Simon's.

"You're not—by any chance—that fellow they call the Saint?"

"Yes." The Saint smiled. "But I'm just a tourist."

He disengaged himself pleasantly; but as he went down the steps he could feel Netlord's eyes on his back, and remembered that for one instant he had seen in them the kind of fear from which murder is born.

III

In telling so many stories of Simon Templar, the chronicler runs a risk of becoming unduly preoccupied with the reactions of various characters to the discovery that they have met the Saint, and it may fairly be observed that there is a definite limit to the possible variety of these responses. One of the most obvious of them was the shock to a guilty conscience which could open a momentary crack in an otherwise impenetrable mask. Yet in this case it was of vital importance.

If Theron Netlord had not betrayed himself for that fleeting second, and the Saint had not been sharply aware of it, Simon might have quickly dismissed the panty potentate from his mind; and then there might have been no story to tell at all.

Instead of which, Simon only waited to make more inquiries about Mr. Netlord until he was able to corner his host, Atherton Lee, alone in the bar that night.

He had an easy gambit by casually relating the incident of Sibao.

"Theron Netlord? Oh, yes, I know him," Lee said. "He stayed

here for a while before he rented that house up on the hill. He still drops in sometimes for a drink and a yarn."

"One of the original rugged individualists, isn't he?" Simon remarked.

"Did he give you his big tirade about wages and taxes?"

"I got the synopsis, anyway."

"Yes, he's a personality all right. At least he doesn't make any bones about where he stands. What beats me is how a fellow of that type could get all wrapped up in voodoo."

Simon did not actually choke and splutter over his drink because he was not given to such demonstrations, but he felt as close to it as he was ever likely to.

"He what?"

"Didn't he get on to that subject? I guess you didn't stay very long."

"Only for one drink."

"He's really sold on it. That's how he originally came up here. He'd seen the voodoo dances they put on in the tourist spots down in Port-au-Prince, but he knew they were just a night-club show. He was looking for the McCoy. Well, we sent the word around, as we do sometimes for guests who're interested, and a bunch from around here came up and put on a show in the patio. They don't do any of the real sacred ceremonies, of course, but they're a lot more authentic than the professionals in town. Netlord lapped it up; but it was just an appetizer to him. He wanted to get right into the fraternity and find out what it was all about."

"What for?"

"He said he was thinking of writing a book about it. But half the time he talks as if he really believed in it. He says that the trouble with Western civilization is that it's too practical—it's never had enough time to develop its spiritual potential."

"Are you pulling my leg or is he pulling yours?"

"I'm not kidding. He rented that house, anyway, and set out to get himself accepted by the natives. He took lessons in Creole so that he could talk to them, and he speaks it a hell of a lot better than I do—and I've lived here a hell of a long time. He hired that girl Sibao just because she's the daughter of the local *houngan*, and she's been instructing him and sponsoring him for the *houm-*

fort. It's all very serious and legitimate. He told me some time ago that he'd been initiated as a junior member, or whatever they call it, but he's planning to take the full course and become a graduate witch-doctor."

"Can he do that? I mean, can a white man qualify?"

"Haitians are very broad-minded," Atherton Lee said gently. "There's no color bar here."

Simon broodingly chain-lighted another cigarette.

"He must be dreaming up something new and frightful for the underwear market," he murmured. "Maybe he's planning to top those perfumes that are supposed to contain mysterious smells that drive the male sniffer mad with desire. Next season he'll come out with a negligee with a genuine voodoo spell woven in, guaranteed to give the matron of a girls' reformatory more sex appeal than Cleopatra."

But the strange combination of fear and menace that he had caught in Theron Netlord's eyes came back to him with added vividness, and he knew that a puzzle confronted him that could not be dismissed with any amusing flippancy. There had to be a true answer, and it had to be of unimaginable ugliness: therefore he had to find it, or he would be haunted for ever after by the thought of the evil he might have prevented.

To find the answer, however, was much easier to resolve than to do. He wrestled with it for half the night, pacing up and down his room; but when he finally gave up and lay down to sleep, he had to admit that his brain had only carried him around in as many circles as his feet, and gotten him just as close to nowhere.

In the morning, as he was about to leave his room, something white on the floor caught his eye. It was an envelope that had been slipped under the door. He picked it up. It was sealed, but there was no writing on it. It was stiff to his touch, as if it contained some kind of card, but it was curiously heavy.

He opened it. Folded in a sheet of paper was a piece of thin bright metal, about three inches by two, which looked as if it might have been cut from an ordinary tin can, flattened out and with the edges neatly turned under so that they would not be sharp. On it had been hammered an intricate symmetrical design.

Basically, a heart. The inside of the heart filled with a precise network of vertical and horizontal lines, with a single dot in the center of each little square that they formed. The outline of the heart trimmed with a regularly scalloped edge, like a doily, with a similar dot in each of the scallops. Impaled on a mast rising from the upper V of the heart, a crest like an ornate letter M, with a star above and below it. Two curlicues like skeletal wings swooping out, one from each shoulder of the heart, and two smaller curlicues tufting from the bottom point of the heart, on either side of another sort of vertical mast projecting down from the point and ending in another star—like an infinitely stylized and painstaking doodle.

On the paper that wrapped it was written, in a careful childish script:

> *Pour vous protéger.*
> *Merci.*
> > *Sibao*

Simon went on down to the dining room and found Atherton Lee having breakfast.

"This isn't Valentine's Day in Haiti, is it?" asked the Saint.

Lee shook his head.

"Or anywhere else that I know of. That's sometime in February."

"Well, anyhow, I got a valentine."

Simon showed him the rectangle of embossed metal.

"It's native work," Lee said. "But what is it?"

"That's what I thought you could tell me."

"I never saw anything quite like it."

The waiter was bringing Simon a glass of orange juice. He stood frozen in the act of putting it down, his eyes fixed on the piece of tin and widening slowly. The glass rattled on his service plate.

Lee glanced up at him.

"Do you know what it is?"

"*Vêver,*" the man said.

He put the orange juice down and stepped back, still staring.

Simon did not know the word. He looked inquiringly at his host, who shrugged helplessly and handed the token back.

"What's that?"

"*Vêver,*" said the waiter. "Of Maîtresse Erzulie."

"Erzulie is the top voodoo goddess," Lee explained. "I guess that's her symbol, or some sort of charm."

"If you get good way, very good," said the waiter obscurely. "If you no should have, very bad."

"I believe I dig you, Alphonse," said the Saint. "And you don't have to worry about me. I got it the good way." He showed Lee the paper that had enclosed it. "It was slid under my door sometime this morning. I guess coming from her makes it pretty special."

"Congratulations," Lee said. "I'm glad you're officially protected. Is there anything you particularly need to be protected from?"

Simon dropped the little plaque into the breast pocket of his shirt.

"First off, I'd like to be protected from the heat of Port-au-Prince. I'm afraid I've got to go back down there. May I borrow the jeep again?"

"Of course. But we can send down for anything you want."

"I hardly think they'd let you bring back the Public Library," said the Saint. "I'm going to wade through everything they've got on the subject of voodoo. No, I'm not going to take it up like Netlord. But I'm just crazy enough myself to lie awake wondering what's in it for him."

He found plenty of material to study—so much, in fact, that instead of being frustrated by a paucity of information he was almost discouraged by its abundance. He had assumed, like any average man, that voodoo was a primitive cult that would have a correspondingly simple theology and ritual: he soon discovered that it was astonishingly complex and formalized. Obviously he wasn't going to master it all in one short day's study. However, that wasn't necessarily the objective. He didn't have to write a thesis on it, or even pass an examination. He was only looking for something, anything, that would give him a clue to what Theron Netlord was seeking.

He browsed through books until one o'clock, went out to lunch, and returned to read some more. The trouble was that he didn't know what he was looking for. All he could do was expose himself to as many ideas as possible, and hope that the same one would catch his attention as must have caught Netlord's.

And when the answer did strike him, it was so far-fetched and monstrous that he could not believe he was on the right track. He thought it would make an interesting plot for a story, but could not accept it for himself. He felt an exasperating lack of accomplishment when the library closed for the day and he had to drive back up again to Kenscoff.

He headed straight for the bar of the Châtelet des Fleurs and the long relaxing drink that he had looked forward to all the way up. The waiter who was on duty brought him a note with his drink.

Dear Mr. Templar,
 I'm sorry your visit yesterday had to be so short. If it wouldn't bore you too much, I should enjoy another meeting. Could you come to dinner tonight? Just send word by the bearer.

       Sincerely,
       Theron Netlord

Simon glanced up.
"Is someone still waiting for an answer?"
"Yes, sir. Outside."
The Saint pulled out his pen and scribbled at the foot of the note:

 Thanks. I'll be with you about 7.

       S.T.

He decided, practically in the same instant in which the irresponsible impulse occurred to him, against signing himself with the little haloed stick figure which he had made famous. As he handed the note back to the waiter he reflected that, in the circumstances, his mere acceptance was bravado enough.

IV

There were drums beating somewhere in the hills, faint and far-off, calling and answering each other from different directions, their sound wandering and echoing through the night so that it was impossible ever to be certain just where a particular tattoo had come from. It reached inside Netlord's house as a kind of vague vibration, like the endless thin chorus of nocturnal insects, which was so persistent that the ear learned to filter it out and for long stretches would be quite deaf to it, and then, in a lull in the conversation, with an infinitesimal retuning of attention, it would come back in a startling crescendo.

Theron Netlord caught the Saint listening at one of those moments, and said, "They're having a *brûler zin* tonight."

"What's that?"

"The big voodoo festive ceremony which climaxes most of the special rites. Dancing, litanies, invocation, possession by *loas,* more dances, sacrifice, more invocations and possessions, more dancing. It won't begin until much later. Right now they're just telling each other about it, warming up and getting in the mood."

Simon had been there for more than an hour, and this was the first time there had been any mention of voodoo.

Netlord had made himself a good if somewhat overpowering host. He mixed excellent rum cocktails, but without offering his guest the choice of anything else. He made stimulating conversation, salted with recurrent gibes at bureaucratic government and the Welfare State, but he held the floor so energetically that it was almost impossible to take advantage of the provocative openings he offered.

Simon had not seen Sibao again. Netlord had opened the door himself, and the cocktail makings were already on a side table in the living room. There had been subdued rustlings and clinkings behind a screen that almost closed a dark alcove at the far end of the room, but no servant announced dinner: presently Netlord had announced it himself and led the way around the screen and switched on a light, revealing a damask-covered table set for two and burdened additionally with chafing dishes, from which he himself served rice, asparagus, and a savory chicken stew rather like *coq au vin.* It was during one of the dialogue breaks induced by eating that Netlord had caught Simon listening to the drums.

"*Brûler*—that means 'burn,' " said the Saint. "But what is *zin?*"

"The *zin* is a special earthenware pot. It stands on a tripod, and a fire is lighted under it. The *mambo* kills a sacrificial chicken by sticking her finger down into its mouth and tearing its throat open." Netlord took a hearty mouthful of stew. "She sprinkles blood and feathers in various places, and the plucked hens go into the pot with some corn. There's a chant:

> *'Hounsis là yo, levez, nous domi trope:*
> *Hounsis là yo, levez, pour nous laver yeux nous:*
> *Gadé qui l'heu li yé.'*

Later on she serves the boiling food right into the bare hands of the *hounsis*. Sometimes they put their bare feet in the flames too. It doesn't hurt them. The pots are left on the fire till they get red hot and crack, and everyone shouts *'Zin yo craqués!'* "

"It sounds like a big moment," said the Saint gravely. "If I could understand half of it."

"You mean you didn't get very far with your researches today?"

Simon felt the involuntary contraction of his stomach muscles, but he was able to control his hands so that there was no check in the smooth flow of what he was doing.

"How did you know about my researches?" he asked, as if he were only amused to have them mentioned.

"I dropped in to see Atherton Lee this morning, and asked after you. He told me where you'd gone. He said he'd told you about my interest in voodoo, and he supposed you were getting primed for an argument. I must admit, that encouraged me to hope you'd accept my invitation tonight."

The Saint thought that that might well qualify among the great understatements of the decade, but he did not let himself show it. After their first reflex leap his pulses ran like cool clockwork.

"I didn't find out too much," he said, "except that voodoo is a lot more complicated than I imagined. I thought it was just a few primitive superstitions that the slaves brought with them from Africa."

"Of course, some of it came from Dahomey. But how did it get there? The voodoo story of the Creation ties up with the myths of ancient Egypt. The Basin of Damballah—that's a sort of font at the foot of a voodoo altar—is obviously related to the blood trough at the foot of a Mayan altar. Their magic uses the Pentacle —the same mystic figure that medieval European magicians believed in. If you know anything about it, you can find links with eighteenth-century Masonry in some of their rituals, and even the design of the *vêvers*——"

"Those are the sacred drawings that are supposed to summon the gods to take possession of their devotees, aren't they? I read about them."

"Yes, when the *houngan* draws them by dripping ashes and corn meal from his fingers, with the proper invocation. And doesn't that remind you of the sacred sand paintings of the Navajos? Do you see how all those roots must go back to a common source that's older than any written history?"

Netlord stared at the Saint challengingly, in one of those rare pauses where he waited for an answer.

Simon's fingertips touched the hard shape of the little tin plaque that was still in his shirt pocket, but he decided against showing it, and again he checked the bet.

"I saw a drawing of the *vêver* of Erzulie in a book," he said. "Somehow it made me think of Catholic symbols connected with the Virgin Mary—with the heart, the stars, and the 'M' over it."

"Why not? Voodoo is pantheistic. The Church is against voodoo, not voodoo against the Church. Part of the purification prescribed for anyone who's being initiated as a *hounsis-canzo* is to go to church and make confession. Jesus Christ and the Virgin Mary are regarded as powerful intermediaries to the highest gods. Part of the litany they'll chant tonight at the *brûler zin* goes: *Grâce, Marie, grâce, Marie grâce, grâce, Marie grâce, Jésus, pardonnez-nous!*"

"Seriously?"

"The invocation of Legba Atibon calls on St. Anthony of Padua: *Par pouvoir St.-Antoine de Padoue*. And take the invocation of my own patron, Ogoun Feraille. It begins: *Par pouvoir St.-Jacques Majeur . . .*"

"Isn't that blasphemy?" said the Saint. "I mean, a kind of deliberate sacrilege, like they're supposed to use in a Black Mass, to win the favor of devils by defiling something holy?"

Netlord's fist crashed on the table like a thunderclap.

"No, it isn't! The truth can't be blasphemous. Sacrilege is a sin invented by bigots to try to keep God under contract to their own exclusive club. As if supernatural facts could be alerted by human name-calling! There are a hundred sects all claiming to be the only true Christianity, and Christianity is only one of thousands of religions, all claiming to have the only genuine divine revelation. But the real truth is bigger than any one of them and includes them all!"

"I'm sorry," said the Saint. "I forgot that you were a convert."

"Lee told you that, of course. I don't deny it." The metallic grey eyes probed the Saint like knives. "I suppose you think I'm crazy."

"I'd rather say I was puzzled."

"Because you wouldn't expect a man like me to have any time for mysticism."

"Maybe."

Netlord poured some more wine.

"That's where you show your own limitations. The whole trouble with Western civilization is that it's blind in one eye. It doesn't believe in anything that can't be weighed and measured or reduced to a mathematical or chemical formula. It thinks it knows all the answers because it invented airplanes and television and hydrogen bombs. It thinks other cultures were backward because they fooled around with levitation and telepathy and raising the dead instead of killing the living. Well, some mighty clever people were living in Asia and Africa and Central America, thousands of years before Europeans crawled out of their caves. What makes you so sure that they didn't discover things that you don't understand?"

"I'm not so sure, but—"

"Do you know why I got ahead of everybody else in business? Because I never wore a blinker over one eye. If anyone said he could do anything, I never said 'That's impossible.' I said 'Show me how.' I don't care who I learn from, a college professor or a ditch-digger, a Chinaman or a nigger—so long as I can use what he knows."

The Saint finished eating and picked up his glass.

"And you think you'll find something in voodoo you can use?"

"I have found it. Do you know what it is?"

Simon waited to be told, but apparently it was not another of Netlord's rhetorical questions. When it was clear that a reply was expected, he said: "Why should I?"

"That's what you were trying to find out at the Public Library."

"I suppose I can admit that," Simon said mildly. "I'm a seeker for knowledge, too."

"I was afraid you would be, Templar, as soon as I heard your name. Not knowing who you were, I'd talked a little too much last night. It wouldn't have mattered with anyone else, but as the Saint you'd be curious about me. You'd have to ask questions. Lee would tell you about my interest in voodoo. Then you'd try to find out what I could use voodoo for. I knew all that when I asked you to come here tonight."

"And I knew you knew all that when I accepted."

"Put your cards on the table, then. What did your reading tell you?"

Simon felt unwontedly stupid. Perhaps because he had let Netlord do most of the talking, he must have done more than his own share of eating and drinking. Now it was an effort to keep up the verbal swordplay.

"It wasn't too much help," he said. "The mythology of voodoo was quite fascinating, but I couldn't see a guy like you getting a large charge out of spiritual trimmings. You'd want something that meant power, or money, or both. And the books I got hold of today didn't have much factual material about the darker side of voodoo—the angles that I've seen played up in lurid fiction."

"Don't stop now."

The Saint felt as if he lifted a slender blade once more against a remorseless bludgeon.

"Of course," he said, and meant to say it lightly, "you might really have union and government trouble if it got out that Netlord Underwear was being made by American zombies."

"So you guessed it," Netlord said.

V

Simon Templar stared.

He had a sensation of utter unreality, as if at some point he had slipped from wakeful life into a nightmare without being aware of the moment when he fell asleep. A separate part of his brain seemed to hear his own voice at a distance.

"You really believe in zombies?"

"That isn't a matter of belief. I've seen them. A zombie prepared and served this dinner. That's why he was ordered not to let you see him."

"Now I really need the cliché: this I have got to see!"

"I'm afraid he's left for the night," Netlord said matter-of-factly.

"But you know how to make 'em?"

"Not yet. He belongs to the *houngan*. But I shall know before the sun comes up tomorrow. In a little while I shall go down to the *houmfort,* and the *houngan* will admit me to the last mysteries. The *brûler zin* afterwards is to celebrate that."

"Congratulations. What did you have to do to rate this?"

"I've promised to marry his daughter, Sibao."

Simon felt as if he had passed beyond the capacity for surprise. A soft blanket of cotton wool was folding around his mind.

"Do you mean that?"

"Don't be absurd. As soon as I know all I need to, I can do without both of them."

"But suppose they resent that."

"Let me tell you something. Voodoo is a very practical kind of insurance. When a member is properly initiated, certain parts of a sacrifice and certain things from his body go into a little urn called the *pot de tête,* and after that the vulnerable element of his soul stays in the urn, which stays in the *houmfort.*"

"Just like a safe deposit."

"And so, no one can lay an evil spell on him."

"Unless they can get hold of his *pot de tête.*"

"So you see how easily I can destroy them if I act first."

The Saint moved his head as if to shake and clear it. It was like trying to shake a ton weight.

"It's very good of you to tell me all this," he articulated mechanically. "But what makes you so confidential?"

"I had to know how you'd respond to my idea when you knew it. Now you must tell me, truthfully."

"I think it stinks."

"Suppose you knew that I had creatures working for me, in a factory—zombies, who'd give me back all the money they'd nominally have to earn, except the bare minimum required for food and lodging. What would you do?"

"Report it to some authority that could stop you."

"That mightn't be so easy. A court that didn't believe in zombies couldn't stop people voluntarily giving me money."

"In that case," Simon answered deliberately, "I might just have to kill you."

Netlord sighed heavily.

"I expected that too," he said. "I only wanted to be sure. That's why I took steps in advance to be able to control you."

The Saint had known it for some indefinite time. He was conscious of his body sitting in a chair, but it did not seem to belong to him.

"You bastard," he said. "So you managed to feed me some kind of dope. But you're really crazy if you think that'll help you."

Theron Netlord put a hand in his coat pocket and took out a small automatic. He leveled it at the Saint's chest, resting his forearm on the table.

"It's very simple," he said calmly. "I could kill you now, and easily account for your disappearance. But I like the idea of having you work for me. As a zombie, you could retain many of your unusual abilities. So I could kill you, and, after I've learned a little more tonight, restore you to living death. But that would impair your usefulness in certain ways. So I'd rather apply what I know already, if I can, and make you my creature without harming you physically."

"That's certainly considerate of you," Simon scoffed.

He didn't know what unquenchable spark of defiance gave him the will to keep up the hopeless bluff. He seemed to have no contact with any muscles below his neck. But as long as he didn't try to move, and fail, Netlord couldn't be sure of that.

"The drug is only to relax you," Netlord said. "Now look at this."

He dipped his left hand in the ashtray beside him, and quickly began drawing a pattern with his fingertips on the white tablecloth —a design of crisscross diagonal lines with other vertical lines rising through the diamonds they formed, the verticals tipped with stars and curlicues, more than anything like the picture of an ornate wrought-iron gate. And as he drew it he intoned in a strange chanting voice:

"*Par pouvoir St.-Jacques Majeur, Ogoun Badagris nèg Baguidi,*

*Bago, Ogoun Feraille nèg fer, nèg feraille, nèg tagnifer nago,
Ogoun batala, nèg, nèg Ossagne malor, ossangne aquiquan, Os-
sange agouelingui, Jupiter tonnerre, nèg blabla, nèg oloncoun,
nèg vantè-m pas fie'm. . . . Aocher nago, aocher nago, aocher
nago!"*

The voice had risen, ending on a kind of muted shout, and
there was a blaze of fanatic excitement in Netlord's dilated eyes.

Simon wanted to laugh. He said: "What's that—a sequel to the
Hutsut Song?" Or he said: "I prefer *'Twas brillig and the slithy
toves.'*" Or perhaps he said neither, for the thoughts and the
ludicrousness and the laugh were suddenly chilled and empty,
and it was like a hollowness and a darkness, like stepping into
nothingness and a quicksand opening under his feet, sucking him
down, only it was the mind that went down, the lines of the
wrought-iron gate pattern shimmering and blinding before his
eyes, and a black horror such as he had never known rising
around him.

Out of some untouched reserve of will power he wrung the
strength to clear his vision again for a moment, and to shape
words that he knew came out, even though they came through
stiff clumsy lips.

"Then I'll have to kill you right now," he said.

He tried to get up. He had to try now. He couldn't pretend
any longer that he was immobile from choice. His limbs felt like
lead. His body was encased in invisible concrete. The triumphant
fascinated face of Theron Netlord blurred in his sight.

The commands of his brain went out along nerves that swallowed them in enveloping numbness. His mind was drowning in
the swelling dreadful dark. He thought: "Sibao, your Maîtresse
Erzulie must be the weak sister in this league."

And suddenly, he moved.

As if taut wires had snapped, he moved. He was on his feet.
Uncertainly, like a thawing out, like a painful return of circula-
tion, he felt connections with his body linking up again. He saw
the exultation in Netlord's face crumple into rage and incredulous
terror.

"Fooled you, didn't I?" said the Saint croakily. "You must still
need some coaching on your hex technique."

Netlord moved his hand a little, rather carefully, and his

knuckle whitened on the trigger of the automatic. The range was point-blank.

Simon's eardrums rang with the shot, and something struck him a stunning blinding blow over the heart. He had an impression of being hurled backwards as if by the blow of a giant fist; and then with no recollection of falling he knew that he was lying on the floor, half under the table, and he had no strength to move any more.

VI

Theron Netlord rose from his chair and looked down, shaken by the pounding of his own heart. He had done many brutal things in his life, but he had never killed anyone before. It had been surprisingly easy to do, and he had been quite deliberate about it. It was only afterwards that the shock shook him, with his first understanding of the new loneliness into which he had irrevocably stepped, the apartness from all other men that only murderers know.

Then a whisper and a stir of movement caught his eye and ear together, and he turned his head and saw Sibao. She wore the white dress and the white handkerchief on her head, and the necklaces of threaded seeds and grain, that were prescribed for the ceremony that night.

"What are you doing here?" he snarled in Creole. "I said I would meet you at the *houmfort*."

"I felt there was need for me."

She knelt by the Saint, touching him with her sensitive hands. Netlord put the gun in his pocket and turned to the sideboard. He uncorked a bottle of rum, poured some into a glass, and drank.

Sibao stood before him again.

"Why did you want to kill him?"

"He was—he was a bad man. A thief."

"He was good."

"No, he was clever." Netlord had had no time to prepare for questions. He was improvising wildly, aware of the hollowness of his invention and trying to bolster it with truculence. "He must have been waiting for a chance to meet you. If that had not happened, he would have found another way. He came to rob me."

"What could he steal?"

Netlord pulled out his wallet, and took from it a thick pad of currency. He showed it to her.

"He knew that I had this. He would have killed me for it." There were twenty-five crisp hundred-dollar bills, an incredible fortune by the standards of a Haitian peasant, but only the amount of pocket money that Netlord normally carried and would have felt undressed without. The girl's dark velvet eyes rested on it, and he was quick to see more possibilities. "It was a present I was going to give to you and your father tonight." Money was the strongest argument he had ever known. He went on with new-found confidence: "Here, take it now."

She held the money submissively.

"But what about—him?"

"We must not risk trouble with the police. Later we will take care of him, in our own way. . . . But we must go now, or we shall be late."

He took her compellingly by the arm, but for a moment she still held back.

"You know that when you enter the *sobagui* to be cleansed, your *loa,* who sees all things, will know if there is any untruth in your heart."

"I have nothing to fear." He was sure of it now. There was nothing in voodoo that scared him. It was simply a craft that he had set out to master, as he had mastered everything else that he made up his mind to. He would use it on others, but it could do nothing to him. "Come along, they are waiting for us."

Simon heard their voices before the last extinguishing wave of darkness rolled over him.

VII

He woke up with a start, feeling cramped and bruised from lying on the floor. Memory came back to him in full flood as he sat up. He looked down at his shirt. There was a black-rimmed hole in it, and even a grey scorch of powder around that. But when he examined his chest, there was no hole and no blood, only a pronounced soreness over the ribs. From his breast pocket he drew out the metal plaque with the *vêver* of Erzulie. The bullet had scarred and bent it, but it had struck at an angle and glanced off without even scratching him, tearing another hole in the shirt under his arm.

The Saint gazed at the twisted piece of tin with an uncanny tingle feathering his spine.

Sibao must have known he was unhurt when she touched him. Yet she seemed to have kept the knowledge to herself. Why?

He hoisted himself experimentally to his feet. He knew that he had first been drugged, then over that lowered resistance almost completely mesmerized; coming on top of that, the deadened impact of the bullet must have knocked him out, as a punch over the heart could knock out an already groggy boxer. But now all the effects seemed to have worn off together, leaving only a tender spot on his chest and an insignificant muzziness in his head. By his watch, he had been out for about two hours.

The house was full of the silence of emptiness. He went through a door to the kitchen, ran some water, and bathed his face. The only other sound there was the ticking of a cheap clock.

Netlord had said that only the two of them were in the house. And Netlord had gone—with Sibao.

Gone to something that everything in the Saint's philosophy must refuse to believe. But things had happened to himself already that night which he could only think of incredulously. And incredulity would not alter them, or make them less true.

He went back through the living room and out on to the front verandah. Ridge beyond ridge, the mysterious hills fell away from before him under a full yellow moon that dimmed the stars; and there was no jeep in the driveway at his feet.

The drums still pulsed through the night, but they were no longer scattered. They were gathered together, blending in unison and counterpoint, but the acoustical tricks of the mountains still masked their location. Their muttering swelled and receded with chance shifts of air, and the echoes of it came from all around the horizon, so that the whole world seemed to throb softly with it.

There was plenty of light for him to walk down to the Châtelet des Fleurs.

He found Atherton Lee and the waiter starting to put out the lights in the bar. The innkeeper looked at him in a rather startled way.

"Why—what happened?" Lee asked.

Simon sat up at the counter and lighted a cigarette.

"Pour me a Barbancourt," he said defensively, "and tell me why you think anything happened."

"Netlord brought the jeep back. He told me he'd taken you to the airport—you'd had some news which made you suddenly decide to catch the night plane to Miami, and you just had time to make it. He was coming back tomorrow to pick up your things and send them after you."

"Oh, that," said the Saint blandly. "When the plane came through, it turned out to have filled up at Ciudad Trujillo. I couldn't get on. So I changed my mind again. I ran into someone downtown who gave me a lift back."

He couldn't say: "Netlord thought he'd just murdered me, and he was laying the foundation for me to disappear without being missed." Somehow, it sounded so ridiculous, even with a bullet hole in his shirt. And if he were pressed for details, he would have to say: "He was trying to put some kind of hex on me, or make me a zombie." That would be assured of a great reception. And then the police would have to be brought in. Perhaps Haiti was the only country on earth where a policeman might feel obliged to listen seriously to such a story; but the police were still the police. And just at those times when most people automatically turn to the police, Simon Templar's instinct was to avoid them.

What would have to be settled now between him and Theron Netlord, he would settle himself, in his own way.

The waiter, closing windows and emptying ashtrays, was singing to himself under his breath:

> "*Moin pralé nan Sibao,*
> *Chaché, chaché, lolé-o——*"

"What's that?" Simon asked sharply.

"Just Haitian song, sir."

"What does it mean?"

"It mean, *I will go to Sibao*—that holy place in voodoo, sir. *I take oil for lamp*, it say. *If you eat food of Legba you will have to die:*

> '*Si ou mangé mangé Legba*
> *Ti ga çon onà mouri, oui.*
> *Moin pralé nan Sibao——*' "

"After spending an evening with Netlord, you should know all about that," Atherton Lee said.

Simon downed his drink and stretched out a yawn.

"You're right. I've had enough of it for one night," he said. "I'd better let you go on closing up—I'm ready to hit the sack myself."

But he lay awake for a long time, stretched out on his bed in the moonlight. Was Theron Netlord merely insane, or was there even the most fantastic possibility that he might be able to make use of things that modern materialistic science did not understand? Would it work on Americans, in America? Simon remembered that one of the books he had read referred to a certain American evangelist as *un houngan insuffisamment instruit;* and it was a known fact that that man controlled property worth millions, and that his followers turned over all their earnings to him, for which he gave them only food, shelter, and sermons. Such things *had* happened, and were as unsatisfactory to explain away as flying saucers. . . .

The ceaseless mutter of the distant drums mocked him till he fell asleep.

> "*Si ou mangé mangé Legba*
> *Ti ga çon onà mouri, oui!*"

He awoke and still heard the song. The moonlight had given way to the grey light of dawn, and the first thing he was conscious of was a fragile unfamiliar stillness left void because the drums were at last silent. But the voice went on—a flat, lifeless, distorted voice that was nevertheless recognizable in a way that sent icy filaments crawling over his scalp.

> "*Moin pralé nan Sibao,*
> *Moin pralé nan Sibao,*
> *Moin pralé nan Sibao,*
> *Chaché, chaché, lolé-o . . .*"

His window overlooked the road that curved up past the inn, and he was there while the song still drifted up to it. The two of them stood directly beneath him—Netlord, and the slender black girl dressed all in white. The girl looked up and saw Simon, as if she had expected to. She raised one hand and solemnly made a pattern in the air, a shape that somehow blended the outlines of a heart and an ornate letter M, quickly and intricately, and her lips moved with it.

It was curiously like a benediction.

Then she turned to the man beside her, as she might have turned to a child.

"*Venez*," she said.

The tycoon also looked up, before he obediently followed her. But there was no recognition, no expression at all, in the grey face that had once been so ruthless and domineering; and all at once Simon knew why Theron Netlord would be no problem to him or to anyone, any more.

In "The Darker Drink" (1949), Simon Templar's hideout in the high Sierras is invaded by a man called Big Bill Holbrook who claims to be the dreamworld creation of a sleeping bank clerk in Glendale, California. It is perhaps the Saint's strangest adventure, beginning as a screwball send-up of The Maltese Falcon *and ending as a nightmare.*

THE DARKER DRINK

So when that Angel of the Darker Drink
At last shall find you by the river-brink,
And, offering his Cup, invite your Soul
Forth to your lips to quaff—you shall not shrink.
          —Omar Khayyam

Simon Templar looked up from the frying pan in which six mountain trout were developing a crisp golden tan. Above the gentle sputter of grease, the sound of feet on dry pine needles crackled through the cabin window.

It didn't cross his mind that the sound carried menace, for it was twilight in the Sierras, and the dusky calm stirred only with the rustlings of nature at peace.

The Saint also was at peace. In spite of everything his enemies would have said, there actually were times when peace was the main preoccupation of that fantastic freebooter; when hills and blue sky were high enough adventure, and baiting a hook was respite enough from baiting policemen or promoters. In such a mood he had jumped at the invitation to join a friend in a week of hunting and fishing in the High Sierras—a friend who had been recalled to town on urgent business almost as soon as they arrived, leaving the Saint in by no means melancholy solitude, for Simon Templar could always put up with his own company.

The footsteps came nearer with a kind of desperate urgency. Simon moved the frying pan off the flames and flowed, rather than walked, to where he could see through windows in two directions.

A man came out of the pines. He was travelling on the short side of a dead run, but straining with every gasping breath to step up his speed. He came, hatless and coatless, across the pine-carpeted clearing toward the cabin door.

He burst through it; and in spite of his relaxation the Saint felt a kind of simmer of anticipating approval. If his solitude had to be intruded on, this was the way it should happen. Unannounced. At a dead run.

The visitor slammed the door, shot the bolt, whirled around, and seemed about to fold in the middle. He saw the Saint. His jaw sagged, swung adrift on its hinges for a moment, then imitated a steel trap.

After the sharp click of his teeth, he said: "How did you get in here? Where's Dawn?"

"Dawn?" Simon echoed lazily. "If you're referring to the rosy-fingered goddess who peels away the darkness each morning, she's on the twelve-hour shift, chum. She'll be around at the regular time."

"I never dreamed you here," the man said. "Who are you?"

"You dropped a word," the Saint said. " 'I never dreamed you *were* here' makes more sense."

"Nuts, brother. You're part of my dream, and I never saw you before. You don't even have a name. All the others have, complete with backgrounds. But I can't place you. Funny, I——Look here, you're not real, are you?"

"The last time I pinched myself, I yelped."

"This is crazy," the man muttered.

He walked across the pine floor to within a couple of feet of the Saint. He was breathing easier now, and the Saint examined him impassively.

He was big, only a shade under the Saint's six feet two, with sandy hair, a square jaw, and hard brown eyes.

"May I?" he said, and pinched the Saint. He sighed. "I was afraid this was happening. When I put my arms around Dawn Winter in my dreams, she——"

"Please," the Saint broke in. "Gentlemen don't go into lurid detail after the lady has a name."

"Oh, she's only part of my dream." The stranger stared into space, and an almost tangible aura of desire formed about him. "God!" he whispered. "I really dreamed up something in her."

"We must swap reminiscences someday," the Saint said. "But at the moment the pine-scented breeze is laden with threshings in the underbrush."

"I've got to hide. Quick! Where can I get out of sight?"

The Saint waved expressively at the single room. In its 400 square feet, one might hide a large bird if it were camouflaged as an atlas or something, but that would be about the limit.

The two bunk beds were made with hospital precision, and even a marble would have bulged under their tight covers. The deck chairs wouldn't offer sanctuary for even an undernourished mouse, the table was high and wide open beneath the rough top, and the bookcase was small and open.

"If we had time," the Saint mused, "I could candy-stripe you— if I had some red paint—and put on a barber's smock. Or—er— you say you're dreaming all this?"

"That's right."

"Then why don't you wake up—and vanish?"

The Saint's visitor unhappily gnawed his full underlip.

"I always have before, when the going got tough, but——Oh, hell, I don't know what's going on, but I don't want to die—even in my dream. Death is so—so——"

"Permanent?"

"Mmm, I guess. Listen, would you be a pal and try to steer these guys away? They're after me."

"Why should I?"

"Yeah," the man said. "You don't owe me a damn thing, but I'm trying to help Dawn. She——"

He broke off to fish an object out of his watch pocket. This was a small chamois bag, and out of it he took something that pulsed with incredible fires. He handed it to the Saint.

"That's Dawn."

The circular fire opal blazed with living beauty—blue, green, gold, cerise, chartreuse—and the Saint gasped with reverent wonder as he looked at the cameo head carved on the unbelievable gem.

There is beauty to which one can put a name. There is beauty that inspires awe, bravery, fear, lust, greed, passion. There is beauty that softens the savage blows of fate. There is beauty that drives to high adventure, to violence.

That stone, and above all the face cut eternally on its incandescent surface, was beauty beyond belief. No man could look on that face and ever know complete peace again.

She was the lily maid of Astolat, the lost loveliness that all men seek and never find, the nameless desire that haunts the ragged edge of sleep, that curls a lonely smile and sends vacant eyes searching far spaces.

Her face was made for—and of? The Saint asked himself—dreaming.

"Count me in, old boy."

He went outside. Through the dusky stillness the far-off unseen feet pounded nearer.

The feet were four. The men, with mathematical logic, two. One might be a jockey, the other a weight lifter. They tore out of the forest.

"Did you see a kind of big dopey-lookin' lug?" the jockey asked.

The Saint pointed to the other side of the clearing where the hill pitched down.

"He went that way—in a hell of a rush."

"Thanks, pal."

They were off, hot on the imaginary trail, and the sounds of their passage soon faded. The Saint went inside.

"They'll be back," he said. "But meanwhile we can clear up a few points. Could you down a brace of trout? They've probably cooled enough to eat."

"What do you mean, they'll be back?"

"It's inevitable," Simon pointed out as he put coffee on, set the table, and gathered cutlery. "They won't find you. They want to find you. So they'll be back with questions. Since those questions will be directed at me, I'd like to know what not to answer."

"Who are you?"

"Who are you?" the Saint countered.

"I'm—oh, blast it to hell and goddam. The guy you're looking at is Big Bill Holbrook. But he's only something I dreamed up. I'm really Andrew Faulks, and I'm asleep in Glendale, California."

"And I am the queen of Rumania."

"Sure, I know. You don't believe it. Who would? But since you've got me out of a tight spot for the time being, I'd like to tell you what I've never told anybody. But who am I telling?"

"I'm Simon Templar," said the Saint, and waited for a reaction.

"No!" Holbrook-Faulks breathed. "The Saint! What beautiful, wonderful luck. And isn't it just like a bank clerk to work the Saint into his dream?" He paused for breath. "The Robin Hood of Modern Crime, the Twentieth Century's brightest buccaneer, the devil with dames, the headache of cops and crooks alike. What a sixteen-cylinder dream this is."

"Your alliterative encomia," the Saint murmured, "leave me as awed as your inference. Don't you think you'd better give out with this—er—bedtime story? Before that unholy pair return with gun-lined question marks?"

The strange man rubbed his eyes in a dazed helpless way.

"I don't know where to begin," he said conventionally.

But after a while, haltingly, he tried.

Andrew Faulks, in the normal course of events, weathered the slingshots and arrows of outrageous playmates and grew up to be a man.

As men will, he fixed his heart and eyes on a girl and eventually married her. As women will, she gave birth in due course to a boy, Andy Jr., and later a girl, Alexandria.

He became a bank clerk, and went to and from home on an immutable schedule. He got an occasional raise; he was bawled out at times by the head teller; he became a company man, a white-collar worker, and developed all the political ills that white-collared flesh is heir to.

And he dreamed. Literally.

This was what Big Bill Holbrook told the Saint in the mountain cabin to which Simon had retired to await the blowing over of a rather embarrassing situation which involved items duly registered on police records.

"In the first dream, I was coming out of this hotel, see. And whammo! Bumping into her woke me——Oh, the hell with it.

Whoever was dreaming woke up, but it was me bumped into her. And I was sorry as hell, because, brother, she was something."

Some two weeks later, Big Bill said, he bumped into her again. The dream started exactly as its predecessor, progressed exactly to the point of collision.

"But I didn't awaken this time. We each apologized all over the place and somehow we were walking along together. Just as I was about to ask her to have dinner, I woke up again."

"Or Andy did," the Saint supplied.

"Yeah. Whoever. Now this is what happened. Every ten days or two weeks, I'd be back in this dream, starting out of the hotel, crashing into her, walking along, having dinner, getting to know her better each dream. Each one started exactly the same, but each one went a little further into her life. It was like reading the same book over and over, always starting back at the beginning, but getting one chapter further every time. I got so used to it that I'd say to myself, 'This is where I woke up last time,' and then after the dream had gone a bit further I'd begin to think, 'Well, I guess this must be getting near the end of another installment,' and sure enough, about that time I'd wake up again."

The accidental encounter began to develop sinister ramifications, picked up unsavory characters, and put Big Bill Holbrook in the role of a Robin Hood.

"Or a Saint," he amended, "rescuing a dame from a bunch of lugs."

And there was, of course, the jewel.

It had a history. The fire opal, which seemed to be eternal yet living beauty, had carved upon it the likeness of Dawn's great-great-grandmother, of whom the girl was the living image.

The talented Oriental craftsman who had chiseled those features which were the essence of beauty—that wily fellow had breathed upon the cameo gem a curse.

The curse: It must not get out of the possession of the family— or else.

Death, deprivation, and a myriad other unpleasantries were predicted if the stone fell into alien hands.

The name of Selden Appopoulis sort of slithered into the tale. This was a fat man, a lecherous fat man, a greedy fat man, who wanted—not loved—Dawn; and who wanted—*and* loved—the cameo opal. In some fashion that was not exactly clear to the Saint, the fat man was in a position to put a financial squeeze on her. In each succeeding dream of Andrew Faulks, Glendale bank clerk, Dawn's position became more and more untenable. In desperation she finally agreed to turn the jewel over to Appopoulis. The fat man sent for the jewel by the two henchmen whom the Saint had directed off into the Holbrook-bare woods.

"Now in this dream—this here *now* dream," Holbrook said, "I took it away from him, see? Andy Faulks went to sleep in Glendale Saturday night and—say, what day is it now?"

"Tuesday."

"Yeah, that's the way it seems to me too. And that's funny. If you're really part of this dream you'd naturally think it was Tuesday, because your time and my time would be the same. But you don't seem like part of a dream. I pinched you and—oh, nuts, I'm all mixed up."

"Let's try and be clear about this," said the Saint patiently. "You know that it's Tuesday here, but you think you're dreaming all this in Glendale on Saturday night."

"I don't know," said the other wearily. "You see, I never dreamed more than one day at a stretch before. But tonight it's been going on and on. It's gone way past the time when I ought to have woken up. But I don't seem to be able to wake up. I've tried . . . My God, suppose I don't wake up! Suppose I never *can* wake up? Suppose I never can get back, and I have to go on and on with this, being Big Bill Holbrook——"

"You could take a trip to Glendale," Simon suggested gravely, "and try waking Faulks up."

Holbrook-Faulks stared at him with oddly unfocused eyes.

"I can't," he said huskily. "I thought of that—once. But I couldn't make myself do it. I—I'm scared . . . of what I might find. . . . Suppose——"

He broke off, his pupils dilated with the formless horror of a glimpse of something that no mind could conceive.

Simon roused him again, gently: "So you took the jewel——"

Holbrook snapped out of his reverie.

"Yeah, and I lammed out for this cabin. Dawn was supposed to meet me here. But I guess I can't control all these characters.

Say," he asked suddenly, "who do you suppose I am? Faulks or Holbrook?"

"I suggest you ask your mother, old boy."

"This ain't funny. I mean, who do you *really* suppose I am? Andy Faulks is asleep and dreaming me but I've got all his memories, so am I a projection of Andy or am I me and him both? None of these other characters have any more memories than they need."

Simon wondered if the two men chasing Holbrook were his keepers; he could use a few. In fact, Simon reflected, keepers would fit into the life of Holbrook-Faulks like thread in a needle. But he sipped his brandy and urged the man to continue.

"Well, something's happened," Holbrook-Faulks said. "It never was like this before. I never could smell things before. I never could really feel them. You know how it is in a dream. But now it seems like as if you stuck a knife in me I'd bleed real blood. You don't suppose a—a reiterated dream could become reality?"

"I," said the Saint, "am a rank amateur in that department."

"Well, I was too—or Andy was, whichever of us is me—but I read everything I could get my hands on about dreams—or Andy did—and it didn't help a bit."

Most men wouldn't have heard the faint far-off stirring in the forest. But the Saint's ears, attuned by long practice to detect sound that differed from what should be there, picked up evidence of movement toward the cabin.

"Some one," he said suddenly, "and I mean one, is coming. Not your pursuers—it's from the opposite direction."

Holbrook-Faulks listened.

"I don't hear anything."

"I didn't expect you to—yet. Now that it's dark, perhaps you'd better slip outside, brother, and wait. I don't pretend to believe your yarn, but that some game is afoot is so obvious that even Sherlock Holmes could detect it. I suggest that we prepare for eventualities."

The eventuality that presently manifested itself was a girl. And it was a girl who could have been no one but Dawn Winter.

She came wearily into the cabin, dishevelled, her dress torn provocatively so that sun-browned flesh showed through, her cloud of golden hair swirled in fairy patterns, her dark eyes brooding, her mouth a parted dream.

The Saint caught his breath and began to wonder whether he could really make Big Bill Holbrook wake up and vanish.

"Do you belong to the coffee and/or brandy school of thought?" he asked.

"Please." She fell carelessly into a chair, and the Saint coined a word.

She was glamorous beyond belief.

"Miss Winter, pull down your dress or I'll never get this drink poured. You've turned me into an aspen. You're the most beautiful hunk of flesh I've ever seen. Have your drink and go, please."

She looked at him then, and took in the steel-cable leanness of him, the height of him, the crisp black hair, the debonair blue eyes. She smiled, and a brazen gong tolled in the Saint's head.

"Must I?" she said.

Her voice caught at the core of desire and tangled itself forever there.

"Set me some task," the Saint said uncertainly. "Name me a mountain to build, a continent to sink, a star to fetch you in the morning."

The cabin door crashed open. The spell splintered into shining shards. Holbrook-Faulks stood stony-faced against the door.

"Hello, Bill," the girl said, her eyes still on the Saint. "I came, you see."

Bill's gaze was an unwavering glance, with the Saint pinioned on its blazing tip.

"Am I gonna have trouble with you too, Saint?"

The Saint opened his mouth to answer, and stiffened as another sound reached his ears. Jockey and weight lifter were returning.

"We'll postpone any jousting over the fair lady for the moment," Simon said. "We're about to have more company."

Holbrook stared wildly around.

"Come on, Dawn. Out the window. They'll kill us."

Many times before in his checkered career the Saint had had to make decisions in a fragment of time—when a gun was levelled and a finger whitening on the trigger, when a traffic accident roared toward consummation, when a ship was sinking, when a knife flashed through candlelight. His decision now was compounded of several factors, none of which was the desire for self-preservation. The Saint rarely gave thought room to self-preservation—never when there was something more important to preserve.

He did not want this creature of tattered loveliness, this epitome of what men live for, to get out of his sight. He must therefore keep her inside the cabin. And there was no place to hide. . . .

His eyes narrowed as he looked at the two bunks. He was tearing out the mattresses before his thought was fully formed. He tossed the mattresses in a corner where shadows had retreated from the candle on the table. Then he motioned to Holbrook.

"Climb up. Make like a mattress."

He boosted the big man into the top bunk, and his hands were like striking brown snakes as he packed blankets around him and remade the bed so that it only looked untidily put together.

"Now you," he said to the girl.

She got into the lower bunk and lay flat on her back, her disturbing head in the far corner. The Saint deposited a swift kiss upon her full red lips. They were cool and soft, and the Saint was adrift for a second.

Then he covered her. He emptied a box of pine cones on the mattresses and arranged the whole to appear as a corner heap of cones.

He was busy cleaning the dishes when the pounding came on the door.

As he examined the pair, Simon Templar was struck by the fact that these men were types, such types as B pictures had imprinted upon the consciousness of the world.

The small one could be a jockey, but one with whom you could make a deal. For a consideration, he would pull a horse in the stretch or slip a Mickey into a rival rider's sarsaparilla. In the dim light that fanned out from the door, his eyes were small and ratlike, his mouth a slit of cynicism.

His heavier companion was a different but equally familiar type. This man was Butch to a T. He was large, placid, oafish, and an order taker. His not to reason why; his but to do—or cry. He'd be terribly hurt if he failed to do what he was ordered; he'd apologize, he'd curse himself.

It crossed the Saint's mind that a bank clerk such as Andrew Faulks had been described would dream such characters.

"So you lied to us," the little man snarled.

The Saint arched an eyebrow. At the same time he reached out and twisted the little man's nose, as if he were trying to unscrew it.

"When you address me, Oswald, say 'sir.' "

The little man sprang back in outraged fury. He clapped one hand to his injured proboscis, now turning a deeper purple than the night. The other hand slid under his coat.

Simon waited until he had the gun out of the holster, then leaped the intervening six feet and twisted it from the little man's hand. The Saint let the gun swing from his finger by its trigger guard.

"Take him, Mac!" grated the disarmed man.

Mac vented a kind of low growl, but did nothing but fidget as the Saint turned curious blue eyes on him. The tableau hung frozen for a long moment before the little man shattered the silence.

"Well? Ya afraid of 'im?"

"Yup," Mac said unhappily. "Criminy, Jimmy, 'f he c'n get the best uh you, well, criminy, Jimmy."

Jimmy moaned: "You mean you're gonna stand there and let just one guy take my gun away from me? Cripes, he ain't a army."

"No," Mac agreed, growing more unhappy by the second, "but he kind of seems like one, Jimmy. Didja see that jump? Criminy, Jimmy."

The Saint decided to break it up.

"Now, Oswald——"

"Didn'ja hear Mac? Name's Jimmy."

"Oswald," the Saint said firmly, "is how I hold you in my heart. Now, Oswald, perhaps you'll pour oil on these troubled waters, before I take you limb from muscle and throw you away."

"We don't want no trouble," Jimmy said. "We want Big Bill. You got him, but we got to take him back with us."

"And who is Big Bill, and why do you want him, and why do you think I have him?"

"We know you got him," Jimmy said. "This here's Trailer Mac."

The Saint nodded at Mac.

"Charmed, I'm sure."

"Hey, Jimmy," Mac broke in, "this guy's a phony."

Jimmy blinked.

"Owls," Mac explained, "can't swim."

"What the damblasted hell has owls to do with it?" Jimmy demanded.

"He said pour owls on the something waters. So that," Mac said in triumph, "proves it."

This, the Saint thought, wanders. He restrained Jimmy from assaulting Mac, and returned to the subject.

"Why should the revelation of this gent's identity be regarded as even an intimation that I have—what was the name?—Big Bill?"

"Holbrook," Jimmy said. "Why, this is Trailer Mac. Ain't you never heard of him? He follered Loopie Louie for eighteen years and finally caught 'im in the middle of Lake Erie."

"I never heard of him," Simon said, and smiled at Mac's hurt look. "But then there are lots of people I've never heard of."

This, he thought as he said it, was hardly true. He had filed away in the indexes of his amazing memory the dossiers of almost every crook in history. He was certain that he'd have heard of such a chase if it had ever occurred.

"Anyway," Jimmy went on, "we didn't go more'n a coupla miles till Mac he says Big Bill ain't here, 'n he ain't been here, neither. Well, he come this far, 'n he didn't go no farther. So you got him. He's inside."

"The cumulative logic in that series of statements is devastating," the Saint said. "But logicians veer. History will bear me out. Aristotle was a shining example. Likewise all the boys who gave verisimilitude to idiocy by substituting syllogisms for thought processes, who evaded reality by using unsemantic verbalisms for fact-racing and, God save the mark, fact-finding."

Mac appealed to the superior intellect in his crowd.

"Whut'n hell's he talkin' about, Jimmy?"

"I mean," the Saint said, "Big Bill ain't here. Come in and case the joint."

"Whyn't cha say so?" Mac snarled, and pushed inside.

They searched nook and cranny, and Mac fingered a knothole

hopefully once. They gave the bunk beds a passing glance, and were incurious about the seeming pile of pine cones in the corner. Mac boosted Jimmy up on the big central beam to peer into ceiling shadows, and they scanned the fireplace chimney.

Then they stood and looked at the Saint with resentment.

"Sump'n's fishy," Jimmy pronounced. "He's got to be here. This here"—he pointed—"is Trailer Mac."

"Maybe we better go get the boss, huh, Jimmy?"

"Yeah," Jimmy agreed. "He'll find Big Bill."

"Who," the Saint inquired, "is the boss?"

"You'll see," Jimmy promised. "He won't be scared of you. He's just down the hill in the town. Stopped off to play a game of billiards. So we'll be seein' ya, bub."

They went off into the night, and the Saint stood quite still for a moment in a little cloud of perplexity.

Never before had he been faced with a situation that was so full of holes.

He added up known data: a man who had a fabulous jewel, who claimed to be the projected dream of his alter ego; a girl of incredible beauty said to be another creation of that dream; and two characters who were after the man and/or the jewel and/or —perhaps—the girl.

Mac and Jimmy had searched the cabin. They professed to have overlooked an object the size of Big Bill Holbrook. Their proof that they had overlooked him: "This here's Trailer Mac." They assumed he would remain here while they walked four miles to the settlement and back with their boss who was said to have stopped off to shoot a game of billiards.

But would a man on the trail of that fire opal stop off to play billiards? Would two pseudo-tough guys go away and leave their quarry unguarded?

No, the Saint decided. These were the observable facts, but they were unimportant. They masked a larger, more sinister pattern. Great forces must be underlying the surface trivia. Undeniably, the jewel was a thing to drive men to madness. It could motivate historic bloodshed. The girl, too, possessing the carven features of the gem, could drive men to—anything. But for the life of him, the Saint could not get beneath the surface pattern to what must be the real issues. He could only cling to the conviction that they had to exist, and that they must be deadly.

He turned back to the bunk beds.

"Come on out, kids," he said. "The big bad wolves have temporarily woofed away."

Fear lingered in the dark depths of Dawn Winter's eyes, making her even more hauntingly beautiful. The Saint found strange words forming on his lips, as if some other being possessed them.

He seemed to be saying: "Dawn . . . I've seen the likeness of every beauty in history or imagination. Every one of them would be a drab shadow beside you. You are so beautiful that the world would bow down and worship you—if the world knew of your existence. Yet it's impossible that the world doesn't know. If one single person looked at you, the word would go out. Cameramen would beat a path to your door, artists would dust off their palettes, agents would clamor with contracts. But somehow this hasn't happened. Why? Where, to be trite, have you been all my life?"

He couldn't define the expression which now entered her eyes. It might have been bewilderment, or worry, or fear, or an admixture.

"I—I——" She put a hand as graceful as a calla lily against her forehead. "I—don't know."

"Oh, don't let's carry this too far." It sounded more like himself again. "Where were you born, where did you go to school, who are your parents?"

She worried at him with wide, dark eyes.

"That's just the trouble. I—don't remember any childhood. I remember only my great-great-grandmother. I never saw her, of course, but she's the only family I know about."

Big Bill's facial contortions finally caught the Saint's eye. They were something to watch. His mouth worked like a corkscrew, his eyebrows did a cancan.

"I gather," said the Saint mildly, "that you are giving me the hush-hush. I'm sorry, comrade, but I'm curious. Suppose you put in your two cents."

"I told you once," Big Bill said. "I told you the truth."

"Pish," Simon said. "Also, tush."

"It's true," Big Bill insisted. "I wouldn't lie to the Saint."

The girl echoed this in a voice of awe.

"The Saint? The Robin Hood of Modern Crime, the Twentieth Century's brightest buccaneer, the"—she blushed—"the devil with dames."

It occurred to Simon, with a shock of remembrance, that her phrases were exactly those of Big Bill's when he learned his host's identity. And even then they had been far from new. The Saint thought of this for a moment, and rejected what it suggested. He shook his head.

"Let's consider that fire opal then, children. It's slightly fabulous, you know. Now, I don't think anybody knows more than I do about famous jools. Besides such well-known items as the Cullinan and the Hope diamonds, I am familiar with the history of almost every noteworthy bauble that was ever dug up. There's the Waters diamond, for example. No more than a half dozen persons know of its existence, its perfect golden flawless color. And the Chiang emerald, that great and beautiful stone that has been seen by only three living people, myself included. But this cameo opal is the damn warp of history. It couldn't be hidden for three generations without word of it getting out. In the course of time, I couldn't have helped hearing about it. But I didn't. . . . So it doesn't exist. But it does. I know it exists; I've held it in my hand——"

"And put it in your pocket," Big Bill said.

The Saint felt in his jacket.

"So I did." He pulled out the chamois bag with its precious contents and made as if to toss it. "Here."

Big Bill stopped him with flared hands.

"Please keep it for me, Mr. Templar. Things will get rather bad around here soon. I don't want Appopoulis to get his fat hands on it."

"Soon? Surely not for a couple of hours."

Big Bill frowned.

"Things happen so quickly in dreams. This may *seem* real, but it'll still hold the screwy pattern you'd expect."

The Saint made a gesture of annoyance.

"Still sticking to your story? Well, maybe you're screwy or maybe you just think I am. But I'd rather face facts. As a matter of fact, I insist on it." He turned back to the girl. "For instance, darling, I know that you exist. I've kissed you."

Big Bill growled, glared, but did nothing as the Saint waited calmly.

Simon continued: "I have the evidence of my hands, lips, and eyes that you have all the common things in common with other women. In addition you have this incredible, unbelievable loveliness. When I look at you, I find it hard to believe that you're real. But that's only a figure of speech. My senses convince me. Yet you say you don't remember certain things that all people remember. Why?"

She repeated her gesture of confusion.

"I—don't know. I can't remember any past."

"It would be a great privilege and a rare pleasure," the Saint said gently, "to provide you with a past to remember."

Another low growl rumbled in Big Bill's chest, and the Saint waited again for developments. None came, and it struck the Saint that all the characters in this muddled melodrama had one characteristic in common—a certain cowardice in the clutch. Even Dawn Winter showed signs of fear, and nobody had yet made a move to harm her. It was only another of the preposterous paradoxes that blended into the indefinable unreality of the whole.

Simon gave it up. If he couldn't get what he thought was truth from either of these two, he could watch and wait and divine the truth. Conflict hung on the wind, and conflict drags truth out of her hiding place and casts her naked before watching eyes.

"Well, souls," he said, "what now? The unholy three will be back sometime. You could go now. There is the wide black night to wander in."

"No," Big Bill said. "Now that you're in this, give us your help, Saint. We need you."

"Just what, then," Simon asked, "are we trying to prevent, or accomplish?"

"Selden Appopoulis must not get his hands on the opal or Dawn. He wants both. He'll stop at nothing to get them."

"I believe you mentioned a curse breathed on this gewgaw by some Oriental character."

Dawn Winter's voice once more tangled itself in Simon's heart.

As long as he could remember that quality—of far-off bells at dusk, of 'cellos on a midnight hill—time would never again pass slowly enough.

"Death shall swoop on him," she chanted, "who holds this ancient gem from its true possessor, but all manner of things shall plague him before that dark dread angel shall come to rest at his shoulder. His nights shall be sleepless with terror, and hurts shall dog his accursed steps by day. Beauty shall bring an end to the vandal."

The mood of her strange incantation, far more than the actual words, seemed to linger on the air after she had finished, so that in spite of all rationality the Saint felt spectral fingers on his spine. He shook off the spell with conscious resolution.

"It sounds very impressive," he murmured, "in a gruesome sort of way. Reminds me of one of those zombie pictures. But where, may I ask, does this place me in the scheme of dire events? I have the jewel."

"You," Big Bill Holbrook said, "will die, as I must, and as Trailer Mac and Jimmy must. They stole it from Dawn; I stole it from them."

The Saint smiled.

"Well, if that's settled, let's pass on to more entertaining subjects bordering on the carnal. Miss Winter, my car is just down the hill. If Bill is resigned to his fate, suppose we leave him and his playmates to their own fantastic devices and drift off into the night."

Her face haloed with pleasure.

"I'd like it," she said. "But I—I just can't."

"Why not? You're over three years old. Nobody is sitting on your chest."

"I can't do what I like, somehow," she said. "I can only do what I must. It's always that way."

"This," the Saint said to nobody in particular, "sounds like one of those stories that fellow Charteris might write. And what's the matter with you?" he demanded of Holbrook. "A little earlier you were eager to get banged about because I admired the lady. Now you sit with disgusting indifference to my indecent proposal. I assure you it was indecent, from your viewpoint."

Big Bill grinned.

"It just occurred to me. She can't go with you. She must do what she must. She can't get out of my sight. Good old Andy," he added.

The Saint turned his eyes away and stared into space, wondering. His wandering gaze focused on a small wall mirror that reflected Dawn Winter. Her features were blurred, run together, an amorphous mass. Simon wondered what could have happened to that mirror.

He swung back to face Bill Holbrook.

"I'm afraid," he said softly, but with the iron will showing through his velvet tones, "that we must have some truth in our little séance. Like the walrus, I feel the time has come to speak of many things. From this moment, you are my prisoners. The length of your durance vile depends on you. Who are you, Miss Winter?"

The look she turned on him made his hands tingle. Hers was a face for cupping between tender palms. Dark and troubled, her eyes pleaded for understanding, for sympathy.

"I told you all I know," she pleaded. "I've tried and tried, ever since I could remember anything, to think of—well, all those things you think of at times."

Again she passed a hand across her face, as if wiping away veils.

"I don't ever remember snagging a stocking on the way to an important appointment," she said. "And I know that girls do. I never had to fight for my"—she colored—"my honor, whatever that is. And I know that girls like me have fought for this something I don't understand, by the time they've reached my age. Whatever that is," she added pensively. "I don't even know how old I am, or where I've been."

A pattern suddenly clicked into place in the Saint's brain, a pattern so monstrous, so inhuman as to arouse his destructive instincts to the point of homicidal mania. The look he turned on Big Bill Holbrook was ice and flame.

His voice was pitched at conversational level, but each word fell from his lips like a shining sword.

"Do you know," he said, "I'm beginning to get some new ideas. Not very nice ideas, chum. And if I'm guessing right about what you and your fellow scum have done to this innocent girl, you are liable to cost your insurance company money."

He moved toward Holbrook with a liquid grace that had all the co-ordination of a panther's movement—and the menace. Big Bill Holbrook leaned back from it.

"Stop acting the knight in armor," he protested. "What in hell you talking about?"

"It should have been obvious before," Simon Templar said. "Up on your feet, Holbrook."

Holbrook remained at ease.

"If you've got an explanation for all this that doesn't agree with mine, I want to know it."

The Saint paused. There was honest curiosity in the man's voice—and no fear. That cowardice which had characterized him before was replaced with what seemed an honest desire to hear the Saint's idea.

"This girl," the Saint said, "whoever she is, has breeding, grace, and beauty out of this world. She has been brought up under expensive and sheltered surroundings. You can see that in her every gesture, every expression. She was bred to great wealth, perhaps nobility, or even royalty."

Big Bill leaned forward in almost an agony of concentration. Every word of Simon Templar's might have been a $20 gold piece, the way he reached for it with every sense.

The Saint patted his jacket pocket.

"This jewel is the symbol of her position—heiress, princess, queen, or what have you. You and your unsavory companions kidnaped her, and are holding her for ransom. That would be wicked enough; but you've done worse. Somewhere in the course of your nasty little scheme, it seemed like a good idea to destroy a part of her beauty that could be dangerous to you and your precious pals. So you destroyed her mind. With drugs, I have no doubt—drugs that have dulled her mind until she has no memory. Your reasons are clear enough—it was just a sound form of insurance. And now your gang has split up, fighting over the spoils. I don't know who would have come out on top, if you hadn't happened to run into me. But I know what the end is going to be now—and you aren't going to like it. Get on your feet!"

The command was like a pistol shot, and Big Bill Holbrook jumped. Then he leaned back again and chuckled in admiration.

"Everything that's been said about you is true. There's nobody like you. That's so much better than Andy Faulks did there's no comparison. Say, that really would have been something, and look, it'd have explained why she couldn't remember who she was. Saint, I got to hand it to you. Too bad you're not in bed in Glendale."

For once of a very few times in his life, the Saint was taken aback. The words were spoken with such ease, such sincerity, that Simon's deadly purpose cooled to a feeling of confusion. While it is true that a man who is accustomed to danger, to gambling for high stakes with death as a forfeit could simulate feelings he did not actually feel, it is seldom that a man of Big Bill Holbrook's obvious I.Q. can look annihilation in the face with an admiring grin.

Something was still wrong, but wrong in the same way that everything in the whole episode was wrong—wrong with that same unearthly off-key distortion that defeated logical diagnosis.

The Saint took out a cigarette and lighted it, slowly; and over the hiss of the match he heard other sounds, which resolved themselves into a blur of footsteps.

Simon glanced at his watch. Jimmy and Mac had been gone less than half an hour. It was impossible for them to be returning from the village four miles away.

What had Holbrook said? Something about everything happening faster in dreams? But that was in the same vein of nonsense. Maybe they'd met the boss at the foot of the hill.

Holbrook said: "What is it? Did you hear something?"

"Only your friends again."

Fear came once more to Holbrook and Dawn Winter. Their eyes were wide and dark with it, turning instantly toward the bunk beds.

"No," Simon said. "Not this time. We'll have this out in the open."

"But he'll kill us!" Holbrook began to babble. "It's awful, the things he'll do. You don't know him, Saint. You can't imagine, you couldn't——"

"I can imagine anything," said the Saint coldly. "I've been

doing that for some time, and I'm tired of it. Now I'd prefer to know."

He crossed the room as the footsteps outside turned into knuckles at the door.

"Welcome to our study club," the Saint said.

Trailer Mac and Jimmy preceded an enormous hulk through the door and, when they saw Holbrook and Dawn, charged like lions leaping on paralyzed gazelles.

The Saint moved in a lightning blur. Two sharp cracks of fist on flesh piled Mac in one corner, Jimmy in another. They lay still.

A butter chuckle caused the Saint to turn. He was looking into a small circular hole. A .38, he computed. He raised his eyes to twins of the barrel, but these were eyes. They lay deep in flesh that swelled in yellowish-brown rolls, flowing fatly downward to describe one of the fattest men the Saint had ever seen. They could only have belonged to a man called Selden Appopoulis.

"Mr. Sydney Greenstreet, I presume?" Simon drawled.

The buttery chuckle set a sea of flesh ebbing and flowing.

"A quick action, sir, and an efficient direction of action. I compliment you, and am saddened that you must die."

The Saint shrugged. He knew that this fat man, though butter-voiced, had a heart of iridium. His eyes were the pale expressionless orbs of a killer. His mouth was thin with determination, his hand steady with purpose. But Simon had faced all those indications before.

"I hate to disappoint you, comrade," he said lightly, "but that line has a familiar ring. And yet I'm still alive."

Appopoulis appraised and dismissed the Saint, though his eyes never wavered. He spoke to Holbrook.

"The opal. Quickly!"

The butter of his voice had frozen into oleaginous icicles; and Holbrook quailed under the bite of their sharp edges.

"I haven't got it, Appopoulis. The Saint has it."

Simon was astonished at the change in the fat man. It was subtle, admittedly, but it was there nonetheless. Fear came into the pale grey eyes which had been calmly contemplating murder as a climax to unspeakable inquisitions. Fear and respect. The voice melted butter again.

"So," he said warmly. "Simon Templar, the Robin Hood of Modern Crime, the Twentieth Century's brightest buccaneer, the —ah—devil with dames. I had not anticipated this."

Once more it struck the Saint that the descriptive phrases were an exact repetition of Holbrook's. And once more it struck him that the quality of fear in this weird quintet was not strained. And once more he wondered about Holbrook's fantastic tale. . . .

"You are expecting maybe Little Lord Feigenbaum?" Simon asked. "Or what do you want?"

"The cameo opal, for one thing," Appopoulis said easily. "For the other, the girl."

"And what do you intend to do with them?"

"Cherish them, sir. Both of them."

His voice had encyclopaedic lust and greed, and the Saint felt as if small things crawled on him.

Before he could make an answer, stirrings in their respective corners announced the return of Mac and Jimmy to another common plane of existence. Without a word they got groggily to their feet, shook their heads clear of trip hammers, and moved toward the Saint.

"Now, Mr. Templar," said Appopoulis, "you have a choice. Live, and my desires are granted without violence, or die, and they are spiced with emotions at fever heat."

Mac and Jimmy had halted: one small and thunderstruck, one large and paralyzed.

"Boss," quavered Jimmy, "did youse say Templar? Da Saint?"

"The same." Simon bowed.

"Chee!" Mac breathed. "Da Saint. Da Robin Hood of Modern Crime, da——"

"Please," Simon groaned. "Another record, if you don't mind."

"Boss, we ain't got a chanct," Jimmy said.

Appopoulis turned his eyes on the little man.

"He," the boss said, "has the opal."

This news stiffened their gelatinous spines long enough to set them at the Saint in a two-directional charge.

The Saint swerved to meet it. He held Jimmy between himself and the unwavering gun of Appopoulis with one hand. With the other he wrought havoc on the features of Mac.

It was like dancing, like feathers on the breeze, the way the

Saint moved. Even to himself it had the kind of exhilaration that a fighter may only experience once in a lifetime. He had a sense of power, of supernatural co-ordination, of invincibility beyond anything he had ever known. He cared nothing for the knowledge that Appopoulis was skipping around on the outskirts of the fray, trying to find an angle from which he could terminate it with a well-placed shot. Simon knew that it was no fear of killing Jimmy that stayed the fat man's finger on the trigger—it was simply the knowledge that it would have wasted a shot, that the Saint could have gone on using Jimmy as a shield, alive or dead. The Saint knew this coolly and detachedly, as if with a mind separate from his own, while he battered Mac's face into a varicolored pulp.

Then Mac's eyes glazed and he went down; and the Saint's right hand snaked hipwards for his own gun while his left flung Jimmy bodily at the paunch of Appopoulis.

And that was when the amazing, the incredible and impossible thing went wrong. For Jimmy didn't fly away from the Saint's thrust, as he should have, like a marble from a slingshot. Somehow he remained entangled with the Saint's arm, clinging to it as if bogged in some indissoluble birdlime, with a writhing tenacity that was as inescapable as a nightmare. And Simon looked down the barrel of Appopoulis's gun and saw the fat man's piggy eyes brighten with something that might have been lust. . . .

The Saint tried to throw a shot at him, but he was off balance, and the frenzied squirming of his erstwhile shield made it like trying to shoot from the back of a bucking horse. The bullet missed by a fraction of an inch, and buried itself in the wall beside the mirror. Then Appopoulis fired back.

The Saint felt a jar, and a flame roared inside his chest. Somehow, he couldn't pull the trigger any more. The gun fell from his limp fingers. His incredulous eyes looked full in the mirror and saw a neat black hole over his heart, saw it begin to spread as his life's blood gushed out.

It was strange to realize that this was it, and it had happened to him at last, as it had always been destined to happen someday, and in an instant he was going to cheat to the back of the book for the answer to the greatest mystery of all. Yet his last conscious thought was that his image was sharp and clear in the mir-

ror. When he had seen Dawn's reflection, it had been like one
seen in an agitated pool. . . .

When he opened his eyes again it was broad daylight, and the
intensity of the light told him that it must have been more than
twelve hours since he had been shot.

He was lying on the floor of the cabin. He felt for his heart. It
was beating strongly. His hand did not come away sticky with
blood.

His eyes turned hesitantly down to his shirt. There was no hole
in it. He jumped to his feet, felt himself all over, examined himself in the mirror. He was as whole as he'd ever been; and he felt
fine.

He looked around the cabin. The mattresses were piled in the
corner under the pine cones, the bunks unmade. Otherwise there
were no signs of the brawl the night before. No trace of Jimmy
and Mac, or Appopoulis. No Big Bill Holbrook. No Dawn. . . .

And no hole in the wall beside the mirror where his hopeless
shot at Appopoulis had buried itself.

The Saint shook his head. If it had all been a dream, he might
have to seriously consider consulting a psychiatrist. Dreams reach
only a certain point of vividness. What he remembered was too
sharp of definition, too coherent, too consecutive. Yet if it wasn't
a dream, where were the evidences of reality, the bullet hole in
his chest, in the wall?

Simon reached for a cigarette, and suddenly sniffed it suspiciously before he put it in his mouth. If some joker either in fun
or malice, had adulterated his tobacco with some more exotic
herb . . . But that, too, was absurd. A jag of those dimensions
would surely bequeath a hangover to match.

He fumbled in his pockets for a match. Instead, his questing
fingers touched something solid, a shape that was oddly familiar
—yet impossibly alien. The tactile sensation lasted only for an instant, before his hand recoiled as if the thing had been red hot.
He was afraid, actually afraid, to take it out.

The address of Andrew Faulks was in the Glendale directory.
The house was a modest two-bedroom affair on a side street near
Forest Lawn Memorial Park. A wreath hung on the door. A sol-

emn gentleman who looked like, and undoubtedly was, an under-taker opened the door.

"Mr. Faulks passed on last night," he said in answer to the Saint's query. Unctuous sorrow overlaid the immediate landscape.

"Wasn't it rather sudden?"

"Ah, not exactly, sir. He went to sleep last Saturday, passed into a coma, and never awakened."

"At what time," Simon asked, "did he die?"

"At 10:40," the man replied. "It was a sad death. He was in a delirium. He kept shouting about shooting someone, and talked about a saint."

Simon had moved into the house while listening to the tale of death and found himself looking off the hallway into a well-lighted den. His keen eyes noted that while most of the shelves were gay with the lurid jackets of adventure fiction, one section was devoted to works on psychology and psychiatry.

Here were the tomes of Freud, Adler, Jung, Brill, Bergson, Krafft-Ebing, and lesser lights. A book lay open on a small read-ing table.

The Saint stepped inside the room to look at it. It was titled *In Darkest Schizophrenia,* by William J. Holbrook, Ph.D.

Simon wondered what the psychic-phenomena boys would do with this one. This, he thought, would certainly give them a shot in the aura.

"Mrs. Faulks is upstairs, sir," the professional mourner was saying. "Are you a friend of the family?"

"I wish you'd just show her this." Simon forced one hand into a pocket. "And ask her———"

He never finished the question. Never.

There was nothing in the pocket for his hand to find. Nothing to meet his fingertips but a memory that was even then darkening and dying out along his nerves.

Finally, 1962's "The Convenient Monster" introduces a wearier but more mature Saint. Before he used to enjoy people's reactions to his name. Now he feels embarrassment and irritation. And while he still reminisces about the good old days, he sees them as behind him. Even the establishment is viewing him as more respectable. In fact, a baffled Scottish inspector solicits Simon's help in solving this classic whodunit, in which the leading suspect is the Loch Ness Monster.

THE CONVENIENT MONSTER

"Of course," said Inspector Robert Mackenzie, of the Inverness-shire Constabulary, with a burr as broad as his boots seeming to add an extra R to the word, "I know ye're only in Scotland as an ordinary visitor, and no' expectin' to be mixed up in any criminal business."

"That's right," said the Saint cheerfully.

He was so used to this sort of thing that the monotony sometimes became irritating, but Inspector Mackenzie made the conventional gambit with such courteous geniality that it almost sounded like an official welcome. He was a large and homely man with large red hands and small twinkling grey eyes and sandy hair carefully plastered over the bare patch above his forehead, and so very obviously and traditionally a policeman that Simon Templar actually felt a kind of nostalgic affection for him. Short of a call from Chief Inspector Claud Eustace Teal in person, nothing could have brought back more sharply what the Saint often thought of as the good days; and he took it as a compliment that even after so many years, and even as far away as Scotland itself, he was not lost to the telescopic eye of Scotland Yard.

"And I suppose," Mackenzie continued, "ye couldna even be bothered with a wee bit of a local mystery."

"What's your problem?" Simon asked. "Has somebody stolen the haggis you were fattening for the annual Police Banquet?"

The Inspector ignored this with the same stony dignity with

which he would have greeted the hoary question about what a Scotsman wore under his kilt.

"It might be involvin' the Loch Ness Monster," he said with the utmost gravity.

"All right," said the Saint good-humouredly. "I started this. I suppose I had it coming. But you're the first policeman who ever tried to pull my leg. Didn't they tell you that I'm the guy who's supposed to do the pulling?"

"I'm no' makin' a joke," Mackenzie persisted aggrievedly, and the Saint stared at him.

It was in the spring of 1933 that a remarkable succession of sober and reputable witnesses began to testify that they had seen in Loch Ness a monstrous creature whose existence had been a legend of region since ancient times, but which few persons in this century had claimed to have seen for themselves. The descriptions varied in detail, as human observations are prone to do, but they seemed generally to agree that the beast was roughly 30 feet long and could swim at about the same number of miles per hour; it was a dark grey in colour, with a small horse-like head on a long tapering neck, which it turned from side to side with the quick movements of an alert hen. There were divergencies as to whether it had one or more humps in its back, and whether it churned the water with flippers or a powerful tail; but all agreed that it could not be classified with anything known to modern natural history.

The reports culminated in December with a photograph showing a strange reptilian shape thrashing in the water, taken by a senior employee of the British Aluminum Company, which has a plant nearby. A number of experts certified the negative to be unretouched and unfaked, and the headline writers took it from there.

Within a fortnight a London newspaper had a correspondent on the scene with a highly publicized big-game authority in tow; some footprints were found and casts made of them—which before the New Year was three days old had been pronounced by the chief zoologists of the British Museum to have all been made by the right hind foot of a hippopotamus, and a stuffed hippopotamus at that. In the nation-wide guffaw which followed the exposure of this hoax, the whole matter exploded into a theme for cartoonists and comedians, and that aura of hilarious incredulity still coloured the Saint's vague recollections of the subject.

It took a little while for him to convince himself that the Inspector's straight face was not part of an elaborate exercise in Highland humour.

"What has the Monster done that's illegal?" Simon inquired at length, with a gravity to match Mackenzie's own.

"A few weeks ago, it's thocht to ha' eaten a sheep. And last night it may ha' killed a dog."

"Where was this?"

"The sheep belonged to Fergus Clanraith, who has a farm by the loch beyond Foyers, and the dog belongs to his neighbours, a couple named Bastion from doon in England who settled here last summer. 'Tis only aboot twenty miles away, if ye could spairr the time with me."

The Saint sighed. In certain interludes, he thought that everything had already happened to him that could befall a man even with his exceptional gift for stumbling into fantastic situations and being offered bizarre assignments, but apparently there was always some still more preposterous imbroglio waiting to entangle him.

"Okay," he said resignedly. "I've been slugged with practically every other improbability you could raise an eyebrow at, so why should I draw the line at dog-slaying monsters. Lay on, Macduff."

"The name is Mackenzie," said the Inspector seriously.

Simon paid his hotel bill and took his own car, for he had been intending to continue his pleasantly aimless wandering that day anyhow, and it would not make much difference to him where he stopped along the way. He followed Mackenzie's somewhat venerable chariot out of Inverness on the road that takes the east bank of the Ness River, and in a few minutes the slaty grimness of the town had been gratefully forgotten in the green and gold loveliness of the countryside.

The road ran at a fairly straight tangent to the curves of the river and the Caledonian Canal, giving only infrequent glimpses of the seven locks built to lift shipping to the level of the lake, until at Dores he had his first view of Loch Ness at its full breadth.

The Great Glen of Scotland transects the country diagonally

from north-east to south-west, as if a giant had tried to break off
the upper end of the land between the deep natural notches
formed by Loch Linnhe and the Beauly Firth. On the map which
Simon had seen, the chain of lochs stretched in an almost crow-
flight line that had made him look twice to be sure that there was
not in fact a clear channel across from the Eastern to the Western
Sea. Loch Ness itself, a tremendous trough 24 miles long but only
averaging about a mile in width, suggested nothing more than an
enlargement of the Canal system which gave access to it at both
ends.

But not many vessels seemed to avail themselves of the passage, for there was no boat in sight on the lake that afternoon.
With the water as calm as a mill-pond and the fields and trees rising from its shores to a blue sky dappled with soft woolly clouds,
it was as pretty as a picture postcard and utterly unconvincing to
think of as a place which might be haunted by some outlandish
horror from the mists of antiquity.

For a drive of twenty minutes, at the sedate pace set by
Mackenzie the highway paralleled the edge of the loch a little way
up its steep stony banks. The opposite shore widened slightly into
the tranquil beauty of Urquhart Bay with its ancient castle standing out grey and stately on the far point, and then returned to the
original almost uniform breadth. Then, within fortunately brief
sight of the unpicturesque aluminium works, it bore away to the
south through the small stark village of Foyers and went winding
up the glen of one of the tumbling streams that feed the lake.

Several minutes further on, Mackenzie turned off into a narrow
side road that twisted around and over a hill and swung down
again, until suddenly the loch was spread out squarely before
them once more and the lane curled past the first of two houses
that could be seen standing solitarily apart from each other but
each within a bowshot of the loch. Both of them stood out with
equal harshness against the gentle curves and colours of the landscape with the same dark graceless austerity as the last village or
the last town or any other buildings Simon had seen in Scotland,
a country whose unbounded natural beauty seemed to have inspired no corresponding artistry in its architects, but rather to
have goaded them into competition to offset it with the most contrasting ugliness into which bricks and stone and tile could be as-

sembled. This was a paradox to which he had failed to fit a plausible theory for so long that he had finally given up trying.

Beside the first house a man in a stained shirt and corduroy trousers tucked into muddy canvas leggings was digging in a vegetable garden. He looked up as Mackenzie brought his rattletrap to a stop, and walked slowly over to the hedge. He was short but powerfully built, and his hair flamed like a stormy sunset.

Mackenzie climbed out and beckoned to the Saint. As Simon reached them, the red-haired man was saying: "Aye, I've been over and seen what's left o' the dog. It's more than they found of my sheep, I can tell ye."

"But could it ha' been the same thing that did it?" asked the Inspector.

"That' no' for me to say, Mackenzie. I'm no' a detective. But remember, it wasna me who said the Monster took my sheep. It was the Bastions who thocht o' that, it might be to head me off from askin' if *they* hadn't been the last to see it—pairhaps on their Sunday dinner table. There's nae such trick I wouldna put beyond the Sassenach."

Mackenzie introduced them: "This is Mr. Clanraith, whom I was tellin' ye aboot. Fergus, I'd like ye to meet Mr. Templar, who may be helpin' me to investigate."

Clanraith gave Simon a muscular and horny grip across the untrimmed hedge, appraising him shrewdly from under shaggy ginger brows.

"Ye dinna look like a policeman, Mr. Templar."

"I try not to," said Saint expressionlessly. "Did you mean by what you were just saying that you don't believe in the Monster at all?"

"I didna say that."

"Then apart from anything else, you think there might actually be such a thing."

"There might."

"Living where you do, I should think you'd have as good a chance as anyone of seeing it yourself—if it does exist."

The farmer peered at Simon suspiciously.

"Wad ye be a reporrter, Mr. Templar, pairhaps?"

"No, I'm not," Simon assured him; but the other remained wary.

"When a man tells o' seein' monsters, his best friends are apt to wonder if he may ha' taken a wee drop too much. If I had seen anything, ever, I wadna be talkin' aboot it to every stranger, to be made a laughin'-stock of."

"But ye'll admit," Mackenzie put in, "it's no' exactly norrmal for a dog to be chewed up an' killed the way this one was."

"I wull say this," Clanraith conceded guardedly. "It's strange that nobody hairrd the dog bark, or e'en whimper."

Through the Saint's mind flickered an eerie vision of something amorphous and loathsome oozing soundlessly out of night-blackened water, flowing with obscene stealth towards a hound that slept unwarned by any of its senses.

"Do you mean it mightn't've had a chance to let out even a yip?"

"I'm no' sayin'," Clanraith maintained cautiously. "But it was a guid watchdog, if naught else."

A girl had stepped out of the house and come closer while they talked. She had Fergus Clanraith's fiery hair and greenish eyes, but her skin was pink and white where his was weatherbeaten and her lips were full where his were tight. She was a half a head taller than he, and her figure was slim where it should be.

Now she said: "That's right. He even barked whenever he heard me coming, although he saw me every day."

Her voice was low and well modulated, with only an attractive trace of her father's accent.

"Then if it was a pairrson wha' killed him, Annie, 'twad only mean it was a body he was still more used to."

"But you can't really believe that any human being would do a thing like that to a dog that knew them—least of all to their own dog!"

"That's the trouble wi' lettin' a lass be brocht up an' schooled on the wrong side o' the Tweed," Clanraith said darkly. "She forgets what the English ha' done to honest Scotsmen no' so lang syne."

The girl's eyes had kept returning to the Saint with candid interest, and it was to him that she explained, smiling: "Father still wishes he could fight for Bonnie Prince Charlie. He's glad to let me do part-time secretarial work for Mr. Bastion because I can live at home and keep house as well, but he still feels I'm guilty of fraternizing with the Enemy."

"We'd best be gettin' on and talk to them ourselves," Mackenzie said. "And then we'll see if Mr. Templar has any more questions to ask."

There was something in Annie Clanraith's glance which seemed to say that she hoped that he would, and the Saint was inclined to be of the same sentiment. He had certainly not expected to find anyone so decorative in the cast of characters, and he began to feel a tentative quickening of optimism about this interruption in his travels. He could see her in his rear-view mirror, still standing by the hedge and following with her gaze after her father had turned back to his digging.

About three hundred yards and a few bends farther on, Mackenzie veered between a pair of stone gateposts and chugged to a standstill on the circular driveway in front of the second house. Simon stopped behind him and then strolled after him to the front door, which was opened almost at once by a tall thin man in a pullover and baggy grey flannel slacks.

"Good afternoon, sir," said the detective courteously. "I'm Inspector Mackenzie from Inverness. Are ye Mr. Bastion?"

"Yes."

Bastion had a bony face with a long aquiline nose, lank black hair flecked with grey, and a broad toothbrush moustache that gave him an indeterminately military appearance. His black eyes flickered to the Saint inquiringly.

"This is Mr. Templar, who may be assistin' me," Mackenzie said. "The constable who was here this morning told me all aboot what ye showed him, on the telephone, but could we ha' a wee look for ourselves?"

"Oh, yes, certainly. Will you come this way?"

The way was around the house, across an uninspired formal garden at the back which looked overdue for the attention of a gardener, and through a small orchard beyond which a stretch of rough grass sloped quickly down to the water. As the meadow fell away, a pebbly beach came into view, and Simon saw that this was one of the rare breaches in the steep average angle of the loch's sides. On either side of the little beach the ground swelled up again to form a shallow bowl that gave an easy natural access to the lake. The path that they traced led to a short rustic pier with a shabby skiff tied to it, and on the ground to one side of the pier was something covered with potato sacking.

"I haven't touched anything, as the constable asked me," Bastion said. "Except to cover him up."

He bent down and carefully lifted off the burlap.

They looked down in silence at what was uncovered.

"The puir beastie," Mackenzie said at last.

It had been a large dog of confused parentage in which the Alsatian may have predominated. What had happened to it was no nicer to look at than it is to catalogue. Its head and hindquarters were partly mashed to a red pulp; and plainly traceable across its chest was a row of slot-like gashes, each about an inch long and close together, from which blood had run and clotted in the short fur. Mackenzie squatted and stretched the skin with gentle fingers to see the slits more clearly. The Saint also felt the chest: it had an unnatural contour where the line of punctures crossed it, and his probing touch found only sponginess where there should have been a hard cage of ribs.

His eyes met Mackenzie's across the pitifully mangled form.

"That would be quite a row of teeth," he remarked.

"Aye," said the Inspector grimly. "But what live here that has a mouth like that?"

They straightened up and surveyed the immediate surroundings. The ground here, only a stride or two from the beach, which in turn was less than a yard wide, was so moist that it was soggy, and pockets of muddy liquid stood in the deeper indentations with which it was plentifully rumpled. The carpet of coarse grass made individual impressions difficult to identify, but three or four shoe-heel prints could be positively distinguished.

"I'm afraid I made a lot of those tracks," Bastion said. "I know you're not supposed to go near anything, but all I could think of at the time was seeing if *he* was still alive and if I could do anything for him. The constable tramped around a bit too, when he was here." He pointed past the body. "But neither of us had anything to do with those marks there."

Close to the beach was a place where the turf looked as if it had been raked by something with three gigantic claws. One talon had caught in the roots of a tuft of grass and torn it up bodily:

the clump lay on the pebbles at the water's edge. Aside from that, the claws had left three parallel grooves, about four inches apart and each about half an inch wide. They dug into the ground at their upper ends to a depth of more than two inches, and dragged back towards the lake for a length of about ten inches as they tapered up.

Simon and Mackenzie stood on the pebbles to study the marks. Simon spanning them experimentally with his fingers while the detective took exact measurements with a tape and entered them in his notebook.

"Anything wi' a foot big enough to carry claws like that," Mackenzie said, "I'd no' wish to ha' comin' after me."

"Well, they call it a Monster, don't they?" said the Saint dryly. "It wouldn't impress anyone if it made tracks like a mouse."

Mackenzie unbent his knees stiffly, shooting the Saint a distrustful glance, and turned to Bastion.

"When did ye find all this, sir?" he asked.

"I suppose it was about six o'clock," Bastion said. "I woke up before dawn and couldn't get to sleep again, so I decided to try a little early fishing. I got up as soon as it was light——"

"Ye didna hear any noise before that?"

"No."

"It couldna ha' been the dog barkin' that woke ye?"

"Not that I'm aware of. And my wife is a very light sleeper, and she didn't hear anything. But I was rather surprised when I didn't see the dog outside. He doesn't sleep in the house, but he's always waiting on the doorstep in the morning. However, I came on down here—and that's how I found him."

"And you didn't see anything else?" Simon asked. "In the lake, I mean."

"No. I didn't see the Monster. And when I looked for it, there wasn't a ripple on the water. Of course, the dog may have been killed some time before, though his body was still warm."

"Mr. Bastion," Mackenzie said, "do *ye* believe it was the Monster that killed him?"

Bastion looked at him and at the Saint.

"I'm not a superstitious man," he replied. "But if it wasn't a monster of some kind, what else could it have been?"

The Inspector closed his notebook with a snap that seemed to be echoed by his clamping lips. It was evident that he felt that the situation was wandering far outside his professional province. He scowled at the Saint as though he expected Simon to do something about it.

"It might be interesting," Simon said thoughtfully, "if we got a vet to do a post-mortem."

"What for?" Bastion demanded brusquely.

"Let's face it," said the Saint. "Those claw marks *could* be fakes. And the dog *could* have been mashed up with some sort of club—even a club with spikes set in it to leave wounds that'd look as if they were made by teeth. But by all accounts, no one could have got near enough to the dog to do that without him barking. *Unless the dog was doped first.* So before we go overboard on this Monster theory, I'd like to rule everything else out. An autopsy would do that."

Bastion rubbed his scrubby moustache.

"I see your point. Yes, that might be a good idea."

He helped them to shift the dog on to the sack which had previously covered it, and Simon and Mackenzie carried it between them back to the driveway and laid it in the boot of the detective's car.

"D'ye think we could ha' a wurrd wi' Mrs. Bastion, sir?" Mackenzie asked, wiping his hands on a clean rag and passing it to the Saint.

"I suppose so," Bastion assented dubiously. "Although she's pretty upset about this, as you can imagine. It was really her dog more than mine. But come in, and I'll see if she'll talk to you for a minute."

But Mrs. Bastion herself settled that by meeting them in the hall, and she made it obvious that she had been watching them from a window.

"What are they doing with Golly Noel?" she greeted her husband wildly. "Why are they taking him away?"

"They want to have him examined by a doctor, dear."

Bastion went on to explain why, until she interrupted him again:

"Then don't let them bring him back. It's bad enough to have seen him the way he is, without having to look at him dissected."

She turned to Simon and Mackenzie. "You must understand how I feel. Golly was like a son to me. His name was really Goliath— I called him that because he was so big and fierce, but actually he was a pushover when you got on the right side of him."

Words came from her in a driving torrent that suggested the corollary of a power-house. She was a big-boned strong-featured woman who made no attempt to minimize any of her probable forty-five years. Her blonde hair was unwaved and pulled back into a tight bun, and her blue eyes were set in a nest of wrinkles that would have been called characterful on an outdoor man. Her lipstick, which needed renewing, had a slapdash air of being her one impatient concession to feminine artifice. But Bastion put a soothing arm around her as solicitously as if she had been a dimpled bride.

"I'm sure these officers will have him buried for us, Eleanor," he said. "But while they're here I think they wanted to ask you something."

"Only to comfairrm what Mr. Bastion told us, ma'am," said Mackenzie. "That ye didna hear an disturrbance last night."

"Absolutely not. And if Golly had made a sound, I should have heard him. I always do. Why are you trying so hard to get around the facts? It's as plain as a pikestaff that the Monster did it."

"Some monsters have two legs," Simon remarked.

"And I suppose you're taught not to believe in any other kind. Even with the evidence under your very eyes."

"I mind a time when some other footprints were found, ma'am," Mackenzie put in deferentially, "which turned oot to be a fraud."

"I know exactly what you're referring to. And that stupid hoax made a lot of idiots disbelieve the authentic photograph which was taken just before it, and refuse to accept an even better picture that was taken by a thoroughly reputable London surgeon about four months later. I know what I'm talking about. As a matter of fact, the reason we took this house was mainly because I'm hoping to discover the Monster."

Two pairs of eyebrows shot up and lowered almost in unison, but it was the Saint who spoke for Mackenzie as well as himself.

"How would you do that, Mrs. Bastion?" he inquired with some circumspection. "If the Monster has been well known around here for a few centuries, at least to everyone who believes in him——"

"It still hasn't been scientifically and officially established. I'd like to have the credit for doing that, beyond any shadow of doubt, and naming it *monstrum eleanoris.*"

"Probably you gentlemen don't know it," Bastion elucidated, with a kind of quaintly protective pride, "but Mrs. Bastion is a rather distinguished naturalist. She's hunted every kind of big game there is, and even holds a couple of world's records."

"But I never had a trophy as important as this would be," his better half took over again. "I expect you think I'm a little cracked—that there couldn't really be any animal of any size in the world that hasn't been discovered by this time. Tell them the facts of life, Noel."

Bastion cleared his throat like a schoolboy preparing to recite, and said with much the same awkward air: "The gorilla was only discovered in 1847, the giant panda in 1869, and the okapi wasn't discovered till 1901. Of course explorers brought back rumours of them, but people thought they were just native fairy tales. And you yourselves probably remember reading about the first coelacanth being caught. That was only in 1938."

"So why shouldn't there still be something else left that I could be the first to prove?" Eleanor Bastion concluded for him. "The obvious thing to go after, I suppose, was the Abominable Snowman; but Mr. Bastion can't stand high altitudes. So I'm making do with the Loch Ness Monster."

Inspector Mackenzie, who had for some time been looking progressively more confused and impatient in spite of his politely valiant efforts to conceal the fact, finally managed to interrupt the antiphonal barrage of what he could only be expected to regard as delirious irrelevancies.

"All that I'm consairned wi', ma'am," he said heavily, "is tryin' to detairrmine whether there's a human felon to be apprehended. If it should turrn oot to be a monster, as ye're thinkin', it wadna be in my jurisdeection. However, in that case, pairhaps Mr. Templar, who is no' a police officer, could be o' more help to ye."

"Templar," Bastion repeated slowly. "I feel as if I ought to recognize that name, now, but I was rather preoccupied with something else when I first heard it."

"Do you have a halo on you somewhere?" quizzed Mrs. Bastion, the huntress, in a tone which somehow suggested the aiming of a gun.

"Sometimes."

"Well, by Jove!" Bastion said. "I should've guessed it, of course, if I'd been thinking about it. You didn't sound like a policeman."

Mackenzie winced faintly, but both the Bastions were too openly absorbed in re-appraising the Saint to notice it.

Simon Templar should have been hardened to that kind of scrutiny, but as the years went on it was beginning to cause him a mixture of embarrassment and petty irritation. He wished that new acquaintances could dispense with the reactions and stay with their original problems.

He said, rather roughly: "It's just my bad luck that Mackenzie caught me as I was leaving Inverness. I was on my way to Loch Lomond, like any innocent tourist, to find out how bonnie the banks actually are. He talked me into taking the low road instead of the high road, and stopping here to stick my nose into your problem."

"But that's perfectly wonderful!" Mrs. Bastion announced like a bugle. "Noel, ask him to stay the night. I mean, for the weekend. Or for the rest of the week, if he can spare the time."

"Why—er—yes," Bastion concurred obediently. "Yes, of course. We'd be delighted. The Saint ought to have some good ideas about catching a monster."

Simon regarded him coolly, aware of the invisible glow of slightly malicious expectation emanating from Mackenzie, and made a reckless instant decision.

"Thank you," he said. "I'd love it. I'll bring in my things, and Mac can be on his way."

He sauntered out without further palaver, happily conscious that only Mrs. Bastion had not been moderately rocked by his casual acceptance.

They all ask for it, he thought. Cops and civilians alike, as soon as they hear the name. Well, let's oblige them. And see how they like whatever comes of it.

Mackenzie followed him outside, with a certain ponderous dubiety which indicated that some of the joke had already evaporated.

"Ye'll ha' no authorrity in this, ye underrrstand," he emphasized, "except the rights o' any private investigator—which are no' the same in Scotland as in America, to judge by some o' the books I've read."

"I shall try very hard not to gang agley," Simon assured him. "Just phone me the result of the P.M. as soon as you possibly can. And while you're waiting for it, you might look up the law about shooting monsters. See if one has to take out a special licence, or anything like that."

He watched the detective drive away, and went back in with his two-suiter. He felt better already, with no official eyes and ears absorbing his most trivial responses. And it would be highly misleading to say that he found the bare facts of the case, as they had been presented to him, utterly banal and boring.

Noel Bastion showed him to a small but comfortable room upstairs, with a window that faced towards the home of Fergus Clanraith but which also afforded a sidelong glimpse of the loch. Mrs. Bastion was already busy there, making up the bed.

"You can't get any servants in a place like this," she explained. "I'm lucky to have a woman who bicycles up from Fort Augustus once a week to do the heavy cleaning. They all want to stay in the towns where they can have what they think of as a bit of life."

Simon looked at Bastion innocuously and remarked: "You're lucky to find a secretary right on the spot like the one I met up the road."

"Oh, you mean Annie Clanraith." Bastion scrubbed a knuckle on his upper lip. "Yes. She was working in Liverpool, but she came home at Christmas to spend the holidays with her father. I had to get some typing done in a hurry, and she helped me out. It was Clanraith who talked her into staying. I couldn't pay her as much as she'd been earning in Liverpool, but he pointed out that she'd end up with just as much in her pocket if she didn't have to pay for board and lodging, which he'd give her if she kept house. He's a widower, so it's not a bad deal for him."

"Noel's a writer," Mrs. Bastion said. "His big book isn't finished yet, but he works on it all the time."

"It's a life of Wellington," said the writer. "It's never been done, as I think it should be, by a professional soldier."

"Mackenzie didn't tell me anything about your background," said the Saint. "What should he have called you—Colonel?"

"Only Major. But that was in the Regular Army."

Simon did not miss the faintly defensive tone of the addendum. But the silent calculation he made was that the pension of a retired British Army Major, unless augmented by some more commercial form of authorship than an unfinished biography of distinctly limited appeal, would not finance enough big-game safaris to earn an ambitious huntress a great reputation.

"There," said Mrs. Bastion finally. "Now, if you'd like to settle in and make yourself at home, I'll have made tea ready in five minutes."

The Saint had embarked on his Scottish trip with an open mind and an attitude of benevolent optimism, but if anyone had prophesied that it would lead to him sipping tea in the drawing-room of two practically total strangers, with his valise unpacked in their guest bedroom, and solemnly chatting about a monster as if it were as real as a monkey, he would probably have been mildly derisive. His hostess, however, was obsessed with the topic.

"Listen to this," she said, fetching a well-worn volume from a bookcase. "It's a quotation from the biography of St. Columba, written about the middle of the seventh century. It tells about his visit to Inverness some hundred years before, and it says *he was obliged to cross the water of Nesa; and when he had come to the bank he sees some of the inhabitants bringing an unfortunate fellow whom, as those who were bringing him related, a little while before some aquatic monster seized and savagely bit while he was swimming. . . . The blessed man orders one of his companions to swim out and bring him from over the water a coble . . . Lugne Mocumin without delay takes off his clothes except his tunic and casts himself into the water. But the monster comes up and moves towards the man as he swam. . . . The blessed man, seeing it, commanded the ferocious monster saying, 'Go thou no further nor touch the man; go back at once.' Then on hearing this word of the Saint the monster was terrified and fled away again more quickly than if it had been dragged off by ropes.*"

"I must try to remember that formula," Simon murmured, "and hope the Monster can't tell one Saint from another."

" 'Monster' is really a rather stupid name for it," Mrs. Bastion said. "It encourages people to be illogical about it. Actually, in the old days the local people called it *an Niseag*, which is simply the name 'Ness' in Gaelic with a feminine diminutive ending. You could literally translate it as 'Nessie'."

"That does sound a lot cuter," Simon agreed. "If you forget how it plays with dogs."

Eleanor Bastion's weathered face went pale, but the muscles under the skin did not flinch.

"I haven't forgotten Golly. But I was trying to keep my mind off him."

"Assuming this beastie does exist," said the Saint, "how did it get here?"

"Why did it have to 'get' here at all? I find it easier to believe that it always was here. The loch is 750 feet deep, which is twice the mean depth of the North Sea. *An Niseag* is a creature that obviously prefers the depths and only comes to the surface occasionally. I think its original home was always at the bottom of the loch, and it was trapped there when some prehistoric geological upheaval cut off the loch from the sea."

"And it's lived there ever since—for how many million years?"

"Not the original ones—I suppose we must assume at least a couple. But their descendants. Like many primitive creatures, it probably lives to a tremendous age."

"What do you think it is?"

"Most likely something of the plesiosaurus family. The descriptions sound more like that than anything—large body, long neck, paddle-like legs. Some people claim to have seen stumpy projections on its head, rather like the horns of a snail, which aren't part of the usual reconstruction of a plesiosaurus. But after all, we've never seen much of a plesiosaurus except its skeleton. You wouldn't know exactly what a snail looked like if you'd only seen its shell."

"But if Nessie has been here all this time, why wasn't she reported much longer ago?"

"She was. You heard that story about St. Columba. And if you think only modern observations are worth paying attention to, several reliable sightings were recorded from 1871 onwards."

"But there was no motor road along the loch until 1933," Bastion managed to contribute at last, "and a trip like you made today would have been quite an expedition. So there weren't many witnesses about until fairly recently, of the type that scientists would take seriously."

Simon lighted a cigarette. The picture was clear enough. Like the flying saucers, it depended on what you wanted to believe—and whom.

Except that here there was not only fantasy to be thought of. There could be felony.

"What would you have to do to make it an official discovery?"

"We have movie and still cameras with the most powerful telephoto lenses you can buy," said the woman. "I spend eight hours a day simply watching the lake, just like anyone might put in at a regular job, but I vary the times of day systematically. Noel sometimes puts in a few hours as well. We have a view for several miles in both directions, and by the law of averages *an Niseag* must come up eventually in the area we're covering. Whenever that happens, our lenses will get close-up pictures that'll show every detail beyond any possibility of argument. It's simply a matter of patience, and when I came here I made up my mind that I'd spend ten years on it if necessary."

"And now," said the Saint, "I guess you're more convinced than ever that you're on the right track and the scent is hot."

Mrs. Bastion looked him in the eyes with terrifying equanimity.

"Now," she said, "I'm going to watch with a Weatherby Magnum as well as the cameras. *An Niseag* can't be much bigger than an elephant, and it isn't any more bullet-proof. I used to think it'd be a crime to kill the last survivor of a species, but since I saw what it did to poor Golly I'd like to have it as a trophy as well as a picture."

There was much more of this conversation, but nothing that would not seem repetitous in verbatim quotation. Mrs. Bastion had accumulated numerous other books on the subject, from any of which she was prepared to read excerpts in support of her convictions.

It was hardly eight-thirty, however, after a supper of cold meat and salad, when she announced that she was going to bed.

"I want to get up at two o'clock and be out at the loch well before daylight—the same time when that thing must have been there this morning."

"Okay," said the Saint. "Knock on my door, and I'll go with you."

He remained to accept a nightcap of Peter Dawson, which seemed to taste especially rich and smooth in the land where they made it. Probably this was his imagination, but it gave him a pleasant feeling of drinking the wine of the country on its own home ground.

"If you're going to be kind enough to look after her, I may sleep a bit later," Bastion said. "I must get some work done on my book tonight, while there's a little peace and quiet. Not that Eleanor can't take care of herself better than most women, but I wouldn't like her being out there alone after what's happened."

"You're thoroughly sold on this monster yourself, are you?"

The other stared into his glass.

"It's the sort of thing that all my instincts and experience would take with a grain of salt. But you've seen for yourself that it isn't easy to argue with Eleanor. And I must admit that she makes a terrific case for it. But until this morning I was keeping an open mind."

"And now it isn't so open?"

"Quite frankly, I'm pretty shaken. I feel it's got to be settled now, one way or the other. Perhaps you'll have some luck tomorrow."

It did in fact turn out to be a vigil that gave Simon goose-pimples, but they were caused almost entirely by the pre-dawn chill of the air. Daylight came slowly, through a grey and leaky-looking overcast. The lake remained unruffled, guarding its secrets under a pale pearly glaze.

"I wonder what we did wrong," Mrs. Bastion said at last, when the daylight was as broad as the clouds evidently intended to let it become. "The thing should have come back to where it made its last kill. Perhaps if we hadn't been so sentimental we should have left Golly right where he was and built a *machan* over him where we could have stood watch in turns."

Simon was not so disappointed. Indeed, if a monster had actually appeared almost on schedule under their expectant eyes, he would have been inclined to sense the hand of a Hollywood B-picture producer rather than the finger of Fate.

"As you said yesterday, it's a matter of patience," he observed philosophically. "But the odds are that the rest of your eight hours, now, will be just routine. So if you're not nervous I'll ramble around a while."

His rambling had brought him no nearer to the house than the orchard when the sight of a coppery-rosy head on top of a shapely free-swinging figure made his pulse fluctuate enjoyably with a reminder of the remotely possible promise of romantic compensation that had started to warm his interest the day before.

Annie Clanraith's smile was so eager and happy to see him that he might have been an old and close friend who had been away for a long time.

"Inspector Mackenzie told my father he'd left you here. I'm so glad you stayed!"

"I'm glad you're glad," said the Saint, and against her ingenuous sincerity it was impossible to make the reply sound even vestigially skeptical. "But what made it so important?"

"Just having someone new and alive to talk to. You haven't stayed long enough to find out how bored you can be here."

"But you've got a job that must be a little more attractive than going back to an office in Liverpool."

"Oh, it's not bad. And it helps to make father comfortable. And it's nice to live in such beautiful scenery, I expect you'll say. But I read books and I look at the TV, and I can't stop having my silly dreams."

"A gal like you," he said teasingly, "should have her hands full, fighting off other dreamers."

"All I get my hands full of is pages and pages of military strategy, about a man who only managed to beat Napoleon. But at least Napoleon had Josephine. The only thing Wellington gave his name to was an old boot."

Simon clucked sympathetically.

"He may have had moments with his boots off, you know. Or

has your father taught you to believe nothing good of anyone who
was ever born south of the Tweed?"

"You must have thought it was terrible, the way he talked
about Mr. Bastion. And he's so nice, isn't he? It's too bad he's
married!"

"Maybe his wife doesn't think so."

"I mean, I'm a normal girl and I'm not old-fashioned, and the
one thing I do miss here is a man to fight off. In fact, I'm beginning to feel that if one did come along I wouldn't even struggle."

"You sound as if that Scottish song was written about you,"
said the Saint, and he sang softly:

> *"Ilka lassie has her laddie,*
> *Ne'er a ane ha' I;*
> *But all the lads they smile at me,*
> *Comin' through the rye."*

She laughed.

"Well, at least you smiled at me, and that makes today look a
little better."

"Where were you going?"

"To work. I just walked over across the fields—it's much
shorter than by the lane."

Now that she mentioned it, he could see a glimpse of the
Clanraith house between the trees. He turned and walked with
her through the untidy little garden towards the Bastions' entrance.

"I'm sorry that stops me offering to take you on a picnic."

"I don't have any luck, do I? There's a dance in Fort Augustus
tomorrow night, and I haven't been dancing for months, but I
don't know a soul who'd take me."

"I'd like to do something about that," he said. "But it rather
depends on what develops around here. Don't give up hope yet,
though."

As they entered the hall, Bastion came out of a back room and
said: "Ah, good morning, Annie. There are some pages I was
revising last night on my desk. I'll be with you in a moment."

She went on into the room he had just come from, and he
turned to the Saint.

"I suppose you didn't see anything."

"If we had, you'd've heard plenty of gunfire and hollering."

"Did you leave Eleanor down there?"

"Yes. But I don't think she's in any danger in broad daylight. Did Mackenzie call?"

"Not yet. I expect you're anxious to hear from him. The telephone's in the drawing-room—why don't you settle down there? You might like to browse through some of Eleanor's collection of books about the Monster."

Simon accepted the suggestion, and soon found himself so absorbed that only his empty stomach was conscious of the time when Bastion came in and told him that lunch was ready. Mrs. Bastion had already returned and was dishing up an agreeably aromatic lamb stew which she apologized for having only warmed up.

"You were right, it was just routine," she said. "A lot of waiting for nothing. But one of these days it won't be for nothing."

"I was thinking about it myself, dear," Bastion said, "and it seems to me that there's one bad weakness in your eight-hour-a-day system. There are enough odds against you already in only being able to see about a quarter of the loch, which leaves the Monster another three-quarters where it could just as easily pop up. But on top of that, watching only eight hours out of the twenty-four only gives us a one-third chance of being there even if it does pop up within range of our observation post. That doesn't add to the odds against us, it multiplies them."

"I know; but what can we do about it?"

"Since Mr. Templar pointed out that anyone should really be safe enough with a high-powered rifle in their hands and everyone else within call, I thought that three of us could divide up the watches and cover the whole day from before dawn till after dusk, as long as one could possibly see anything. That is, if Mr. Templar would help out. I know he can't stay here indefinitely, but——"

"If it'll make anybody feel better, I'd be glad to take a turn that way," Simon said indifferently.

It might have been more polite to sound more enthusiastic, but he could not make himself believe that the Monster would actually be caught by any such system. He was impatient for Mackenzie's report, which he thought was the essential detail.

The call came about two o'clock, and it was climactically negative.

"The doctor canna find a trrace o' drugs or poison in the puir animal."

Simon took a deep breath.

"What did he think of its injuries?"

"He said he'd ne'er seen the like o' them. He dinna ken anything in the wurruld wi' such crrushin' power in its jaws as yon Monster must have. If 'twas no' for the teeth marrks, he wad ha' thocht it was done wi' a club. But the autopsy mak's that impossible."

"So I take it you figure that rules you officially out," said the Saint bluntly. "But give me a number where I can call you if the picture changes again."

He wrote it down on a pad beside the telephone before he turned and relayed the report.

"That settles it," said Mrs. Bastion. "It can't be anything else but *an Niseag*. And we've got all the more reason to try Noel's idea of keeping watch all day."

"I had a good sleep this morning, so I'll start right away," Bastion volunteered. "You're entitled to a siesta."

"I'll take over after that," she said. "I want to be out there again at twilight. I know I'm monopolizing the most promising times, but this matters more to me than to anyone else."

Simon helped her with the dishes after they had had coffee, and then she excused herself.

"I'll be fresher later if I do take a little nap. Why don't you do the same? It was awfully good of you to get up in the middle of the night with me."

"It sounds as if I won't be needed again until later tomorrow morning," said the Saint. "But I'll be reading and brooding. I'm almost as interested in *an Niseag* now as you are."

He went back to the book he had left in the drawing-room as the house settled into stillness. Annie Clanraith had already departed, before lunch, taking a sheaf of papers with her to type at home.

Presently he put the volume down on his thighs and lay pas-

sively thinking, stretched out on the couch. It was his uniquely
personal method of tackling profound problems, to let himself
relax into a state of blank receptiveness in which half-subcon-
scious impressions could grow and flow together in delicately fluid
adjustments that could presently mould a conclusion almost as
concrete as knowledge. For some time he gazed sightlessly at the
ceiling, and then he continued to meditate with his eyes closed.

He was awakened by Noel Bastion entering the room, humming tunelessly. The biographer of Wellington was instantly apol-
ogetic.

"I'm sorry, Templar—I thought you'd be in your room."

"That's all right." Simon glanced at his watch, and was mildly
surprised to discover how sleepy he must have been. "I was doing
some thinking, and the strain must have been too much for me."

"Eleanor relieved me an hour ago. I hadn't seen anything, I'm
afraid."

"I didn't hear you come in."

"I'm pretty quiet on my feet. Must be a habit I got from com-
mando training. Eleanor often says that if she could stalk like me
she'd have a lot more trophies." Bastion went to the bookcase,
took down a book, and thumbed through it for some reference.
"I've been trying to do some work, but it isn't easy to concentrate."

Simon stood up and stretched himself.

"I guess you'll have to get used to working under difficulties if
you're going to be a part-time monster hunter for ten years—isn't
that how long Eleanor said she was ready to spend at it?"

"I'm hoping it'll be a good deal less than that."

"I was reading in this book *More Than a Legend* that in 1934,
when the excitement about the Monster was at its height, a chap
named Sir Edward Mountain hired a bunch of men and organized
a systematic watch like you were suggesting, but spacing them all
around the lake. It went on for a month or two, and they got a
few pictures of distant splashings, but nothing that was
scientifically accepted."

Bastion put his volume back on the shelf. "You're still skeptical, aren't you?"

"What I've been wondering," said the Saint, "is why this savage behemoth with the big sharp teeth and the nutcracker jaws chomped up a dog but didn't swallow even a little nibble of it."

"Perhaps it isn't carnivorous. An angry elephant will mash a man to a pulp, but it won't eat him. And that dog could be very irritating, barking at everything——"

"According to what I heard, there wasn't any barking. And I'm sure the sheep it's supposed to have taken didn't bark. But the sheep disappeared entirely, didn't it?"

"That's what Clanraith says. But for all we know, the sheep may have been stolen."

"But that could have given somebody the idea of building up the Monster legend from there."

Bastion shook his head.

"But the dog *did* bark at everyone," he insisted stubbornly.

"Except the people he knew," said the Saint, no less persistently. "Every dog is vulnerable to a few people. You yourself, for instance, if you'd wanted to, could have come along, and if he felt lazy he'd've opened one eye and then shut it again and gone back to sleep. Now, are you absolutely sure that nobody else was on those terms with him? Could a postman or a milkman have made friends with him? Or anyone else at all?"

The other man massaged his moustache.

"I don't know. . . . Well, perhaps Fergus Clanraith might."

Simon blinked.

"But it sounded to me as if he didn't exactly love the dog."

"Perhaps he didn't. But it must have known him pretty well. Eleanor likes to go hiking across country, and the dog always used to go with her. She's always crossing Clanraith's property and stopping to talk to him, she tells me. She gets on very well with him."

"What, that old curmudgeon?"

"I know, he's full of that Scottish Nationalist nonsense. But Eleanor is half Scots herself, and that makes her almost human in his estimation. I believe they talk for hours about salmon fishing and grouse shooting."

"I wondered if he had an appealing side hidden away somewhere," said the Saint thoughtfully, "or if Annie got it all from her mother."

Bastion's deep-set sooty eyes flickered over him appraisingly.

"She's rather an attractive filly, isn't she?"

"I have a feeling that to a certain type of man, in certain circumstances, and perhaps at a certain age, her appeal might be quite dangerous."

Noel Bastion had an odd expression of balancing some answer on the tip of his tongue, weighing it for advisability, changing his mind a couple of times about it, and finally swallowing it. He then tried to recover from the pause by making a business of consulting the clock on the mantelpiece.

"Will you excuse me? Eleanor asked me to bring her a thermos of tea about now. She hates to miss that, even for *an Niseag*."

"Sure."

Simon followed him into the kitchen, where a kettle was already simmering on the black coal stove. He watched while his host carefully scalded a teapot and measured leaves into it from a canister.

"You know, Major," he said, "I'm not a detective by nature, even of the private variety."

"I know. In fact, I think you used to be just the opposite."

"That's true, too, I do get into situations, though, where I have to do a bit of deducing, and sometimes I startle everyone by coming up with a brilliant hunch. But as a general rule, I'd rather prevent a crime than solve one. As it says in your kind of text-books, a little preventive action can save a lot of counter-attacks."

The Major had poured boiling water into the pot with a steady hand, and was opening a vacuum flask while he waited for the brew.

"You're a bit late to prevent this one, aren't you?—if it *was* a crime."

"Not necessarily. Not if the death of Golly was only a stepping-stone—something to build on the story of a missing sheep, and pave the way for the Monster's next victim to be a person. If a person were killed in a similar way now, the Monster explanation would get a lot more believers than if it had just happened out of the blue."

Bastion put sugar and milk into the flask, without measuring, with the unhesitating positiveness of practice, and took the lid off the teapot to sniff and stir it.

"But, good heavens, Templar, who could treat a dog like that, except a sadistic maniac?"

Simon lighted a cigarette. He was very certain now, and the certainty made him very calm.

"A professional killer," he said. "There are quite a lot of them around who don't have police records. People whose temperament and habits have developed a great callousness about death. But they're not sadists. They're normally kind to animals and even to human beings, when it's normally useful to be. But fundamentally they see them as expendable, and when the time comes they can sacrifice them quite impersonally."

"I know Clanraith's a farmer, and he raises animals only to have them butchered," Bastion said slowly. "But it's hard to imagine him doing what you're talking about, much as I dislike him."

"Then you think we should discard him as a red herring?"

Bastion filled the thermos from the teapot, and capped it.

"I'm hanged if I know. I'd want to think some more about it. But first I've got to take this to Eleanor."

"I'll go with you," said the Saint.

He followed the other out of the back door. Outside, the dusk was deepening with a mistiness that was beginning to do more than the failing light to reduce visibility. From the garden, one could see into the orchard but not beyond it.

"It's equally hard for the ordinary man," Simon continued relentlessly, "to imagine anyone who's lived with another person as man and wife, making love and sharing the closest moments, suddenly turning around and killing the other one. But the prison cemeteries are full of 'em. And there are plenty more on the outside who didn't get caught—or who are still planning it. At least half the time, the marriage has been getting a bit dull, and someone more attractive has come along. And then, for some idiotic reason, often connected with money, murder begins to seem cleverer than divorce."

Bastion slackened his steps, half turning to peer at Simon from under heavily contracted brows, then spoke slowly.

"I'm not utterly dense, Templar, and I don't like what you seem to be hinting at."

"I don't expect you to, chum. But I'm trying to stop a murder.

Let me make a confession. When you and Eleanor have been out or in bed at various times, I've done quite a lot of prying. Which may be a breach of hospitality, but it's less trouble than search warrants. You remember those scratches in the ground near the dead dog which I said could've been made with something that wasn't claws? Well, I found a gaff among somebody's fishing tackle that could've made them, and the point had fresh shiny scratches and even some mud smeared on it which can be analyzed. I haven't been in the attic and found an embalmed shark's head with several teeth missing, but I'll bet Mackenzie could find one. And I haven't yet found the club with the teeth set in it, because I haven't yet been allowed down by the lake alone; but I think it's there somewhere, probably stuffed under a bush, and just waiting to be hauled out when the right head is turned the wrong way."

Major Bastion had come to a complete halt by that time.

"You unmitigated bounder," he said shakily. "Are you going to have the impertinence to suggest that I'm trying to murder my wife, to come into her money and run off with a farmer's daughter? Let me tell you that I'm the one who has the private income, and——"

"You poor feeble egotist," Simon retorted harshly. "I didn't suspect that for one second after she made herself rather cutely available to me, a guest in your house. She obviously wasn't stupid, and no girl who wasn't would have gambled a solid understanding with you against a transient flirtation. But didn't you ever read *Lady Chatterly's Lover?* Or the Kinsey Report? And hasn't it dawned on you that a forceful woman like Eleanor, just because she isn't a glamour girl, couldn't be bored to frenzy with a husband who only cares about the campaigns of Wellington?"

Noel Bastion opened his mouth, and his fists clenched, but whatever was intended to come from either never materialized. For at that moment came the scream.

Shrill with unearthly terror and agony, it split the darkening haze with an eldritch intensity that seemed to turn every hair on the Saint's nape into an individual icicle. And it did not stop, but ululated again and again in weird cadences of hysteria.

For an immeasurable span they were both petrified; and then

Bastion turned and began to run wildly across the meadow, towards the sound.

"Eleanor!" he yelled, insanely, in a voice almost as piercing as the screams.

He ran so frantically that the Saint had to call on all his reserves to make up for Bastion's split-second start. But he did close the gap as Bastion stumbled and almost fell over something that lay squarely across their path. Simon had seen it an instant sooner, and swerved, mechanically identifying the steely glint that had caught his eye as a reflection from a long gun-barrel.

And then, looking ahead and upwards, he saw through the blue fogginess something for which he would never completely believe his eyes, yet which would haunt him for the rest of his life. Something grey-black and scaly-slimy, an immense amorphous mass from which a reptilian neck and head with strange protuberances reared and swayed far up over him. And in the hideous dripping jaws something of human shape, from which the screams came, that writhed and flailed ineffectually with a peculiar-looking club. . . .

With a sort of incoherent sob, Bastion scooped up the rifle at his feet and fired it. The horrendous mass convulsed; and into Simon's eardrums, still buzzing from the heavy blast, came a sickening crunch that cut off the last shriek in the middle of a note.

The towering neck corkscrewed with frightful power, and the thing that had been human was flung dreadfully towards them. It fell with a kind of soggy limpness almost at their feet, as whatever had spat it out lurched backwards and was blotted out by the vaporous dimness with the sound of a gigantic splash while Bastion was still firing again at the place where it had been. . . .

As Bastion finally dropped the gun and sank slowly to his knees beside the body of his wife, Simon also looked down and saw that her hand was still spasmodically locked around the thinner end of the crude bludgeon in which had been set a row of shark's teeth. Now that he saw it better, he saw that it was no home-made affair, but probably a souvenir of some expedition to the South Pacific. But you couldn't be right all the time, about every last detail. Just as a few seconds ago, and until he saw Bas-

tion with his head bowed like that over the woman who had plot-
ted to murder him, he had never expected to be restrained in his
comment by the irrational compassion that finally moved him.

"By God," he thought, "now I know I'm ageing."

But aloud he said: "She worked awful hard to sell everyone on
the Monster. If you like, we can leave it that way. Luckily I'm a
witness to what happened just now. But I don't have to say anything about—this."

He released the club gently from the grip of the dead fingers,
and carried it away with him as he went to telephone Mackenzie.

AFTERWORD

Until the present collation was suggested by Drs. Greenberg and Waugh, it had not occurred to my simple little mind that the Saint stories could be segregated into categories according to subject matter. Certainly I hoped, and believed, that they encompassed a fair range of themes—the straight-line adventure, the whodunit, the whatisit, the big and the little swindle, the espionage bit, even the threat of international or cosmic catastrophe—but these variations were dictated only by a desire to avoid monotony, to avoid the perpetual repetition of a recognizable formula, a methodology which seems to me to have been consciously cultivated by certain other writers who shall here be nameless.

In trying to exploit the Saint's versatile potential as a "hero," it was inevitable that my plots should occasionally spill over into the realm of the fantastic. But after all, where exactly does remote possibility end and fantasy begin? In my young days, the idea of a nuclear bomb that could destroy the earth would have been dismissed as fantastic. Three hundred years ago, to claim that you had a box with a window through which you could see something actually happening on the other side of the world (if anyone would believe in such a place) would have got you burnt at the stake. Today, as our horizons draw progressively closer, the fantastic fictional death ray is already in sight.

All right, you might say that by purest definition the adjective "fantastic" should only be applied to imaginings of absolute impossibility, no matter how entertaining, such as the story of Aladdin's lamp. But any slightly less rigorous requirement would have to admit tales in the hazy fringe of the supranormal, of things not clearly related to accepted natural laws or human invention. There are many otherwise realistic people who believe in ghosts, and extrasensory phenomena are still being subjected to serious scientific investigation. Nobody is yet in a position to announce whether they are absolute impossibilities or not.

It is into this marginal field that the Saint has occasionally trespassed, I had not thought with any intention of mine to take sides or to make them an integral part of his way of life. To my mind, these stories were only additional exercises in legitimate imagination. If the Saint could plausibly encounter some "fantastic" new weapon of war (as he did in *The Saint Closes the Case*) why couldn't he just as plausibly encounter some inexplicable demonstration of voodoo magic, as he did in this collection?

Which is not to say that my approach to such imaginings gave me unlimited license to invent anything that would help a story along. On the contrary, my self-imposed discipline for such conceits imposes some quite rigid rules within which fantasy must operate: the backgrounds must be strictly authentic.

Thus, before writing "The Man Who Liked Ants," I read three or four serious books about them. Which doesn't make me an entomologist, but at least gives the story some scientific support. "The Questing Tycoon" was inspired by a visit to Haiti, where I was fortunate enough to be able to witness a couple of genuine voodoo ceremonies—not the kind that are laid on for the tourists. I was also lucky enough to meet a local resident, a lifelong student of the cult and the author of important monographs on the subject: thanks to him, I can vouch that the details and the actual incantation and the song quoted are literally exact. And so on.

I still make haste to concede that my own scientific and occult researches have been superficial compared with those of many distinguished exponents of the genre. Nevertheless, I had to do my homework. I was not taking a quick and easy cop-out from the limitations of believable fiction.

I learned quite a lot from it. I hope that you too may have picked up a few odd items of unusual information, and material for interesting speculation, from . . . *The Fantastic Saint*.

L.C.

Dublin
November 1980

DATE DUE